T0006698

KNIFE RIVER

KNIFE RIVER

A TY DAWSON MYSTERY

BARON BIRTCHER

OPEN ROAD

INTEGRATED MEDIA
NEW YORK

All rights reserved, including without limitation the right to reproduce
this book or any portion thereof in any form or by any means, whether
electronic or mechanical, now known or hereinafter invented, without the
express written permission of the publisher.

This is a work of fiction. Names, characters, places, events, and incidents
either are the product of the author's imagination or are used fictitiously.
Any resemblance to actual persons, living or dead, businesses, companies,
events, or locales is entirely coincidental.

Copyright © 2024 by Rosemeadow Holdings, LLC

ISBN: 978-1-5040-8637-0

Published in 2024 by Open Road Integrated Media, Inc.
180 Maiden Lane
New York, NY 10038
www.openroadmedia.com

For Christina

KNIFE RIVER

"Those who cannot remember the past are condemned to repeat it."

—George Santayana

"That men do not learn very much from the lessons of history is the most important of all the lessons of history."

—Aldous Huxley

PRELUDE

FACING WEST

SOME SAY THAT to be born into a thing is to be blind to half of it. Oftentimes, the things we seek and discover for ourselves are those we hold most dear.

Any cattleman will tell you that a ranch is a living thing. Not only the livestock that graze the meadowland, but the blood that nourishes the hungry soil, the trees that inhale the wind, and the rain that carves runnels into the hardpan that, in time, grow into rivers. The Diamond D is no different in that respect; some would even say it was the beating heart of Meriwether County, Oregon. As both a stockman and the sheriff of this county, I believe this to be true.

But the events that unfolded in the autumn of 1964 cast a cloud across this land. Not just across my ranch, but the entire valley, though they didn't bear their terrible fruit until nearly a dozen years later, in the spring of 1976. The incidents still haunt me, though others paid a steeper price than me, some with their lives, or the lives of their loved ones, while some forfeited their sanity, and still others their souls.

That is where this story begins.

CHAPTER ONE

LAMBS AND LIONS hold no sway over the springtime here in Meriwether County. Some years it will snow through mid-May; other times the golden sun rides high and bright, and the river flows fast, clear, and deep with high-country melt on the first day of March. Most years, it's both, with Mother Nature keeping her whims to herself until she alone decides to turn them loose upon us.

But this particular Saturday morning was unusually quiet, not even a breath of breeze stirring the leaves of the cotton-woods that grew thick and untamed along the creekbank. I was standing outside on the gallery, sipping my coffee as I leaned on the porch rail, watching my wife, Jesse, hammer the last nail into a bird box she had made. She must have felt my eyes on her, as she looked up from her work and smiled. A few moments later, she stepped up the stairs to where I stood and kissed me on the cheek, smelling of sawdust and lemongrass tea.

"The bluebirds are back," she said. "I just saw them."

"You haven't lost your knack for building those things."

"Plenty of practice. You got home late last night."

I had spent the previous day transporting a man all the way from Lewiston up to the Portland lockup to await his trial. He stood accused of murdering his own wife and young child. It had been a long, depressing day, and by the time I completed the intake paperwork, locked up the substation in Meridian, and finally drove home to the ranch, Jesse was already asleep.

But this morning, everything in her expression seemed overflowing with hope and expectation. Springtime was her season and always had been.

"Want a hand putting that thing up?" I asked.

She replied by handing it to me, together with the hammer.

Jesse watched me hang the bird box on a post beside the vegetable garden from the kitchen window where I knew she'd spend her quiet mornings secretly observing the bluebirds as they built their nest and reared their brood.

"You plan on helping Caleb pick the new cowboys today?" she asked me when I came back inside.

It was the time of year when we hired a few temporary hands for Spring Works, when we'd round up the cattle and calves from every corner of the ranch; we'd vet, brand, and sort the livestock and mend a perpetual string of breaks in the wire along miles of fence line before we turned the herd out to the pastures for summer grazing. The Diamond D employed three permanent cowboys in addition to me and old Caleb Wheeler—our foreman for more than three decades—but with sixty-three thousand deeded acres and another fourteen thousand under a Bureau of Land Management lease, Spring Works was more work than the five of us could handle in the short span of time required to get it done. Every year a couple dozen hopeful itinerant riders, ropers, rodeo bums, and saddle tramps would answer the call for a temporary employment opportunity, and every year Caleb Wheeler got more riled up about what he viewed as the eroding quality of the contemporary American cowboy. He'd cuss and grump and holler about it, but he'd end up settling on three or four hands he reckoned could help us get the job done with a minimum of aggravation.

"I'm staying out of it this year," I said, and Jesse grinned. "Figured I'd lay in a cord or two for the woodshed instead, before the weather gets too hot."

"I saw some deadfall down by the Corcorans," she said.

"That's where I was headed."

"Make you some lunch to take with you?"

"I don't intend to be out that long."

"Good to hear," she said, winking at me before she turned and stepped inside the house.

HALF AN HOUR LATER, I was straddling a fallen spruce, angling the chain saw to buck the trunk into three-foot rounds that I'd later split into quarters with the long-handled axe. The solitary labor, the sweat staining my shirt, and the burn down deep inside my muscles were a welcome balm after the week I'd had, and the air was rife with the smell of pine tar, sap, and chain oil. I looked up and caught some movement in the distance, where the BLM forest gave onto an open range already knee-deep with wildflowers and whipgrass. I recognized Tom Jenkins's roping horse moving hellbent-for-leather across the flats, with young Tom leaning across its withers, one hand on the reins and the other holding his hat in place on top of his head. His mount was an admirable animal, a grulla quarter horse that stood nearly seventeen hands, fast and thick through the chest. Tom Jenkins handled it well, and he was beelining in my direction like he had something on his mind.

I killed the power on the chain saw and set it in the bed of the military surplus jeep I use when I do ranch work, stepped over to the fence, and took a splash of water from the canteen I'd hung in the shade of a young cedar. I didn't have to wait long before Tom pulled up in a skidding stop inside a cloud of dust, throwing a cascade of torn earth and pebbles through the barbed strands of the wire.

"Mr. Dawson," he said and touched a finger to his hat brim, sounding nearly as breathless as his horse. "I was hoping that was you."

"What are you doing out here all by yourself?" I asked but suspected I already knew the answer.

When I'd first met Tom Jenkins, he was nothing but a kid with a limp handshake, no eye contact, and the familiar slope-shouldered gait and posture of the typical aimless teenaged slacker. At that time, he'd been well on his way to serious trouble, the variety and scope of which would have landed him in a six-by-eight jail cell where the other inmates would have eaten him alive.

He is the nephew of my neighbor to the south of me, Snoose Corcoran, whose sister had sent the kid up here from California's central valley to his uncle's ranch in southeastern Oregon in hopes of putting some distance between young Tom and his unquestionably poor choices of acquaintances. Ill-equipped to deal with the boy himself, Snoose begged me to take the kid on as a maverick, and I'd reluctantly agreed. After six months working side by side with trail-hardened cowboys on the Diamond D, young Tom Jenkins's attitude had been readjusted, straightening both his spine and fortitude. Now, at barely eighteen years of age, Tom had assumed the reins of the floundering Corcoran cattle operation from his uncle Snoose, who had been gradually disappearing into a bottle.

"Cow and a calf went missing from my place," Tom answered. "Fence busted by the westward line, and I figured them two mighta headed for the water."

My ranch hands ended up nicknaming the kid "Silver" after he'd astonished us all by stepping up and winning a silver buckle for the Diamond D in the team roping event at the annual rodeo. I knew Tom secretly treasured the handle they'd bestowed, wore it like a medal, but I never spoke it; that was between my men and him.

"Where's your uncle?" I asked.

His shrug spoke sorrowful volumes.

"So what set you hightailing over here to see me, son?" I asked. "What's the trouble? Besides the missing beeves."

"I was up there on the other side of the tree line," he said— Tom twisted sideways in his saddle, took off his hat, and gestured with it toward a distant stretch of blue sky—"and there was an eagle making low passes over the meadow, so I stopped to watch it for a minute. It was so still and quiet out there, I could hear the eagle calling out while it was gliding on the thermals."

"You don't see something like that every day," I said. "Not even out here in the boondocks."

"No, sir, that's a fact," Tom said. "But while I sat there watching that creature flying, all of a sudden and out of nowhere, a helicopter come buzzing across the ridge, you know the one . . ."

"Big stone bluff, looks like somebody cut it down the middle with a KA-BAR knife."

"That's the one," he said. "Well, that chopper came in fast and went straight toward that bird . . ." The young man's voice trailed off, his face contorted like he'd encountered a foul odor. "They circled it as it flew, like they were teasing it. Two men inside the—whattaya call it?"

"Cockpit."

"Yeah, the cockpit. Then they started closing in on him, chasing it. The guy in the passenger seat had a rifle in his hands. I could see the barrel sticking out."

What Tom was describing to me was not only a despicable and loathsome act, it was a serious crime. The mere harassment of a protected species is a federal offense; hunting and killing one merely for the sick thrill of it was another matter entirely.

"What happened, Tom?"

He swallowed drily, shook his head, and looked down at the ground between us.

"He shot that bird right out of the sky, sir," he said. "That eagle wasn't even doing nothing, just gliding circles on the wind, and those assholes—sorry, sir—they shot him cold dead."

I could imagine the creature's confused and lonely cry as it spiraled down, bleeding, terrified and helpless, to the earth.

"You pretty sure about the location, Tom?"

"About four, five miles thataway, near the bluff, where the river makes that sharp bend to the south."

"Did you get a look at either of the men?"

"Naw, they were too far away and moving pretty fast. But I got a good look at the whirlybird."

I asked him for a description of the helicopter, and I knew right away he was referring to a Bell H-13, known to soldiers as a "Sioux." They'd been in common use as scouting and medical evacuation aircraft by the military. I'd seen them every day when I was stationed in Korea.

"Like the choppers on that TV show?" I asked.

"Yes, sir. Exactly like on *M*A*S*H*."

"Big glass bubble on the front? No doors? Looks kinda like a dragonfly?"

"Yes, sir."

"Did you see any numbers written on it? On the tail? Or maybe on the underside?"

Tom Jenkins pressed his hat back on his head and gazed up at the empty sky beyond the forest, like he could return that beautiful animal to where it rightfully belonged through sheer force of his will. The high peaks beyond the meadow were streaked with deep blue shadows in the sunlight, their cloughs and gorges washed in purple and topped with snow so white it hurt your eyes.

"I'm sorry, sir," he said. "I don't remember seeing numbers or anything like that."

His face took on the aspect of defeat, as though some personal failure had cost the animal its life.

"You did good, Tom. You did the right thing coming to me straightaway. There was nothing else you could have done."

He nodded once, his lips pressed tight, and he leaned down to adjust a stirrup that needed no adjustment.

"You want some help finding your cows?" I asked, thinking he might appreciate the company.

"I can do it, sir, but thank you. I can haze 'em back home on my own."

"You gotta get eyeballs on the critters first. I can help you, son."

"Thank you just the same, Mr. Dawson . . . Sheriff . . . Hell, I don't even know what to call you."

His expression softened for the first time since he'd showed up, a brief and fleeting smile, then his focus drifted far away again.

"Something else, Tom?"

"Just wondering."

"Wondering what?"

"Do you think you can catch those guys who shot that bird?"

"I'm going to try my damnedest."

His eyes remained fixed on the horizon.

"What'll happen to 'em if you do?"

I drew a bandanna from the back pocket of my jeans, removed my hat, and dried the sweat that had been leaking from beneath the band.

"It's been against the law to kill an eagle since the 1940s. If you're not an Indian, you can't even possess a single feather. If you get caught, you pay a steep fine and then they send you off to jail. If you're a rancher, you could lose the leases on your land."

Tom turned his gaze back on me, and I noted for the hundredth time that this young man no longer bore any resemblance to the person he had been on the day he first arrived here from California.

"That punishment don't seem tough enough," Tom said. "Not for what I seen 'em do."

"No, it doesn't."

He clucked softly to his horse and reined her back in the direction from which they'd come.

"I'd better get a move on," he said.

"Be careful out there, son," I said to his retreating back, but my words were lost in the distance.

CHAPTER TWO

I STOPPED BACK at the ranch to swap the old jeep for my pickup truck, grabbed my badge and Colt Peacemaker, and drove in the direction of the meadow Tom Jenkins had described to me. I had a vague familiarity with the place, though I hadn't been out there in quite a while, the split granite cliff being a local landmark of sorts, which would sometimes appear to glow from within when the rising sun touched it just so.

It wasn't easy to gain access to the place from the ground, except on horseback through dense woodland or over unpaved washboard roads irregularly maintained by the US Forest Service, held locked and gated from the public. Local fire departments and law enforcement agencies, including mine, possessed keys for our use in the case of an emergency. Which is exactly what I considered this to be.

I parked the truck beside a copse of redbud and vine maple, climbed out and smelled the sweet scent of bog moss and the coldness of the river, tasted the mineral content on my tongue. The watercourse ran wide and deep where I was standing, forming a broad arc that altered its trajectory sharply southward.

Knife River.

Stepping deliberately along the rocky bank, I followed the flow of water, the silence of midday broken only by the whisper of clear currents sluicing across the surface of flat stones. Tom Jenkins, in his search for his lost livestock, would have entered this marshland from the opposite direction, which meant that his field of vision would have encompassed the area in which I was standing. The wounded eagle would have spiraled down and landed somewhere inside the semicircle bordered by the riverbank. By necessity, to retrieve the creature, the helicopter would have had to put down here as well.

I took my time pacing an imaginary grid I'd laid out in my mind's eye, the vegetation underneath my boots spongy from spring rain and the absence of sunshine in the vast shadow cast by the steep cliff. I stopped moving for a moment to watch a single redband trout lurking inside a dappled eddy, resting in the lee of an ancient snag. A young plover dropped down from the trees just then, skimmed the water's surface, and disappeared into the bulrushes.

I knew eagles to be territorial in nature, extremely protective of their domain. This would have been its hunting ground—and likely had been for untold generations of its ancestry. But this one's life had been extinguished for no reason at all, apart from human avarice and narcissism, a hubristic and grossly unfair ambush in sole service of the acquisition of a nauseating trophy for somebody's game room.

After several circuits of the meadow, I identified the indentations made from a helicopter's skids near the center of my search area, a pair of parallel inclusions compacted deep into the spongy topsoil. I stepped off a rough estimate of their length, which I'd compare against a Bell chopper's factory specs once I returned to the substation. Now that I knew where the aircraft had landed, I scanned my surroundings to identify any type of foreign material that may have been dislodged out of the cockpit, cast off by the occupants themselves or by the prop wash of the Sioux's rotor blades. A crisp wind gust channeled into the gap out of the west and shook loose an object that had been caught inside a cluster of cattails. I crouched down in the marshy water and extracted a feather, white with black tips, long and perfectly symmetrical. I found another one a few feet away, together with a small contour feather marked in the same hues of black and white. This second tail feather was damaged, with a bloodstain on the calamus, where it had once been attached to flesh and bone—the feather had been pulled loose in a struggle, the same way the contour feather had.

It was clear the gunshot had not been a clean one, and the creature had likely suffered at the hands of the amateur hunter, in an act that was as cruel as it was senseless. What made my discovery all the worse was that I could tell that this eagle had been a juvenile, not even two years old. The tail feathers told the story. Adults of the species have tails of solid white.

I continued my grid search for another hour, covered every square foot of the area, hoping against hope to locate a shell casing, but found nothing else of any use to an investigation. I cast a final glance upward at the looming peak and imagined the animal's death cry echoing against the wall of stone as I picked my way back to the truck.

TOM JENKINS had described the aircraft as having flown in from the back side of the ridge. The only developed property I was aware of on that side was a secluded resort recording studio that had been constructed on the carcass of an old trading post, two or three miles off the state route. Beyond that property were miles of BLM, National Forest, and wilderness land, and little else between it and the Idaho state line.

With a cruising range of roughly two hundred fifty miles, a Sioux chopper would have had to take off from somewhere within a prescribed circle with a maximum radius of a hundred twenty-five miles to allow for its departure and safe return. Either that, or it could have leapfrogged from practically anywhere else inside the lower forty-eight, refueling as it made its way from one airfield to the next. The latter possibility was deeply troubling to me for two reasons: it offered no practical starting point to search for the pilot and definitely placed the case in federal hands. But this atrocity had been committed on my watch in my backyard, and I'd be damned if I gave the case away. Regardless of the aircraft's origin, given its heading and trajectory into the secluded crime scene, I needed to speak to someone on the far side of the bluff, someone at the studio, and see what I could learn.

It was nearly two o'clock that afternoon by the time I pulled off the state road and stopped at the base of an enormous lodge-pole entry structure fitted with iron cantilever gates and palisade fence. It stood at least twenty feet in height, with a crossbeam more than twice that length, fashioned from the trunk of a single Contorta pine. I leaned out from the window of my truck and pressed the button on an intercom box bearing an engraved sign that read HALF MOUNTAIN STUDIO.

I waited for a full minute without reply and punched the button again. Moments later, I announced myself to a man with a polite and officious speaking voice and waited as the gates slowly swung open. A single-lane paved road wound through a dense forest of juniper, fern, and piñon, natural in their distribution and spatial arrangement but meticulously maintained. I clocked the odometer at nearly one full winding mile before I emerged out of the foliage. A sprawling treeless expanse of gently rolling hillocks opened before me, carpeted in emerald fescue that undulated like sea currents in the slow drift of the breeze. A half-dozen outbuildings and workshops dotted the near horizon to the south, where an aviation windsock dangled listlessly from a steel pole and a tractor pulling a box blade worked back and forth smoothing the natural contours of undeveloped tillage. A cloud of fine dust passed overhead as I drove in and parked beside a three-story structure that resembled an old western movie hotel and saloon. I climbed down from the cab and strode to the back of my truck to take in the view from the opposite direction. I counted seven guest cottages as I scanned the property, together with a massive gambrel barn, each of which was constructed of rustic logs and situated around a lake at least five acres in size.

"You must be Sheriff Dawson," a voice said from behind me. It was the same voice I'd heard over the intercom at the gate. "My name's Len Kaanan. I'm the owner of this place."

He offered me his hand and we stepped into the shade of the saloon. He was dressed in khaki slacks, a purple polo shirt, and canvas deck shoes; his smile seemed unforced and natural. Kaanan appeared to be roughly my age, though his hair was prematurely silver, of average height, and athletically built.

"Is that a helicopter pad I noticed out there?" I asked.

His smile remained intact, but the warmth of his initial greeting leached from his eyes.

"What brings you out here, Sheriff?"

"A pair of poachers used a helicopter to hunt and kill an eagle on the wing. It happened not far from here."

"That's appalling."

"Yes, it is. Immoral and illegal, as well."

He ran his fingers through his hair and shook his head.

"This place looks like a resort, Mr. Kaanan. Do you keep any weapons out here? A little recreational hunting, trapshooting, that sort of thing? You know, so your guests can blow off a little steam."

"I don't appreciate the implication, Sheriff."

"I'm simply asking whether you might have seen or heard anything that could help me identify the man who shot that eagle."

"Or if somebody on my staff is capable of doing it."

"That too."

Kaanan gestured toward the split-log barn and squinted into the glare.

"That building is the recording studio," he said. "We've been working in there all morning long. In fact, I wouldn't have interrupted the session when you buzzed me from the gate, except we'd just taken our lunch break. The structure we're standing next to is the mess hall. Upstairs are the accommodations for the crew. Most everyone is having lunch in there at the moment. We don't kill things here."

"You're saying nobody saw or heard anything like a helicopter."

"We work in a recording studio," he repeated. "It's soundproofed."

"I don't see an aircraft on your helipad."

He slid his hands into the pockets of his slacks and rocked back on his heels.

"I don't own a helicopter, Sheriff Dawson."

"Then what do you have a landing pad for?"

"The pad is there to accommodate the artists who record here at Half Mountain. They'll fly into Portland or Eugene from wherever they come from, and oftentimes will hire a private helicopter to shuttle them out here to the studio rather than making the long drive."

His words could have sounded defensive, but his tone carried no trace of it.

"I didn't come out here just to complicate your life," I said.

"Listen, we have a high-end clientele," he said. "I'm not bragging. I'm only telling you that we've been here for less than two years now, and we've already had Elton record an album with us; Billy Joel, John Lennon, Joe Walsh, and a dozen others, too. They expect a certain quality of amenities and privacy. McCartney's booked us for the month of September. We've been very lucky."

"In my experience," I said, "the harder I work, the luckier I get."

Kannan's expression softened.

"I appreciate your saying so," he said.

A young man stepped out of the mess hall and sat down on a bench in the sunshine. He cast his eyes in our direction momentarily, then turned away and tipped his face toward the sky. He had the look of a rock musician, dark hair to his shoulders, heavy beard and mustache, wearing faded dungaree bell-bottom trousers, chambray shirt, and Mexican leather sandals on his otherwise bare feet.

Kaanan saw me looking at the young man.

"That's Ian Swann," he said. "He's the artist whose album we're working on at the moment. Singer-songwriter type. You might have heard of him. He's a bit like Jackson Browne or Fogelberg, the Eagles every now and then. I'm producing his record."

"I'm familiar with Mr. Swann's music."

"Really?"

"My daughter is a senior at Colorado State," I said. "I try to keep current with popular culture. I like to know what I'm up against."

Kaanan eyed the passing clouds reflected in the surface of his lake, compressed his lips into the shape of a cone, a look of concentration wrinkling his forehead.

"Ian's a good kid," he said after a moment. "His first album went platinum. Second one did more than twice that number in sales. This new record's going to launch him into the stratosphere."

I glanced at the young artist again, sitting by himself in the soft sunshine, gazing across the timber land that stretched for miles beyond the confines of the studio property, lost in thought or silent composition. I watched him draw a cigarette out of his shirt pocket and light it with a disposable plastic lighter.

In my peripheral vision, I could see Kaanan watching me take a visual inventory of the young man.

"Ian's a good lad," he said again. "Most guys in his position are nothing but cabooses to their pricks. Not this guy. He's the real deal."

The sweet and unmistakable scent of marijuana carried over to us on the breeze, and I turned to face Kaanan.

"I can't have that happening right in front of me," I said. "Possession of an ounce or more is still a class-B felony."

"I thought pot was legal here."

"Decriminalized, not legalized," I said. "There's a difference. Like I told you before, I'm not here to make your life difficult."

"I'm a record producer, not a den mother, Sheriff."

"Why would a man as smart as you appear to be somehow conclude that arguing with the county sheriff—who's trying to let you off the hook, by the way—is a wise idea?"

I cut my eyes toward the tractor in the distance, saw the driver kill the engine and climb down from the cab.

"Here's what I'm going to do," I said to Kaanan. "I'm going to stroll over there and have a word or two with your groundskeeper. When I come back, I will assume that unusual aroma will be gone, and we won't have to repeat this conversation ever again."

* * *

THE TRACTOR operator squinted as he watched me cross the open field. He was drinking from a can of cola he'd withdrawn from a cooler box and wicking sweat off his face with a soiled kerchief. I don't choose to wear a uniform, but my deputies usually do; I noticed his change of expression when I adjusted the fall of my three-quarter Carhartt and his focus landed on the shiny badge clipped to my gun belt.

"Hello, Officer," he said.

"Sheriff," I corrected. "Sheriff Ty Dawson. And you are. . . ?"

"Ned Teely."

"When's the last time somebody used your helicopter pad, Mr. Teely?"

He looked into the distance somewhere behind me and shrugged.

"I don't know," he said. "It don't get used too often from what I've seen."

"Was it used today?"

"No, sir. Definitely not. I been driving that tractor up and down these hills all day."

"You see anything fly over? Anything at all?"

He sucked air through his teeth then turned and spat into the dirt.

"This place is way the hell out here in the middle of nowhere, Sheriff. You don't tend to see much air traffic at all. Come to think of it, we don't really see much of any kind of traffic, if you don't count the raccoons, ducks, and deer."

I couldn't tell if he was lying.

"Mind if I take a look inside your tractor for a minute?"

"Help yourself."

I climbed into the cramped cab of the machine and looked out through the dusty windshield. Given the noise and the poor visibility inside, it would have been easy to miss a Bell Sioux chopper zipping overhead. I handed him my card anyway.

"Do me a favor, Ned? Give me a call if you remember anything or see anything unusual. We've got people poaching protected animals out this way."

He slid the card into the pocket of his jeans and hoped I was finished talking with him. I started to step away but dashed his hopes when I turned back and addressed him again.

"What are you working on out here, anyway?" I asked.

"Smoothing out the field to build an amphitheater."

"What for?"

"Big grass area for seating and a stage for concerts," he said.

"I know what an amphitheater *is*," I said. "What is it doing *here*?"

"Boss says when Swann's new album's finished, they're going to film a live performance out here. They've been filming the studio sessions, too. Stephen Stills was in there cutting a guest track yesterday. Saw him myself. I guess they plan on making a big movie out of it."

"Seems like a big job for just one man."

"Won't be for long. Boss says he's got a huge crew coming. Good thing, too. We don't have a heap of time to get it done, just a few weeks. Anyways . . ."

"You've been very helpful, Ned. Don't forget to call me if you remember anything I should know."

He patted the pocket where he'd put my card and nodded to me, crushed the cola can beneath his boot, and sighed in relief as I turned to go back to the mess hall.

LEN KAANAN was seated alone on the bench where I'd last witnessed Ian Swann lighting up a joint. I was about to inquire about the new concert venue he was constructing when two men stepped out of the commissary building and approached us. One of them was Ian Swann. The other man was short and stocky, with a pie plate for a face, long black hair pulled tightly across his round head and tied into a ponytail, his predatory eyes backlit with hostility.

"I'm Ian Swann," he said, addressing me. "This is my manager, Mickey London."

Swann reached across to shake my hand while the manager looked on with passive enmity, arms crossed on his chest. The musician's grip was firm, his manner deferential. There was something vaguely familiar about him, but people often feel that way about celebrities. Up close, I could see that his eyes were an unusual shade of blue, almost turquoise, with a skin tone that hinted at Cajun heritage.

"I apologize for my behavior earlier, Sheriff Dawson," Swann said. "I meant no disrespect. I didn't see your badge. I would have never—"

"I don't know what you're referring to, Mr. Swann," I interrupted. "But whatever it was, I'm sure you had no ill intention."

Swann studied me for a moment, searched my face for duplicity and found none, then he broke into a grin, his expression alive with gratitude and humor.

"That's very understanding of you, Sheriff," he said.

For reasons I failed to comprehend, his manager was still glaring at me like he could melt the skin off my face.

"I usually don't allow people to stare at me that way," I said to Mickey London. "Do we have some kind of problem I don't know about?"

"Not yet," he said.

"Care to tell me what that means?"

Rather than reply, he simply turned and stomped away.

"Your manager appears to be a very unhappy man," I said to Ian Swann.

"He has a low opinion of law enforcement."

"That sort of attitude can turn around and bite you in the ass when you least expect it," I said. "I'd recommend he keep it to himself while he's in town—that advice is free of charge, by the way. It's been a pleasure to meet you, Ian."

"Likewise," he said. "I guess I better get back to it. Got music to make."

Kaanan stood and walked me to my truck with no further mention of my interaction with Mickey London.

"I'm genuinely sorry to hear about the poachers," he said. "It's despicable."

"Let me know if you hear anything at all. What they did is not okay with me, and I don't intend to let it pass."

"You can find your own way out, I assume. I need to get back in there with Ian and create some more good luck."

"You do that, Mr. Kaanan. I'll try and do the same."

CHAPTER THREE

IT WAS EMPTY inside the Meridian substation when I stepped through the back door and hung my Resistol on the hat rack, called out the names of my deputies, Sam Griffin and Jordan Powell, but received no reply.

I walked upstairs and found the detainment area vacant, the holding cells all thankfully unoccupied. When I went back downstairs, I located Powell in the supply room. He was standing at the photocopier in the back room, waiting for a report to print, and obviously had not heard me come in. The room was stuffy and overly warm, reeking of toner chemicals and scorched coffee. I moved into the main office, unbolted a window to let in some outside air, and dropped into the rolling chair behind my desk. I shuffled through a stack of message slips, leafed through the mail that had accumulated in my inbox, and put it all back where it came from, unopened.

I leaned into my chair, looked out the window beside the front door, and watched late afternoon descend upon Meridian. The trees along the sidewalk wept tiny blossoms of pink and white onto the street, scattering in the wakes of passing cars and banked in pastel drifts along the curb.

"Oh, hey, Captain," Jordan said when he came out from the back room. "I didn't hear you. Damn Xerox machine's noisy as hell."

His use of my old army rank was an affectation I allowed only to him. It was an appellation he intended as a compliment, from one veteran to another. We'd fought in different wars and returned to even more disparate Americas. When my unit came home from Korea, we were largely ignored, forgotten; invisible centurions from battles nobody knew or cared about, from a conflict the politicians had never even bothered to declare as a real war.

But Jordan Powell and his fellow soldiers rotated home alone, no platoon-mates to help diffuse the shock of returning to a country that had transmuted in their absence. If I had been insulted by having been ignored by the America I returned home to, Powell would have undoubtedly preferred what I got to the treatment *he* received; it was most certainly not the thanks of a grateful nation. Had he not been a lone wolf before he shipped out to southeast Asia, he sure as hell became one when he got home.

Jordan Powell had served as an enlisted man, while I'd been a commissioned officer. If he chose to offer his respect by refer-ring to me as "Captain" from time to time, I was not about to stop him. But that practice began and ended with him alone.

"Where's Sam?" I asked.

"Slow day today, sir. Griffin went back to the ranch to help Caleb sort out the new hands for Spring Works."

"Better him than me," I said. "Caleb gets damned unpleasant after a day talking to applicants."

Powell nodded, not even a shadow of shared humor reaching his eyes.

"I see you're not using your cane," I said.

"No more vertigo. It went away. Doc says I only need one more week of physical therapy."

"That's a huge improvement," I told him. "You should be proud of your progress."

"That's exactly what Shasta said."

"Your fiancée is a wise young woman."

He moved a stack of papers off the long table across from me and took a seat on the open space he'd made. He swung his boots in the empty air and looked out to the street, his expression unreadable, but I could sense that he'd been steeping in the dark side of his own isolation.

"Something on your mind, Jordan?" I asked.

"May I speak freely, sir?"

I gave him a go-ahead gesture.

"You gotta let me out of here, Sheriff. I swear I'm getting barn-sour riding this desk every goddamned day."

"What does Shasta think about that idea?"

"Tell you the truth, I believe she's all for it. I think she's tired of seeing me drag around the house every night when I come home."

"That girl doesn't have a lot of whoa in her, does she?" I said.

It had only been a few months since Powell had been seriously injured by a bullet while on duty. The round had been fired from the rifle of a highly trained sniper—an operative whom we had every reason to believe was in the employ of the federal government at the time—and had left Powell in a coma and very nearly killed him.

"No, sir," he said. "That girl's only got two speeds, and the other one is sleep."

His legs were still swinging back and forth beneath him like a schoolboy waiting for a decision from the principal.

"How long's it been since you sat a horse, Jordan?" I asked.

He looked up from the floor, carefully considering what he thought I wanted to hear. He clenched his teeth, and the livid scar that ran the length of his jaw turned white, but the scar that concerned me most was the one I couldn't see; the one that followed him home at night and stole into his dreams, and worse, had robbed him of his self-confidence. It was a hazardous affliction in our line of work, and one that could be deadly if it wasn't dealt with.

I watched his internal deliberations for long seconds before he finally opted for the truth.

"I haven't been horseback since the accident, Cap."

At Shasta's insistence, they had taken to referring to his injury as an accident. I found it a poignant and endearing defense mechanism, and a testament to their mutual sense of survival. Other than his hitch in Vietnam, Jordan Powell had spent the balance of his adult life either riding rodeo or working for me as a cowboy and a deputy. Any one of those vocations would terrify a normal human being, but Powell was cut from something else entirely and so was his fiancée. That version of the man was the one we needed back.

"How about you come riding with me after your rehab is done," I said. "And we'll see how it goes from there."

"I'd like that very much, sir," he said, a hint of the old Jordan lighting his features.

"In the meantime, I have a case for you."

He looked at me expectantly, as though he'd been handed a new reason to live. I told him about the heartless killing of the young eagle, the poachers in the helicopter, and the investigative steps I had already taken. I handed him the evidence bags containing the feathers I collected at the scene and watched him turn them over in his hands.

"My advice," I said, "is to start local and see if you can get a bead on who that Bell chopper belongs to. Find the pilot, we'll find who chartered it."

"Got a tail number?"

"Nope."

"Gonna be a long shot," he said. "If you ask me, Sheriff, people like that should be chain-dragged and tossed in a hole."

"I don't disagree," I said.

"What if they aren't from around here?"

"You mean from out of state?"

He nodded. I knew what he was asking me, and now it was my turn to tell the truth.

"If that's the case, we'll have to turn it over to the feds. Fact is, I probably ought to do it right now. They murdered that animal on forestry land."

I could see a twitch at the corner of Powell's eye. Between Vietnam and nearly being killed at the hands of a government sniper, Jordan Powell retained no fondness for the feds or their agencies.

"Oh, hell no, sir," he said. "You gotta let me have a crack at this."

CALEB WHEELER was seated at a spool table in a circle of shade beneath the wildwood, unruly tufts of gray hair sneaking out beneath the sweat-stained Stetson he had pulled low on his brow. Caleb was midway through his seventies, tough as boot leather, and had worked for three generations of my family on the Diamond D, holding the positions of foreman and ranch manager for well over a decade.

Sam Griffin, one of my other deputies and finest cowboys, was seated at the table beside Wheeler. He was chewing on a stem of wild honeysuckle and squinting into a patch of sunlight where the last of the Spring Works applicants was standing.

I stepped up quietly, not wanting to interrupt the proceedings, leaned a shoulder against the trunk of the old cedar, and watched. It didn't take long to see that Caleb had reached the end of that day's allotment of tolerance.

"What kind of work do you think we do here?" Caleb asked the applicant.

I figured his age to be twenty-three or so, stocky and strong-looking, but his eyes were landing everywhere but on my foreman's. The kid was wearing blue jeans and a short-sleeved snap-button shirt, with a frayed trucker's cap on his head. Sam Griffin caught sight of me from the corner of his eye, acknowledging my presence with an elevated eyebrow. He turned to look at me, knowing exactly what was coming, the smirk on his face expressing *Here we go again*.

"Go on," Caleb repeated. "Answer me. What kind of work do you think we do around this place?"

"Cattle ranching," the young man replied.

Caleb lifted his eyebrows, cocked his head to one side, and waited for more.

"Sir," the applicant added.

"And what does it say on that hat you've got on?" Caleb asked.

"It says, 'Peterbilt.'"

"What does that mean?"

"It's a company that makes semitrucks, sir."

Caleb sighed deeply and focused somewhere in the distance, sitting in silence for a moment before asking his next question.

"Are you applying for work as a cowboy or a truck driver?"

The kid's eyes drifted first to Sam, then to me, seeking appeal, but found no patronage in either place.

"Are you kidding me right now, sir?" he replied finally.

"Do I give you the impression that I kid a lot?" Caleb asked.

"No, sir, you don't."

Caleb leaned forward, forearms resting on the spool table.

"Then answer my question, son."

"I'm applying for work as a cowboy. I'm pretty good with a string, and I can throw a calf at least as good as anybody I know. Sir."

"I'll tell you what," Caleb said. "Go get you some proper cowboy headgear and come back here tomorrow and we'll see if I still need you."

"Seriously?"

"If you're going to keep asking me if I'm serious, don't bother coming back."

"It's just a thing I say, sir. I didn't mean nothing by it."

"That's a big difference between you and me. 'Cause when I say something, I always mean it."

"I understand."

"Did you mean what you said about your skills with a rope, son?"

"Yes, sir."

"And how 'bout that part about throwing calves?"

"I meant that, too, sir."

Caleb leaned back in his chair and studied the young man, watching him rustle from one foot to the other as Caleb stared at him.

"Get yourself a proper head cover and I'll take a look at you tomorrow and see if I want you. I only have one more slot to fill."

"What time tomorrow, sir?"

"Surprise me," Caleb said. "And make sure and bring your rope and a pair of decent work gloves."

"GODDAMN KIDS, looking for ranch work wearing ball caps," Caleb said. "I swear, I think they're getting dumber every goddamn year."

"You seem a little dragged out, Caleb," I said.

"Perceptive as ever, I see."

"Are you familiar with the myth of Sisyphus?"

"What the hell's that got to do with anything?"

"It's the story of a king who was punished by the gods, forced to push an enormous boulder up a steep hill for all eternity," I said. "I've always seen it as a metaphor for ranching."

"I swear, Tyler," Caleb said after a moment, "sometimes I wish your folks hadn't sent you off to college."

I clapped him on the shoulder and aimed him toward the main house.

"You fellas care to come up for a drink?" I asked. "Appears we could all use one."

"I ain't in a mood to be in the presence of a proper lady," Caleb said. "But I could sure go for a swallow or two of that scamper-juice you keep in the office."

"How about you, Sam? You in?"

"Why not? It's Saturday."

A slow breeze huffed out of the dry creek channel as the three of us moved beneath a canopy of white oak and chinquapin, heard the sounds of the rough stock nickering deep in their throats as we strode past the corral. Caleb stopped to check on the farrier who was working in the shack while I turned the key and unlocked the office.

The room was long and narrow, furnished simply with a pair of desks, one each for Caleb and me, a row of file cabinets, a small sofa, a percolator for our coffee, and a Sparkletts water cooler. I took a seat behind my desk, reached into the bottom drawer, and withdrew a handle of Jim Beam and three juice glasses. I was pouring the last of them as Caleb came inside and grabbed two of the glasses, passed one to Sam, and tossed his back in one smooth motion.

"I was thirstier than I thought," he said, handing it back to me for refilling.

"Did you find any good hires?" I asked Sam as I poured out three more fingers for my foreman.

"Only got one more position to fill," Sam said.

"They as bad as old Caleb says they are?"

Sam Griffin took a seat at the sofa, propped his boots on the coffee table, and swirled the liquid in his glass.

"Lot of young ones, but they seem okay."

"Hell they are," Caleb said. "Buncha coffee-boilers and shavetails."

"I kinda liked the bull rider," Griffin said. "Seemed like he had some experience."

"Are you kidding me? That fella's probably nothing but a skin sack full of busted bones and contusions."

"Seemed pretty handy with a loop," Sam said.

"Maybe so, but I don't trust bull riders. Only good reason to ride a bull is to meet a nurse."

I stood and looked out through the jalousie windows, watching a covey of quail with their hatchlings waddle across the loose dirt in the paddock and hide inside a grove of chokecherry.

"I talked to Jordan at the substation this afternoon," I said. "He's not using his cane, and he says the vertigo is gone."

"He told me the same thing," Sam said.

"Do you believe him?"

"The man's a lot of things," Sam said, "but he ain't a liar."

"Powell seemed pretty down in the mouth still, so I invited him to take a ride with me after he finishes up his rehab. Getting him out of the substation for a change might do him some good. I'll take him up to North Camp and have a look at the pasture grass."

"Got to admit, that boy's got sand," Caleb said. "How long's it been since that cowboy forked a horse?"

"Months."

"You're not thinking—"

"Just trying to get his legs back under him, Caleb."

JESSE STOOD beside the sink in the mudroom as I walked in. She was making an arrangement of daffodils and tulips from the garden, their stalks neatly laid out on the tile.

"What's that on your cheek?" I asked.

"I was pruning dead wood from the rosebushes. They fought back a little."

I kissed her where the thorns had raked her skin and moved into the kitchen while she finished with her flowers. She had already spatchcocked a chicken and had it resting on the counter in a cast-iron skillet. The house was redolent with the smell of fresh cornbread and beans, and the table had been set for two.

Jesse stepped in and placed the vase at the center of the dining table, then turned and looked at me in that way she had that conveyed both irritation and concern.

"Where have you been, Ty? I was beginning to get worried."

"Didn't you get the note I left for you?"

"Yes, but it didn't say where you were going or when you'd be back."

"Because I didn't know."

"You went out to cut a cord of firewood," she said. "Next thing I know, you're MIA."

I debated skipping past some of the more unpleasant details of my afternoon, but that's not how Jesse and I operated. Not anymore. Not after twentysomething years together. I told her about Tommy Jenkins and the fallen eagle, about meeting Ian Swann at the resort recording studio. I filled her in on Jordan Powell's progress with his physical rehabilitation, and that I had invited him to come back to the ranch and ride the fences with me.

She listened with a stoicism she had learned from hard experience and a streak of unwavering faith in me that humbled me to the core. But something in her subdued manner after having heard my story made me feel as though I had dragged something unclean into our home.

WE BROUGHT a quart of ice cream outside to the gallery, sat together on the glider, and shared it as we watched the cottonwoods perform their nightly dance, like a million butterflies descending on their limbs. This time of year, the days grow longer, dawn breaks early, and the sunsets linger long into the night.

The evening air was cool, the darkness folding softly, silently; no birdsong, no fanfare, no color. It felt like benediction. Or perhaps an elegy. I saw Jesse's fingers drumming the seat between us, and I gently held her hand in mine, the way I would an injured bird.

"So many changes, Ty," she breathed. "It's everywhere. I can feel it."

"It's springtime, Jesse."

"It's more than that."

I waited, watched a pair of brown myotis bats describing aimless patterns in the pale night sky.

"I know it," I admitted. "I feel it, too."

She turned and studied me in profile.

"I know you do, Tyler," she said. "I can hear you in your sleep."

INTERLUDE I

(1964)

HEATHER LOMAX SAT by herself at the top row of the bleachers, a small stack of textbooks on the bench beside her. The last of the summer's sunshine had soaked into the wood and felt warm on her thighs through the cotton pedal pushers she was wearing. She stretched her legs, crossed her ankles, and tipped her face toward the sky. The sound of rock and roll blared out from car radios in the high school parking lot behind her, while coaches wearing flattop haircuts shouted curses at their teenaged charges and the smell of fresh-cut grass and sweat drifted across the breeze.

She felt the eyes of someone on her, and she opened hers. She had been blessed with a lithe and lissome body to live in, but she had not yet grown accustomed to the lingering stares of men, the ones that seemed to have begun about the time she entered puberty. Her coiffed hair was the color of harvest-ready wheat and grew nearly to her shoulders, pulled back off her tan forehead by a fabric headband the same shade of violet as the scarf she wore around her neck. Heather had cheekbones like her mother's, though she only knew that from the framed photos on the wall along the staircase in her house and the ones her father had set out along the mantel.

When Heather opened her eyes, she discovered that the gaze she'd felt on her before belonged to her classmate, Paul Swanson. She smiled back at him as he clapped the shoulder of one of his baseball buddies and began to climb the stairs toward her. Heather felt her heart beat faster and a rush of heat inside her ears.

Some people mistook Paul for a troublemaker or a hipster, but that was because they didn't know him, and because he wore his hair in the Arthur cut made recently popular by the Beatles. He drove a hard-used 1958 Chevrolet Brookwood station wagon whose blue factory-applied paint job had gone powdery and faded from neglect, the quarter panels and undercarriage pocked by rust and eroded by salt, but he didn't seem to mind. Like Heather, he was only fourteen years old, but he'd qualified for a hardship driver's license owing to the fact he worked on his family's hog and chicken farm a good half hour out of town.

"Have you given any thought about the homecoming dance this Friday night?" Heather asked.

Paul took a seat one row below her, brushed the hair out of his eyes, and smiled up at her. God, she loved his smile, and the dimple on his right cheek when he grinned that way.

"Are freshmen even allowed to go?" Paul asked, and his focus slid away. She knew that wasn't what was troubling him. The real trouble was money. It seemed to Heather that everything was always about money anymore.

"To heck with the rules," she said and shrugged. Heather had lately come to expect for things to go her way, the natural order, like the seasons. Not only was she smart, young, and attractive, her daddy was becoming a successful building contractor, making a big name for himself in Meriwether County. Some of her friends insisted she was rich, but when she asked her daddy, he just waved it away and said they'd merely been lucky. But Heather thought *luck* was a strange word for him to use, considering the frequent moves, the changing schools, and her daddy's odd work hours. Add the loss of her young mother to an aggressive onset of cancer, and the word *luck* seemed ridiculous.

"Anyway, cheerleaders get dance tickets for free, you know," she said.

"Even freshmen?"

She looked at him sidelong then broke into a grin.

"Yes," she said. "Even lowly freshmen are considered part of the Pep Squad."

"I didn't mean—"

"I know, I'm just teasing you," she said. "Anyway, you have to take me."

Paul showed her the grin and dimple she so adored.

"Is that so?"

"Yes, it is. I already told Daddy that you were coming to our house for dinner Wednesday night so he can meet you."

Paul's complexion colored and he looked off toward the parking lot and the knot of senior boys clustered around a bright red GTO, a gout of silver smoke belching from the tailpipe as the driver revved its engine.

"Say you'll come to dinner," Heather persisted. "Daddy will flip his wig if you don't. He'll never let me go out with you if you don't meet him first."

"He probably won't let you go out with me anyway. Especially after he meets me."

She read the distress in his expression, though he was trying to conceal it. She knew deep down inside that he might well be right. Paul was a good, hardworking boy, in spite of how he looked. Heck, Daddy even told her that he was acquainted with Paul's father—used to employ him as a tradesman for a while. Still, Heather was only fourteen, had never been kissed, and Paul was not the model boyfriend Daddy ever would have chosen for her.

God, why did adults have to make everything so complicated?

PAUL ARRIVED five minutes late that night, a fact not lost on Heather's father. She moved toward the door to greet Paul, but her father headed her off.

"I've got this," he said. "You can finish in the kitchen while I say hello to your friend."

The air inside the house was warm, rich with the aromas of baked chicken and some kind of vegetable Paul could not iden- tify, as Heather's dad opened the door and ushered him into the foyer. Paul offered his hand first, just as Heather had coached him to do, and endured a handshake he was sure was meant to cause him pain.

Her father was of average height, substantial through the chest and thighs, the kind of man who, despite his average build, seemed larger than he was and openly antagonistic and indif- ferent to the estimations of others. His hair was a lifeless blend of brown and gray, though precisely barbered, and his face was square and lean and deeply lined by life in the outdoors. Paul felt the intensity of the man's focus as he took Paul's stock; his irises appeared hazel in the light from the transom, though the whites appeared yellow and threaded with tiny veins.

They shared several awkward moments of small talk before the man finally called out to his daughter and they took their seats at a table in the dining room that had already been set for dinner. Paul had never felt so discomforted and scrutinized in his entire life, enduring a conversation that felt far more like an employment interview than a family meal. It wasn't until Heather brought a freshly baked peach pie in from the kitchen that her father finally changed the subject from Paul's upbringing and his life's goals, and he felt a stream of sweat roll down his spine.

Heather used a silver spatula to serve dessert while her father poured another cocktail for himself from a decanter on a bar shaped like a giant globe tucked into the corner of the room. She met Paul's gaze while her father's back was turned and rolled her eyes, and Paul stifled a relieved grin.

"I know your dad," Heather's father said, still hunched over the bar cart.

"I didn't know that, sir," Paul said, unsure whether he should admit that Heather had already told him.

Heather's father turned and rambled back to his place at the head of the table.

"He can be a little belligerent, can't he? Your dad."

Paul thought that was a somewhat aggressive thing to say, only then taking notice that the man's complexion had been gradually taking on a ruddy hue, his yellow eyes grown moist.

"Yes," Paul said, trying with everything he had to be agreeable. "I suppose he can be pushy sometimes, sir."

"He worked for me for a short while after your family first moved here."

Paul sensed the man's eyes on him again, but this time the evaluation felt openly invasive. It felt to Paul as if an overlay of onion skin had been laid across his visage, a line-by-line comparison to his father, suffering the scrutiny of a man seeking to identify and catalogue the flaws he found.

"I had to fire him," Heather's father said. "Did you know that?"

"Daddy—" Heather said, and Paul felt the heat rise up his neck into his face, felt his ears grow red, certain they were glowing with his shame.

More and more, Paul recognized the similarities between

Mr. Lomax and Paul's own father, men who bore grudges like badges of honor, keeping them fresh, tended like a garden. The more Paul listened to Heather's father speak, it was unmistakable that both he and Heather were living in the shadows of cynical and deeply unhappy widowers, who themselves had been reared in joyless, authoritarian households. To make matters worse, both Paul and Heather had lost their mothers at such early ages, it left a void in their young lives that was impossible to quantify, replace, or even define.

A longcase clock began to chime from somewhere down the hall, and Heather used the distraction to make a break.

"Daddy," she said, "I know Paul has to work before school in the morning. Do you mind if we have a few moments to ourselves before he has to leave?"

For his part, it seemed her father had lost his train of thought and appeared more interested in the contents of his crystal tumbler than in finishing his dialogue with Paul.

"You two can sit out on the porch," Mr. Lomax said. "But I'm keeping the light on, you understand?"

"Yes, sir," Paul answered, as the question seemed to have been directed at him.

"You keep your hands to yourself," he continued, and Heather averted her eyes in embarrassment. "You lay a hand on my daughter or try anything unwholesome, I will peel the bark off you. Believe it."

IT WAS the kind of night when the full moon cast a shadow, and the crickets were still chirping from somewhere in the landscaping, even though the season was on the verge of turning. Nearby, someone had lit a fire in a fireplace, and the atmosphere was laced with the fragrance of applewood, the air threaded with smoke.

"Thank you for being polite with my father," Heather said. "He can be a bully sometimes."

"Yeah, well, I've got one just like him at my house."

They were seated in separate rocking chairs on the front porch, neither of them courageous enough to have suggested sitting together on the glider. Paul looked at Heather and she smiled, but somehow it made her look sad and maybe somewhat fearful.

"Sometimes he drinks and he gets like this," she said. "I'm sorry about what he said about your dad."

"He's not completely wrong."

"I wish you didn't have to leave," she said, glancing at Paul's car parked in the driveway and the road beyond that twisted off into the dark.

"Me too," he said, unable to characterize the meaning behind the expression on her face. "Are you okay?"

"I'll be fine," she said. "Nights like this, I just try to stay out of his way."

A blue reflection from the TV newscast flickered on the living room window, and an eclipse of gypsy moths converged on the porch light. Paul folded his hands into the gap between his knees and looked at Heather in silence, with no idea at all as to how he should reply.

CHAPTER FOUR

SUNDAY MORNING CAME down cold, a film of frost framing the windowpanes, my breath like clouds of steam, and the change in barometric pressure in my ears suggesting the possibility of rain.

I stepped into the kitchen for a cup of coffee, where Jesse stood at the bay window slicing potatoes on a mandoline. A set of casserole dishes was arrayed along the countertop beside a basket of fresh peaches and an unopened box of brown sugar.

"We're having supper with Snoose Corcoran and Tommy after church this afternoon," she said.

"Sweet Jesus."

"Indeed."

BY THE TIME we returned home from church, the clear morning chill had given over to an ash-colored sky, the atmosphere turned close and torpid. A vague odor of ozone infused the air, and gauzy silver clouds slid like listless ripples on the slipstream.

In the corral below, I saw Caleb Wheeler doing groundwork with one of the new rough stock mustangs. Caleb stood at the center of the paddock, controlling the animal with a pair of long reins twenty feet in length, as it trotted out obedient circular orbits around him. Jesse went into the bedroom to change clothes so she could finish preparing her peach cobbler, and I walked down the path to speak with Caleb.

"How's the Lord today?" my foreman asked over his shoulder as I stepped up to the enclosure.

"He misses you."

"He knows where to find me."

The horse's ears pitched forward, but it maintained its pace, and Caleb's eyes remained firmly focused on the horse.

"Fine-looking animal," I said. "Looks like it's got a nice, smooth gait."

"Yep, he's coming around right smartly. Can't say the same about the other'n."

We'd purchased two wild mustangs at auction a month earlier. It was always a crapshoot as to how they would take to the saddle. But when you got a good one, it usually proved worth the gamble.

"The kid come back this morning?" I asked.

"What kid?"

Caleb slowed the horse to a walk, then deliberately stepped toward it and released it from the bridle. The animal snorted once, shook its head vigorously, and trotted off into the shade to join its companion.

"The kid you ran off yesterday," I said. "The one with the Peterbilt cap."

"He sure as hell did come back. Knocked on my door at seven this morning."

"And?"

"I put him through his paces. Turns out he ain't a bad kid. He'll do."

"You hired him?"

46

"He's getting settled in the bunkhouse as we speak."

Which meant we now had a full crew, and as of zero dark thirty tomorrow morning, the ranch would come alive with shouting and cursing and the smell of branded cowhide, fresh-cut hay, and dust. Truth be told, it was one of my favorite times of year.

I told Caleb that Jesse and I were headed to Snoose Corcoran's for supper in a little while and invited him to join us.

"Oh, hell no," he said. "You know I ain't got no patience for that man."

"Snoose just needs a little elbow room to get him through whatever this rough patch is he's going through."

"Don't seem like just a 'patch' to me. Seems like a whole goddamn wilderness he's been stumbling through."

"He's got a drinking problem, Caleb."

"Drinking ain't his problem. He's got a stopping problem is what he's got."

"Come along with us, Caleb," I said. "You don't want to disappoint Jesse."

"Not a chance, pardner. I'd rather take my chances making Jesse unhappy. But thanks to you both just the same."

IT HAD BEEN a long while since the last time Jesse and I had loaded the back of the Bronco with her homemade casseroles and cobbler and shared a table with Snoose Corcoran. Back before his father, Eli, had died, we'd had a standing monthly custom of dining with the old man and his cuckolded son, Snoose.

Snoose's given name was Denman Corcoran, but he'd earned a reputation for uncompromising laziness early in his life. Rarely within earshot when hard work needed to be done, he was frequently discovered in the feed loft, sleeping or simply hiding out when the chores were being divvied. The hired hands had taken to calling him "Snoozer," but over time, it devolved into "Snoose," which had become his handle ever since. I don't believe there could be more than a half-dozen people in the entire county who could accurately relate the name printed on Snoose Corcoran's official birth certificate.

The simplest way to get to the Corcoran ranch was on horseback, using the narrow horse trail that ran the length of the fence that marked off the edge of the BLM acreage and led directly to the Corcorans' postern. But that trail was too narrow to accommodate motor vehicles, so we took the longer route, over a road designed for use by farm equipment, which had been carved out of the clay soil and packed with gravel and caliche.

Jesse rolled down the passenger window, her expression serene as she studied the passing landscape, hair blowing freely around her face. The air smelled of forsythia and juniper berries, and the sky had blanched to a dull gunmetal gray.

We rumbled across the cattle guard and through the entrance of the Corcoran property, a simple pipe-rail gate they'd left unlocked for us, its chain dangling loose from the bolt hook and rattling against the post.

As we drew near the house, we saw bales of last year's hay that had been stacked in loose piles beneath a ragged tarpaulin and had been melted by the weather. A pair of piebald goats balanced themselves on a heap of apple crates, a third one atop an ancient hand-cranked laundry tub that was seamed with rust. The yawning gaze of an abandoned feed shed that Eli and Snoose had built a decade ago had caved in on itself, and the cistern next to it was green with stagnant water. I hadn't been here in more than a year, and I was sickened to see that the Corcorans' property, and nearly all that stood upon it, including the livestock, had fallen into shambles.

We parked beside the walnut tree Eli had planted near the house, where Snoose and Tom Jenkins now sat in handmade rocking chairs at opposite corners of the open porch. As I helped Jesse out of the Bronco and gathered the casserole dishes and freshly cut garden flowers from the back of the truck, she shot a glance at me that told me she was as alarmed as I was at the condition of the place.

We stepped into a grassless yard sliced by the shadows of a picket fence, the gate hanging precariously from a single hinge. Old Eli had built the house with his own hands, adding to it as his family grew, constructing it of river rock and heavy timber he'd harvested from his land. But it, too, had fallen to decrepitude, a once-contented home gilded in disrepair and melancholy.

Tom Jenkins stood and greeted us at the top of the sagging stairs. He looked freshly showered and shaved, in pressed blue jeans and plaid shirt, wearing the polished silver rodeo buckle he'd won when he'd worked at my ranch. Tom was hatless, his hair slicked with pomade, and he smelled like he might have even splashed on some cologne. He relieved Jesse of the things she carried and led her inside the house, while I remained out on the porch where Snoose sat licking the adhesive strip on a hand-rolled cigarette.

"Evening, Snoose" I said.

He acknowledged me with a wordless nod as he completed his task.

He was wearing half-top work boots, denim overalls, and a straw cowboy hat with a hole in the crown. His once-angular face had gone puffy and soft, the sun-darkened complexion of his Black Irish ancestors crisscrossed with the deep lines carved by sixty-five years of hard living and abuse.

Something had crawled under the house and died some time ago, the lingering smell of desiccation in the air, though Snoose didn't appear to notice. The whole place was a shrine to his despondency, suspended in the atmosphere like cobwebs.

WE ATE INDOORS, near the window at a table that I had no doubt had been set by Tom. As inexpert and untrained as the young man was, Jesse and I were touched by Tom's attempt at hospitality. I watched my wife's eyes grow moist as he put Jesse's flowers in a juice pitcher he'd filled with water, and placed them at the center of the table.

During dinner, Snoose remained unusually quiet, his eyes a road map of tiny veins, rheumy and focused somewhere far away and known only to him. His tone and conversation were cordial, but with content of no consequence. At times, I thought I saw his lips moving in such a way that he was either speaking to himself or to a visitor no one else could see.

I helped Tom clear the dishes afterward and stacked them in the sink. As we returned, Snoose made a vague gesture in the direction of the porch and said he wanted to have a private word with me. I didn't like that he was excluding Tom, and I said so.

"This place is as much Tom's as it is yours now, Snoose," I said. "And I don't reckon there's much that goes on around here that he doesn't have his hands on."

Jesse turned away toward the window, not wishing to share further in Snoose's discomfiture, but I could see the smile of understanding on her face in the reflection.

I held the door open for Jesse, but she shook her head and remained inside the house. Tom, Snoose, and I moved out to the porch, the smoke from a slash fire lacing the wind. I propped a hip against the banister and watched Snoose fidget as Tom retook his place in one of the rocking chairs that Snoose's daddy had crafted. Tom glanced at me, looking like a man who was prepared for anything, his uncle's growing unpredictability having become the single unwavering reality of his life.

Snoose remained standing as he leaned his back against the wall near the door to the house, his eyes lighting on everything but my face.

"I've been thinking on it," he said finally. "And I think it's time to sell this place, Dawson. It's just too much for me and Tommy to manage on our own."

Except for Tom's unaided attempts at maintaining appearances, this entire evening had been an exercise in slow-motion resignation and retreat. I had reached my limit of seeing good resources wasted, lost my patience with Snoose's weak and lazy self-indulgence. Our two families had a long history as neighbors on this land, but it had been a decidedly lopsided one for most of it.

"I want to sell it to *you*, Ty," Snoose announced.

I remained silent, not trusting myself with a reply.

The Dawson and Corcoran family histories had been entwined since 1899, a few short years after my grandfather had planted his first stakes in Meriwether County. Old Eli Corcoran, Snoose's father, had shown up from somewhere out in east Wyoming, starting with a few hundred acres that shared a boundary with the Diamond D.

Eli and my grandfather became affable competitors, sharing a mutual respect for each other as well as the land under their care. And as the years went on, both men married good strong women, raised families, and worked their properties with the tirelessness of much younger men. But the Great War came and claimed the older of Eli Corcoran's two sons, blown to pieces somewhere in the Argonne Forest. Blinded by despair and grief, Eli missed the economic boom when the war came to an end, and he was unprepared again when the Depression hit in '29.

My grandfather proved his friendship with Eli by purchasing small parcels of land from him from time to time—parcels my grandfather had no need or use for—so as to provide the Corcoran family enough cash to keep going. Eli continued to work his shrinking holdings with the help of his only remaining son, Denman. But by the time World War II broke out, they were down to their last hundred acres—acreage they'd barely clung to ever since.

"Did you hear what I said to you, Dawson?"

Snoose appeared irritated by my silence.

"We can't do it no more," he repeated. "I'm afraid we might lose everything if we don't get out now."

"Did you know about this, Tom?" I asked finally. "Did you know he was going to tell me this?"

"First I'm hearing of it," he admitted, his tone revealing more hurt than surprise.

"Do you feel the same way, Tom?" I asked him. "You want to hightail it?"

"No, sir," he said. "It's like you taught me, Mr. Dawson: there's no room for fear in the rodeo, 'cause that's when you get hurt. I think the same thing goes for cattle ranching."

"Well, that may be, but it ain't the boy's decision," Snoose said.

"His name's on the deed," I reminded Snoose. "You cut him in for half when he agreed to stay on here with you."

"I'll sell you my half, then, Dawson."

"The hell you will," I said. "Tommy might hold only half of the ranch, but he damn sure does both halves of the work."

Snoose's face went red, eyes shining with tears of indignation.

"What about me? What am I supposed to do?" Snoose said. "It ain't fair. I gave it to him."

"That young man earned every inch of what you gave him," I said finally. "I don't want to buy you out, but here's what

I *will* do. I'll cover your costs for the season, provided Tom keeps running the show. Tom, you can throw in with my crew if you want to, and we can work both herds together. When we go to market, I get my expenses back first, and after that, you keep one hundred percent of whatever you get for your cows. Fair deal?"

Snoose started to say something, but Tom interrupted. He jumped to his feet and shook my hand.

"It's more than fair, sir," Tom said. "And I am obliged. I will not let you down, you have my word."

"That's all I need from you, son."

"And what about me?" Snoose asked again.

"You get the privilege of holding on to your ranch for another year, while Tommy and I take all the risk and do all the work."

"That's not—" Snoose began, but I cut him off before he said something that crossed a line.

"If I were you, Snoose, I would reacquaint myself with ranch labor and stop feeling sorry for yourself. Put down the goddamn bottle and lend a hand to this young man and help him keep what's left of what your family built."

THERE WERE FLICKERS of dry lightning in the clouds as Jesse and I drove home that night. I held her hand as the sky silently raged, and neither of us spoke a word.

CHAPTER FIVE

THE STREETS of Meridian had been washed clean by early morning rain, the wind still raw in the aftermath of the downpour, rich with the stannic scent of damp pavement.

I stopped to check on Jordan Powell at the substation on my way to meet my daughter's train. Cricket was coming home to visit for her spring break.

Powell was seated at his desk, his bootheels resting on a cardboard file box on the floor beside him. He acknowledged me as I came in and slipped out of my coat, his telephone receiver wedged between his shoulder and his ear. Powell was listening intently, scratching notes from time to time on a yellow pad as I poured myself a cup of coffee. I heard him recite the phone number dedicated to our new telefacsimile machine then offer a businesslike farewell to whomever he was speaking with and set down the receiver.

"You're in the office early," I said.

Powell ignored my comment and reached for a half-eaten jelly doughnut that was leaking purple juice onto a soggy napkin, took a bite, and tossed it in the trash.

"That was the Cattlemen's Association on the line," Powell said. "They're going to wire me a list of members. Figure there's a chance that somebody's got a whirlybird or knows someone who does."

"Good move, Jordan," I said. "You might want to do the same with the OSGA."

Oregon Sheep Growers Association. Powell tapped the yellow pad with his pencil eraser.

"Way ahead of you, Cap. I've got their number wrote down right here. They're my next call."

"What're you going to do once you get the lists?"

"Smile and dial, Sheriff."

Powell's tone and demeanor had improved noticeably since I'd last seen him on Saturday. I hoped he wasn't placing too much faith in his own physical progress, or too much hope in how well he'd be able to sit a horse when I took him back out to the Diamond D.

"May I offer a suggestion?" I asked.

"Yes, sir."

"You know the Bell Sioux has a range of about two hundred fifty miles," I began. "I suggest you take a map and locate Half Mountain—the point where the Knife River makes its sharp bend to the south—put it at the center of your grid and draw a circle the diameter of the chopper's range. Any names you get from your association lists that fall within that circle should be your first-priority phone calls."

"Makes sense."

"If you strike out with the first group, move your grid outward using that same distance interval, larger and larger concentric circles with Half Mountain in the center. You follow me?"

"Yes, sir."

"If the pilot leapfrogged his way into the canyon, it's likely he'd choose his friends' ranches to refuel."

"How far out do you want me to search?"

"Until you bump into Idaho or California," I said. "Then go a little further."

He nodded and picked up the receiver as I tossed back the dregs of my coffee and stood up to leave.

"Where you off to, Sheriff, if you don't mind my asking?"

"Going to pick up my daughter from the train and take her to Rowan Boyle's diner for a little father-daughter catch-up."

"Say 'howdy' to her for me, sir."

"Roger that, Jordan."

THE AMTRAK pulled in about half an hour late. I was standing in a patch of sunlight at the edge of the platform, the sound of the airhorn in the distance dopplering closer until I finally heard the crossbuck bells and saw the boom barrier swing down to block the road.

I spotted Cricket's face pressed against the window glass, her hands like twin parentheses shielding the sun glare. She smiled and waved when she spotted me—the way she had when she was just a girl—fully alive and unembarrassed by her spontaneous display of affection. I was struck again by the ephemerality of youth and felt as though a fist had taken hold of my heart and squeezed with all its might.

Cricket jumped down from the doorway onto the station platform with a backpack slung across one shoulder and carrying a canvas duffel bag she'd decorated with stickers of multicolored flowers. She dropped her luggage to the ground, stepped inside my open arms, and hugged me tightly. It was the kind of greeting I had no reason to expect, especially given the capricious and mercurial, often political, exchanges I had stumbled into since she'd gone off to college.

I drove her to Rowan Boyle's diner in Meridian, ate breakfast at the counter while she told me about her trip, her studies, and her renewed interest in American history. When we had finished, I paid the check at the register and returned to collect Cricket, leaving a tip tucked underneath the saltshaker. We had almost reached my truck, which I had parked along the curb, when I heard a voice call out to me from across the street.

Two men were standing on the sidewalk near the front door of the Cottonwood Blossom. A third man was still unfolding himself from the back seat of an electric blue Mustang Cobra with California tags that looked like it had magically appeared there from the showroom floor. I recognized all three of the men from my visit to Half Mountain Studio.

Len Kaanan gestured broadly to me and called out my name a second time, Ian Swann grinning beside him as he watched Mickey London trying to extricate himself from the car's rear seat, slamming the door behind him.

"Sheriff Dawson!"

Cricket gaped at the three men waiting across the street, then turned to me, her expression one of incredulity.

"Do you know who that is?" she whispered to me. "Oh my god. You *know* him?"

"Wait here," I said. "I'll be right back."

I was nearly halfway across the street when I heard Cricket racing up to join me. I shot her a disapproving look, but she ignored it and finger combed her long blonde hair as we joined the three out-of-towners at the curb.

"We were just headed inside for a bite," the record producer said. "Come join us. You can bring your friend."

"This is my daughter, Cricket," I said. "And we just ate. But I thank you just the same."

I could see my daughter's eyes lock onto Ian Swann. He was dressed in the same fashion as when I'd seen him at the studio before, in denim jeans and western shirt, his long chestnut hair framing his face, tossed by the brisk morning breeze. He wore a silver cuff bracelet on his wrist, adorned with turquoise stones that matched the color of his irises, the images of tribal firebirds etched into the metal.

"Don't be rude, Dad," she said.

"Yeah, Dad." Ian's eyes danced playfully, mimicking my daughter as he smiled. "Don't be rude. I'm Ian, by the way."

Cricket's ears turned red as radishes as Ian reached out and touched her hand.

"We really should be getting home," I said. "Cricket's mother is waiting—"

"I'm sure they don't want to hear about that," Cricket interrupted, and she pinched me discreetly, but vigorously, on the fleshy inside of my arm. "Mom'll be just fine."

"I suppose we can spare a few minutes," I complied, and shook my daughter's fingers loose.

I held open the door and followed the four of them inside. Mickey London still had not uttered a word.

I LED the way toward a corner booth in the back with a semi-circular table, in a room that was about half full of patrons. Lankard Downing, the septuagenarian owner of the place, knelt behind the empty bar restocking the beer cooler with longneck bottles. He looked up as we filed past, acknowledging me with a brief, familiar nod before returning to his work.

As was my habit, I took a position at the open end of the table, my back to the wall and my eyes on the entry door. Cricket wedged herself between me and Ian Swann, while Len Kaanan and Mickey London surveyed the other customers as though they were museum exhibits. London leaned in and whispered something to the producer, but I couldn't make it out. They both laughed. A young couple seated near the bar kept staring at our booth.

"Here it comes," London announced to no one in particular.

The young woman who had been staring at us stood, crossed the room, and stepped up to the edge of our table with a napkin and a ballpoint pen in hand. She wore tight hip-hugger jeans and a paisley halter top and stared at Ian Swann like no one else was there. When Ian smiled at her, she beamed in return, cocked a hip, and slid the pen and paper across the table to him.

"Do you mind?" she asked. "I don't mean to bother you."

"It's cool," he said, "I don't mind," and he autographed her napkin, embellishing it with an ornate paraph.

"I'm a huge fan," she said. "So's my boyfriend. He's sitting over there."

"Yeah," Ian said and flashed the guy a peace sign. "I see him."

She waited there expectantly, for what, I didn't know, shifting her weight from one foot to the other.

"Well, I guess I'd better get back to my boyfriend," she said at last.

"Yes, you probably should," Mickey London said, his tone dripping with disdain and contempt.

"Thanks for the . . ." She waved the signed napkin in the air as she turned away.

"Autograph," Ian supplied. "You're welcome."

London made a clucking sound, shook his head, and focused on his menu.

The young woman returned to her table, leaned close to her male companion, and whispered something that caused the young man's face to darken. I had met my wife while I was working as a wrangler for a Hollywood film studio, still raw from having recently returned from Korea and feeling like an outsider in my own country. Jesse was a location scout and production assistant, smart and competent, and entirely out of my league. But she was also beautiful and seemed unfazed by the perceived glamor of the movie business; she likewise was unvexed by my misfit presence in it. Her gentle patience had ushered me back from a war that still remained inside my skin, and when we fell in love, we fell forever.

It had been decades since I had been in close proximity to the demands of the entertainment world, and I was reminded that the public image that Ian Swann occupied was not really his own, living every day inside a mist of whispers.

"This isn't going to become a problem, is it?" I asked.

Len Kaanan cocked his head; his puzzlement seemed feigned and slightly mocking.

"What do you mean?" Kaanan asked.

"The sheriff's worried about drugs, sex, and rock and roll," London answered without looking up from his menu.

"All right—" I said and waited until I had both Kaanan's and London's attention.

"Here we go," London said, casting his gaze around the room.

"I'm the sheriff in this county, gentlemen," I said. "They pay me to worry about everything that happens here. But that's not what I was referring to."

"What *are* you referring to?" Kaanan asked.

Cricket cast a concerned glance at Ian Swann, but Swann's attention was locked on me, something in his eyes hinting at mischief.

"I'm worried about cultures clashing, Mr. London," I said. "Meridian is a very small town. As is Lewiston, at the other end of this valley. In fact, all the towns in this part of the state are small, provincial, and a little bit old-fashioned."

"That's exactly why I built the studio all the way out here," Len Kaanan said, as if he'd won something. "It's a universe apart from Manhattan or Los Angeles."

"My point exactly, Mr. Kaanan," I said. "In my experience,

people can sometimes behave strangely when worlds collide. Jealous. Confrontational. Even violent."

"I don't court trouble any more than you do, Sheriff Dawson."

"I'll take you at your word."

"It's like the man just said, Sheriff," Mickey London added. "We're only here to do our work. We won't bite."

London's air of world-weary cynicism floated like a condescending cloud over our table. To Ian Swann's credit, London's tone appeared to irritate him nearly as much as it had irritated me.

"As I mentioned to you before, Mr. London," I said, "I am the law in Meriwether County. I didn't want the job, but the people who live here trust me to do it."

"Meaning what, exactly?"

London's manner was growing more belligerent, a baseline that I took to be the man's default setting.

"Let me state this plainly for you," I said. "Since we appear to be speaking different languages. What I am saying is that I assume everybody bites until they prove otherwise. You and your entourage are no exception. Am I making myself any clearer for you?"

"We won't be a problem, sir," Ian Swann said. "I like it here."

I could see that Cricket's hands had curled into tiny balls, and her nails dug in to the flesh of her own palms. I saw the tension leach from her expression, though, as Lankard Downing appeared beside our table with a notepad and pencil in hand.

I ordered a cup of coffee and looked past Downing's shoulder at a group of four men entering the bar. They were dressed for outdoor work, blue-collar men whose skin had been burnished like copper, the muscles of their arms and V-shaped backs straining their shirt seams. They appeared to be a loose confederation born out of necessity, and I took them to be sundowners, or rail runners on the move. The oldest-looking of the lot had a round face, and a nose that had been broken at least once, and a distinctly passive demeanor that bordered on invisibility. His eyes were deep-set, hidden by the folds of lids that made him appear half asleep or lost inside of thoughts that only he could see. He had close-cropped hair going to gray along the temples, sideburns sculpted to a point that ran along his jawline and the yellow stains of nicotine between his fingers. The youngest two took seats along the rail and looked around the place, somehow transfixed and jaded at the same time, the story of their lives already written on their vacant faces. The alpha character among them remained standing, blinking as his eyes adjusted to the dimness of the room. He crossed his arms, his expression empty, black jailhouse ink scrolled across his hands and forearms, a man you wouldn't choose to meet a second time. He leaned his back against the bar and scanned the tables one by one until his focus came to rest on ours.

The four newcomers ordered beers from Lankard when he returned to his station behind the stick, and the men took turns making comments to one another as they studied Swann, London, and Kaanan consuming their breakfasts. The men were just starting in on their third round of beers by the time Kaanan paid our tab and we all stood and headed for the door. I waited for my tablemates to move out to the sidewalk so I could have a private word with the new visitors. When the door swung shut behind the rock star and his friends outside, I turned to face the strangers still seated along the bar inside.

I pulled the corner of my coat aside to reveal the badge clipped to my pistol belt and stepped in close to the man with the tattoos, the man who seemed to be in charge. His appearance and demeanor were nearly saurian, his irises the color of something you'd find at the bottom of a wastewater pond.

"You don't want to act on any of the things you're thinking

right now," I said. "In fact, I'd strongly recommend you move on up the road."

The corner of his mouth twitched, but he never took his eyes off my face. Now that I was closer, I could sense that I had been correct about these men. There is a peculiar odor unique to trains and railroad sidings, the tart sharpness of creosote and pine tar, engine oil, grease, and diesel fuel exhaust. All of these had permeated the pores of these four and had collected in the folds of their unlaundered clothing.

"Trying to mad dog me won't work here in the wild," I said. "You're not stalking the yard anymore, chief. Pay the man behind the counter and take your bullshit somewhere else. Hop the next highliner out of here. All four of you. We don't need whatever it is you're selling. Have a nice day."

I stepped out into the sunlight where Cricket, Ian, and Len Kaanan were standing on the sidewalk beside Ian Swann's blue Mustang. Mickey London was hunched over a pay phone on the corner, pumping dimes into the slot. My daughter looked at me with an expression of humiliation and shame, and I didn't understand its cause. When I moved closer to the vehicle, I saw the reason for her reaction.

While we'd all been inside having our breakfasts, someone had snapped off Swann's car radio antennae and used it to carve profanities into the gleaming blue paint job and smear feces across his windshield and door handles.

Halfway down the block, I heard the Blossom's front door slam open, watched the four men from the bar file out in single file, like a chow line in the joint, or a mess tent near the front lines somewhere far downrange. I drew another reckoning from the history I detected in their faces and believed I could see their future written there as well.

* * *

"YOU MUST have taken the long way home," Jesse said as we came inside the house. Cricket hugged her mom and took her belongings into her room, and I stayed behind to tell Jesse what had happened at the Cottonwood Blossom.

"What kind of person does a thing like that?"

"An angry person," I said. "An envious person. A crazy person."

"I don't want to believe we live in a place like that."

"We didn't used to, Jesse. But I think the circus has arrived in town."

I FELL ASLEEP with Jesse's breath against my neck, my mind brimming with images of fallen eagles and the specters of the lonely and the wounded and the lost. That night, I dreamt of a bleak and flattened wasteland five thousand miles from my family home, where the bilious scent of roasted flesh roiled across a frozen field of battle.

In my dream, my ears are ringing from a deafening concussion, dizzy as I retrieve the rifle that had slipped out of my hand when Chinese artillery lit up our position. My eyes feel like they're melting from the heat and smoke; I'm trying vainly to avoid trampling on the disembodied limbs of soldiers and the offal strewn like barnyard waste on steaming tundra, roasted by the chemical hell of Chinese flamethrowers or masticated by grenades. A mortar shell whistles overhead and I stagger and fall into a foxhole, saturating my fatigues in a pool of melted ice and blood and human filth.

I lay shivering, and a familiar thought invades my mind again. Inside the sustained roar of automatic weapons and field cannon, and the rush of blood inside my own ears, I do not feel that I have been singled out. I am simply trapped inside a nightmare war that politicians won't even bother to designate as one, breathless in their oratory and wet-eyed in their pontifications regarding democracy, but without a backward glance concerning those they send to die fighting the devastating wars they themselves initiated.

The far-off whumps of incoming artillery grow nearer. I am too exhausted to feel the terror I know I should feel, and I wonder again how long that final instant lasts. How long does it take for the light to leave one's eyes, or for that twenty-one grams of precious soul to float away?

And what happens if no one tells me when I'm dead?

CHAPTER SIX

I WAS UP before the sun on Tuesday morning and left Jesse snoring softly in our bed as I slipped out to the kitchen. I filled my speckled mug with coffee and took it outside to the porch, the morning air woven with the remnants of late winter chill. A mantle of fog floated above the creek that ran beyond the corral, and I could hear the calves lowing inside the mist.

The cowboys were already stirring in the bunkhouse, a warm yellow glow in the window frames and a narrow stream of smoke rising from the chimney stack. In a short while, the echoes of pounding hoofbeats, the sorting of livestock, and the odors of singed hide would permeate the atmosphere as the rising sun burned through the low ceiling of sky, and the Diamond D would come alive for the new season.

Yesterday's paper still lay folded on the old pine table, and against my better judgment, I picked it up and began reading. The headline story proclaimed that the much-feared resurgence of the 1918 flu virus was proving to be nonexistent, and President Ford's campaign for mass inoculations motivated solely by his reelection hopes. Even with the knowledge the entire panic had been a lie, it appeared neither the president's moral vacuity nor its inherent disingenuity was going to prevent Congress from passing emergency immunization legislation, the implementation of which was serving to confuse and terrify millions of Americans who neither wanted nor needed the damned shot in the first place.

Despite the ginned-up pandemic having failed to materialize, in the end, the real victims of the fiasco were proving to be unsuspecting and innocent citizens who were stricken with a rare neurological disorder determined to be a direct result of having taken the vaccine—as they'd been instructed to do—in the first place. Congressional lapel pins, political ambitions, and white lab coats had proved, yet again, to be a toxic combination. Corporate nihilism.

I folded the newspaper in half, went inside, and tossed it in the rubbish bin, regretting that I didn't have a birdcage.

I was on my third cup of coffee when Cricket came outside to join me on the gallery. She was still wearing her flannel pajamas, a Navajo blanket pulled tight around her shoulders, and cradling a steaming ceramic mug between her palms. She took a seat in the willow chair next to me and angled her face toward a rising sun that appeared slightly out of focus, like a ball of spun cotton glowing softly behind the retreating clouds.

"Smells like horse sweat and juniper out here," she said, her voice still thick from slumber. "Smells like home."

I watched a faint smile appear at the edges of her eyes as she looked at me across the rim of her cup.

Through the window I could see Jesse stirring inside the kitchen, and I was reminded how that woman had swept into my life, shaping it every bit as much as my history on this land and this ranch ever had. Her attitudes were well-defined from the moment I met her, holding fast to an affection for nature and its wildlife and a loathing for anyone who would mistreat or exploit either one of them.

She would hunt wild game with me to stock the smokehouse—a crack shot with both rifle and revolver—and mend a fallen bird's wing that same day and saw no contradiction. She held a permit to carry a concealed firearm, but rarely did so; could ride and rope with my finest cowhands, and break your heart when she got dressed up to go dancing. She was generous and fierce with her love, her loyalty never in question; passionate and opinionated, beautiful and bold.

I returned my attention to Cricket, her face aglow with the diffused sunlight, muted on the planes and angles of her face. While I recognized a few of the traits my daughter had inherited from me, it was clear she had grown to become Jesse's spiritual twin. Which, as her father, scared the hell out of me every single day of my life.

THE PHONE in the house rang at 8:00 a.m. sharp as I was preparing to head down to the corral to watch the new hands drive the first of the calves into the pen for branding, tagging, and castration. Training up a new crew was always a challenge, the bane of Caleb Wheeler's surly existence, but a fine thing to observe when it all came together. By the end of the season, I knew it would resemble nothing short of a ballet on horseback, though one with spitting, swearing, and bloodletting substituting for an orchestral score.

I picked up the telephone receiver and announced myself.

"Hope I'm not calling too early," the caller said.

"We're generally awake by first light around here, Mr. Kaanan," I said.

He hesitated for a moment, and in the background on his end I could hear the muffled noise of table conversation and the resonance of Ian Swann strumming an acoustic guitar.

"Why do I feel like we keep getting off on the wrong foot, Sheriff?"

"I don't know how to reply to that."

"I realize I'm the new guy in this valley," he said. "I understand that. And I understand what you were trying to tell me yesterday about cultures clashing—"

"We both saw what was done to Ian's car."

"Yes, and Ian has no intention to press charges, nor do we have any desire for you to waste your time on that matter. It was a pointless act of vandalism, plain and simple. People with high public profiles like Ian has . . . well, we've come to expect it. It goes with the territory."

"I appreciate the sentiment," I said. "But it happened on my street, where a room full of innocent people were sitting and trying to mind their own business. Surely, you understand my concerns."

"I want you to know I meant what I said before, Sheriff. I don't want any trouble, and I don't want to be the cause of any either. I mean that sincerely."

"And as *I* said before, Mr. Kaanan, I understand your point of view. Is there something else on your mind?"

Outside my kitchen window, I watched the bluebirds foraging sticks and straw and packing them into the bird box Jesse made for them.

"Actually, there is," Kaanan said. "I understand your wife is an experienced production assistant."

"Where did you hear that?" I asked, although I had a very good idea as to where that information had originated.

"I heard you were once in the military, Sheriff Dawson. You know the importance of quality recon."

I have never appreciated a vague answer to a direct question, so I let it sit there, waiting him out in silence.

"It's a small town," Kaanan offered at last.

"My advice is to take anything that Lankard Downing tells you with a grain of salt," I said. "That is the best advice I can offer any newcomer to Meridian."

"The cocktail and dining options are slim in Meriwether County. Plus, it turns out Mr. Downing has been a fountain of useful information to a man such as myself."

"Around here, we refer to that sort of chatter as 'gossip.'"

It was his turn to ignore my remark.

"You may have heard we're making a film of Ian's album as it's being recorded."

"I heard something like that."

"Then I will assume you've also heard that we intend to throw a little concert to kick it off, once we're finished," he added.

"I heard something about that as well."

"Truth is, Sheriff, I could benefit from a little local expertise, and I could really use the help of someone who is organized and familiar with the making of a film."

I leaned on the kitchen counter and looked outside, watched Jesse collect eggs from the nesting box in the coop and place them into a wicker basket dangling from the crook of her arm. She smiled when she caught me looking at her through the window, tucked a tuft of loose hair beneath her hat, and returned to her work.

"You want to hire my wife to assist you with your film production?" I asked.

"Yes, sir, I do."

I don't make Jesse's choices for her and never have. I would have liked to weigh in on this particular decision, but I knew I wouldn't bother trying. As much as I love and admire my wife's independence, it's the stubbornness I could do with a little less of. Nevertheless, you take the whole package when you exchange rings and vows, and that is a bargain we both live with.

"She's feeding the chickens at the moment," I said to Kaanan. "I'll leave her a note to call you back when she's finished."

* * *

I CALLED the substation to tell Jordan and Griffin I would be a couple hours later than usual coming to the office and set out for the horse barn instead. The early morning cloud cover had finally burned away, and fingers of steam rose from the roof as the sun warmed the damp shingles.

I saddled Drambuie, a bay Morgan gelding that had become my most trusted mount in the string. I fitted his bridle, checked the noseband and chinstrap, tightened the girth cinch, climbed up, and settled myself into the cantle. We passed through the barn doors and headed northward, the noise from the ranch growing more distant as I spurred him along the narrow game trail that wound through an old grove of larch and opened onto a field of tall grass cut by a wide, shallow stream. Some years ago, Caleb and I had constructed a footbridge made of stone and deadfall we had reclaimed from the wild as a shortcut for its crossing, the rush of high-country snowmelt flowing clear and cold beneath the freeboard. Boo's hooves clacked the weathered timbers as we crossed and made our way to the paddock I had repurposed as a target-shooting range.

Stacks of baled straw had been piled high along a cutbank, where my spent ordnance would be contained by the natural contour of the land and ricochets were a practical impossibility. Far from the working corrals and activity at the ranch, it was a place where I could expect a certain solitude when I needed to clear my head.

It was no secret in the valley that I was a dead shot—with both pistol and lever-action Winchester rifle—having won a handful of awards at fairs and equestrian exhibitions over the years. I even performed a few trick shots for the cameras back when I worked for the studios.

But that was a long time ago, and my attitudes with respect to gun-handling skills had adapted over the years, having learned to appreciate the considerable difference that a .45-caliber round makes on a human being as opposed to a paper target. And while I do not relish the notion of turning a live firearm on my fellow man, I don't intend to come in second place if the time comes.

I unsaddled Drambuie and allowed him to graze loose in the glade while I laid out my ammo boxes on a stump in the shade of a pair of black oaks. It took a few minutes to bind the targets and ready my weapons while I maintained an eye on my horse as he wandered off in the direction of the trough and feed crib. Drambuie and I had spent hours together, hazing recalcitrant steers from dense tangles of thornbush, bulldogging calves out on the open range, firing a gun at fixed targets inside an arena at a full gallop, and damn near everything else in between. My horse had learned to fear nothing when we were together, not even the reports from my rifle as they echoed inside the arroyo, and he had taught me to trust him the same way.

I was halfway through a third box of ammo when I heard the approach of hoofbeats as they crossed the old bridge. I slid my Peacemaker back into its holster and watched Caleb rein his palomino to a halt inside a patch of marbled sunshine underneath the trees.

"Didn't mean to sneak up on you," he said as he climbed down from his mount.

"You must've learned your sneaking skills inside a sawmill. I heard you coming from a half mile away."

With Spring Works underway, I knew that Caleb hadn't ridden all the way out here for a social visit, but he was also not a man to be hurried along once he got started. Whatever was on his mind would come out in due time, so I peeled off my holster and took a seat on the cut stump. I took a swig of spring water from a blanket canteen and passed it to Caleb.

"How's the crew working out?" I asked.

"They'll do," he said and passed the canteen back to me.

I watched his eyes scan the stacks of straw bales and the mound of spent copper that had piled along the firing line.

"What's all this about?" he asked, eyes squinting at the shredded targets I'd pinned to the bales. "County Fair ain't coming around for months yet. You figuring on getting back in the shooting contest?"

"Just staying sharp," I said. "You know what Wyatt Earp used to say: Fast is fine, but accuracy is final."

"I s'pose old Wyatt oughtta know."

Caleb crouched down on his haunches and tugged the long stem of a wild daisy from the damp earth. He examined the white flower for a protracted moment, the trees overhead alive with birdsong, tucked the culm between his teeth, and tasted the tart nectar. When he turned his attention back on me, I could tell that he was about to come to the point.

"You expecting trouble, Ty?" he asked.

"I'm always expecting trouble."

He cocked his head and studied my face.

"Maybe so," he said. "But this here has a different feel to it."

I saw no point in prevarication.

"It's only a notion, that's all," I said.

"What kind of a notion?"

Living in agrarian Meriwether County, Oregon, was more than a geographical preference. It was an outlook, a lifestyle, an attitude and commitment. The people who settled here were the pioneer survivors of long, deadly trails, wild animal charges, and the savage brutality of bushwhackers and highwaymen; these were the descendants of the Oregon Trail. Hardheaded, self-sufficient, and fiercely independent, they had a tendency to keep to themselves and expected others to do likewise.

"Something's troubling you, Ty," Caleb said. "Spill it."

"What kind of evil drives a man to hire a helicopter so he can shoot a baby eagle out of the sky?" I asked. "What kind of person does something like that?"

Caleb's eyes strayed to the distant hills, soft curves against the horizon, waves of golden mustard weed channeling with the breeze.

"Hunting endangered species is a federal offense, Tyler," Caleb said. "Want my advice? Just let them boys handle it."

I reached for the cigarettes I used to keep in my shirt pocket and remembered I was trying to quit.

"Not a chance," I said. "When the feds get involved, the politicians come right along behind 'em. A flash flood of unemployable morons. Every crisis becomes a fundraising mission, and everything is worse after they finally leave. I've already attended that shit show."

"That ain't all of it, though, is it?"

I'd known the old man since I had been a boy, and he knew me as well as he knew every inch of trail across this ranch, knew me as well as my own family, maybe better.

"You know Jesse and I ate dinner with Snoose Corcoran and Tom Jenkins the other night," I said.

"Yep. And I thank you for not involving me in it."

"Well, I told Tom he could throw his herd in with ours for the season."

"You did *what*?"

"Snoose has that look, Caleb. You know the look I'm talking about. Like he's run out of give-a-damn."

"Snoose Corcoran has always been as useless as a bag of hair, only not quite as smart. He ain't likely to come back from whatever it is he's killing himself about, you know, Ty. You ain't gonna save the man."

"Maybe not," I said. "But the kid deserves a chance."

"Tom Jenkins? I gotta admit he's got some rocks."

"He's not even twenty years old yet, and he's the only thing holding Snoose's place together."

The silence descended like a physical presence, enveloping both of us like a shadow.

"Anything else on your mind, Tyler?"

I turned and strapped on my holster, stepped into the sunlight, drew the Colt, and squeezed off several rounds. Caleb stood and watched, leaned a shoulder on the tree bark, and dropped the chewed-up daisy stem to the dirt between his boots. The smell of burned gunpowder stung my nostrils, and the elkhorn gun butt felt familiar in my grip. A silver cloud of spent propellant tore away on the breeze, the air threaded with the chemical smell of cordite. I thumbed the release tab and flipped open the cylinder, let the blistering shell casings fall to the ground, and the atmosphere seemed to shrink upon itself again.

"I ever tell you I fought in the war?" Caleb asked.

I was shocked by his sudden declaration, a thing I'd never known about Caleb, and I wondered why he had chosen this moment to tell me.

"Which one?" I asked.

"The Cristero War down in Old Mexico."

His eyes drifted skyward, into the tangled branches of the oak, and he swiped a forearm across his face.

"I've never heard that before," I said. "You never talk about it."

"Neither do you."

I searched the open pasture for Drambuie, watched him forage through grass that had already grown to his knees, the air sweet with the smell of fresh water.

"War isn't like the pictures they publish in *Life* magazine," I said.

"That's a fact," he said. "But you ain't the only one who's ever felt it. Won't be the last, neither."

I scanned the glade again and spotted an eight-point stag and two does lingering near the irrigation canals. I saw the buck's ears peak with caution. He lifted his muzzle into the wind and caught our scent, and all three melted into the tree line.

"Well, since we're swappin' confidences, I got another one for you," Caleb said. "I only intend to tell you one time, so listen up."

"I'm listening."

His eyes reflected the directness I had always known in him, but this time I could almost feel the weight of the decades that had accumulated there. He seemed troubled for reasons I could not sufficiently explain.

"You know how much I hate your sheriff job," he said.

"Yes, sir, I believe you have made that clear to me before. Several times."

"Then you also know how much I hate that the damned job takes you away from the Diamond D."

"Yes, sir," I said again.

"Well, there's something I have to admit to you: I might hate that goddamned job, but you're the right man to do it, Tyler Dawson. You're the right man, and I respect you. 'Cause lately it occurs to me that you might not like it any more than I do, but you still do it anyway. I gotta respect a man who does that. Yes, pardner, I certainly do."

His calloused hand felt like a vise as he squeezed my shoulder, then he nodded once and walked away without another word.

CHAPTER SEVEN

THREE DAYS LATER, I was at the substation, filing the last of the week's paperwork, preparing to lock the office for the evening. Jordan Powell was wrapping up a phone call that sounded like another dead end in the eagle poaching case. He'd been striking out where leads were concerned, but to his credit, it hadn't put a dent in his resolve.

He hung up the phone, licked the lead tip of his pencil, and crossed another name off the list he'd obtained from the Cattlemen's Association. He swiveled his chair and faced me, his features tinged with fatigue and frustration.

"Bullet train to nowhere," he said.

"Those aren't words of surrender I'm hearing, are they, Jordan?"

"Oh, hell no, Cap," he said. "Just expressing my opinion on the present condition of the case."

I was about to reply when Sam Griffin pushed through the back door, guiding a gangly man, fitted with handcuffs and wearing a pair of ill-fitting chinos and khaki work shirt with a name patch sewn above the pocket. Griffin had hold of the man by one elbow, as if leading a blind person. He halted at the base of the staircase that led up to the holding cells and displayed an uncharacteristic grin.

"Meet Emmett Burress," Griffin said to Powell and me. "The dumbest criminal in Meriwether County."

Powell and I shot a glance at each other as Griffin turned to address his arrestee. "Lift your eyes off the floor, my man," he said. "This here is the duly elected sheriff of this county, and you're being disrespectful."

Emmett Burress peeled his focus from the linoleum and swiveled his head in Powell's and my general direction.

"What the hell happened to your kisser, Emmett?" Powell asked. "You look like the victim of a botched elementary-school art project."

The suspect's otherwise clean-shaven face had been scrawled upon with a black felt-tip marker—amateurishly, at that—in what appeared to be an attempt at a depiction of a beard, mustache, and garishly arched eyebrows.

"I'm guessing you performed that artwork on yourself," I said.

While most criminals would choose to use a mask, a hood, or even a pair of pantyhose pulled down over their head to obscure facial attributes, this guy had chosen a far less conventional methodology. I placed him in his midtwenties with a lumpy mop of greasy russet-colored hair that looked as though he'd been wearing a hat made from a colander. The veins of the man's arms bulged like blue nightcrawlers had burrowed underneath his nearly translucently pale skin, his eyes lifeless and dull as an old coin. Emmett Burress was not only a poor illustrator, he was obviously intoxicated. He was also an extremely poor planner.

"Folks in your line of work usually prefer a disguise they can remove when they've finished committing the crime," I said. "I guess by now you know why they refer to those felt pens as *permanent markers*."

"What'd you collar him for?" Jordan asked.

"You're going to love this," Griffin said.

"Dude, please—" Emmett Burress complained, the odor of his stale perspiration beginning to permeate the room.

Griffin ignored him.

"Mr. Burress tried to knock over Calhoun's Gun Shop," Griffin said.

"He tried to rob a *gun* shop?"

"Brandishing a baseball bat as his weapon of choice," Griffin added.

"With your face painted like a lunatic rodeo clown?" Jordan said. "Emmett, you are one sorry sonofabitch."

"It wasn't hard for witnesses to pick him out of a crowd, either," Griffin added. "You might notice that his name is stenciled right there on his shirt."

"Damn, man," Jordan said. "You might want to think these things through a little bit before you run off and do 'em."

Burress kept his head down, eyes locked on his filthy, untied sneakers.

"All right, Griffin," I said. "Book this jackass and take him upstairs to the pens."

Powell shook his head in astonishment as he watched the two men ascend the stairs.

"Please don't tell me I have to stay here and look after that guy all night long."

I shook my head.

"Call Dewey before you leave," I said. "Let him know he gets to babysit Shoeless Joe Capone tonight. I'm going home, and so are you and Griffin. It's been a long damn week."

THERE WAS NOBODY at home when I returned to the ranch that evening. Wyatt, my blue heeler, heard my truck pull into the driveway and ran up from the corral to greet me as I stepped down from the cab. I scratched his head and led him into the house, where he circled my ankles beneath the kitchen counter as I prepared a fresh bowl of chow for him. His fur smelled of smoke from the blacksmith's shed, dust from the crowding pen, and the cattle he had been chasing all day long.

Outside on the gallery, I could hear the familiar noises that marked the end of a busy day; the farrier packing his truck, the tuneless whistling of cowboys and their voices in conversation as they stabled their exhausted horses, and the keening of mourning doves perched in the low branches of cedars. The setting sun backlit a sky ribbed with cirrocumulus, spreading out from horizon to horizon like an alluvial plain. The *Farmer's Almanac* calls it a mackerel sky and says that it portends a change in weather. Two hundred years ago, Oregon's indigenous people would have told you that it would be raining by the time morning broke.

A vane of red dust rose into the air from the road leading into the ranch, followed by another one a short distance behind. I expected that the first of the approaching vehicles was Jesse and Cricket, but I circled around to the front of the house to see who the second one might be.

I waited as the two cars arrived in the driveway. The first was Jesse's faux-wood-paneled station wagon, the second an electric blue Mustang with California tags I recognized, only this time, Cricket was behind the wheel.

Jesse had invited our daughter to assist with her new job working for Len Kaanan, which Cricket was unusually quick to accept. I watched as she climbed out of the Mustang's driver's seat, waving at me like a child from the stage of a grammar school play, her teeth shining brightly inside a smile the likes of which I hadn't seen in quite some time.

"Ian let me drive his car," she said as Ian Swann stepped out from the passenger side. He was wearing his signature denim bell-bottom trousers, a shirt decorated with Mexican embroidery on the placket, and a pair of aviator sunglasses with mirrored lenses.

"I can see that," I said. "Very daring of him."

Jesse came over to me, designer tote bag in hand, packed tight with notebooks and cameras, binoculars, pads, pens, and a Dictaphone recorder—the implements of her profession.

She leaned in to kiss me on the ear and whispered, "Be nice."

I led them inside the house, took orders for drinks, and headed to the bar cart in the living room. Jesse took her things to the bedroom, and I heard Cricket splintering ice trays into the silver bucket I'd won as an equestrian trophy for an event I no longer recall.

I mixed our beverages while Cricket showed Ian the view from the living room window, and Jesse took her usual seat beside the fireplace. Animated small talk filled the room as I delivered highballs from the serving tray I was unaccustomed to using. They nearly slipped off when I saw Ian's face as he removed his glasses.

His eye sockets were ringed purple, one of them swollen to the size, color, and texture of a ripening fig, a strip of surgical tape high on his left cheek stained with a pencil-thin line of dried blood. He saw my expression and showed me a lopsided smile that was absent of humor, more an expression of indignity, or even contrition, and all conversation went dead.

He held my gaze as I handed him the whiskey and soda he'd asked for, passed a vodka martini to Jesse and a chilled bottle of Shasta cola to my daughter. I took my time returning the serving tray to its place at the bar and took three fingers of Jim Beam to my leather club chair.

"So," I said. "Anyone have anything new to share with me?"

"I got jumped, sir," Ian said after several long beats of silence so thick you could carry it out the door. I waited, but he offered nothing more.

"Where and when did this happen to you, Ian?"

"Are you asking as a police officer?"

"I don't know yet. Depends on the answer."

"In that case, I would really prefer not to say."

"To tell you the truth, Mr. Swann, after the day I've had, I would prefer not to hear it. But I've discovered that what I *want* is a practically nonexistent part of my job."

He looked at me earnestly, and I was taken aback by his lack of discomfiture.

"Do you mind if I ask you how long you've been sheriff?" Ian asked.

It was an odd turn from the subject at hand, but I decided to go along.

"I'll sum it up for you: I'm forty-three years old, and I've been sheriff for nearly three years now. It is a job I neither wanted nor asked for, but the people elected me to do it, so I do it. I was an MP in the army a lifetime ago, so I suppose I drew the short straw when the position became available—and for other reasons we don't need to go into right now."

"Must have been strange coming back to Meridian after the war. Coming back to a place is not the same as never having left."

He'd surprised me again with the insight of his reply, the depth of his sincerity almost otherworldly. Perhaps this was the blessing and curse Ian carried, a philosopher-king both sad and noble, traveling unceasingly, preaching his wisdom from a revival tent, only to move along again to a new chautauqua.

"I tried to enlist," he said.

"Excuse me," I said. I didn't think I had heard him correctly.

"I wanted to serve," he explained. "But they wouldn't accept me. Bad feet."

"You didn't miss anything. When wars end, nobody cares who fought them."

"Is that true?"

"In my experience, mostly yes."

His eyes raked the room, landed on Cricket for an extra second, an expression I interpreted as a belgard, and I saw the color rise on her throat. He glanced out the living room window, to the ridgeline that had dimmed to a silhouette as the night folded in, and he turned his damaged face back on me.

"I was on my way from The Portman," he said. "I had taken a stroll to clear my head, to have a walk down by the river, when I noticed the old hotel and stopped in for a drink."

"When was this?"

"Couple days ago."

"Go on."

"I'd made it almost all the way back to town—I parked my car there earlier—and three guys came out of the dark and beat holy hell out of me."

"They broke two of his ribs, Dad," Cricket said, then flashed an expression of apology. To whom the apology was directed I was not clear.

"Did you see who it was?" I asked.

"I'd rather not say, sir."

I don't know why I was so profoundly troubled by what he said. Perhaps it was more in the way that he said it, or that something in his comportment did not belong in this century.

AFTER DINNER, Cricket led Ian down to the creek while Jesse and I tended to the dishes. Outside, the ceiling of sky was alight with sunset afterglow, the forest falling swiftly into darkness.

The evening air was unusually warm, swollen with coming rain and the scents of night jasmine and rose blossoms.

"He's an unusual young man," I said as I glanced out the living room window and watched Ian and Cricket recede into the shadows of the trail leading into the woods. "I don't want to see him break our daughter's heart."

"He carries a great deal of responsibility on his shoulders," Jesse said. "A lot of people are depending on him."

"Do any of them give a damn that their golden goose got himself assaulted?"

"Mickey London, his manager, has taken charge of security."

"Terrific. The man's a street thug. What could possibly go wrong?"

Jesse paused as she watched the bluebirds tuck themselves into the nest box for the night, and the chimney swifts flying in circles around the flue.

"Spring's coming early," she said. "The bluebirds are ready to lay."

"You're changing the subject."

Jesse folded the dishtowel she was using, laid it across her shoulder, and looked at me.

"It's a fire drill out there," she said. "A goat rodeo and a shit show all rolled into one, Ty. I've never seen anything quite like it."

Never one inclined toward profanity, I could see that Jesse's stress level was already reaching its peak.

"They're bringing in contractors from all over," she said. "Dozens and dozens of them. Carpenters, electricians, sound people, stagehands . . . and that's just the concert venue. They're still recording tracks for the album. I honestly don't know how they're going to pull it together."

"They've got you," I said. "That's a good start."

A hint of a smile appeared in her eyes, and she leaned up to kiss me. Her lips tasted of the wine she'd had with dinner, and her hair smelled of lavender and honey.

"Is he telling the truth?" I asked.

"Ian? Telling the truth about what?"

"That he was jumped on his way back from the Gold Hotel." I used the name we residents call The Portman, due to its lavish decor.

"Why would he lie?"

"You just said that the studio is swarming with new faces."

"You don't think very highly of people anymore, do you?"

That night as the first raindrops ticked against the window glass, we made love with a passion and urgency that bordered upon desperation.

CHAPTER EIGHT

JORDAN POWELL AND I spent the next morning, even though it was Saturday, interviewing a half-dozen ranchers whose properties included helicopter pads, but with very little useful result. The weather had grounded the aircraft, which offered us the opportunity to inspect the choppers themselves, but we discovered nothing that pointed to illegal hunting. We had hit the road early that morning, driving from the Meridian substation all the way up to Lewiston, across to Dunwood, then southward through the pass to Jericho, with nothing to show but two hundred fifty extra miles on the odometer.

Jordan had grown increasingly silent as we started the long trek back toward Meridian, his idle attention fixed on the smoke from a distant wildfire that hung in the folds of the foothills. I saw his face in the dim reflection of the passenger window. He was absently stroking the crescent-shaped disfigurement that marked the edge of his jawline, the permanent reminder of a nearly fatal ambush.

"You okay, Jordan?" I asked.

"Aces."

His focus remained on the steep cliffs that ascended from the roadside and were forested with conifers and fern. A thin white veil of runoff from a waterfall flowed down from the summit and disappeared behind a stand of old-growth ponderosa.

"That's where it happened," he said. "Right over that ridge."

Neither of us had returned to that place since Jordan had been shot, but I had no doubt it occupied a space inside his brain that would never ebb or melt away.

"You think you want to go back there?" I asked him.

He rubbed his cheek and seemed momentarily perplexed, drifting somewhere far away. Jordan and I had both lost a good friend on that lonely stretch of county road, the victim of duplicitous and avaricious cowards.

"The turnoff is only about a mile ahead," I said.

Jordan seemed as though he was about to say something, then retreated, his reply swept away inside the mechanical thrum of wiper blades. When I turned again to look at him, I could see he had begun to weep.

I OFFERED to drop Jordan off at the house he shared with his fiancée, but he declined, said he had work to finish at the substation and needed to pick up his truck from the lot. We both recognized the pithy excuse for exactly what it was, but he owed me no justification. Still, I was concerned as to why Jordan felt he needed a pretext to avoid returning to the peace and comfort of a warm household and the woman who loved him without precondition.

"You still inclined to join me for a ride next week to check the yearlings?" I asked, changing the subject.

"Think you can still trust me horseback after today? You didn't change your mind?"

"I believe you told me you were born seeing the world between a horse's ears," I said. "Wouldn't be right for me to keep a man from his birthplace."

The specter of a smile touched his eyes, and I was unclear as to whether it was gratitude or uncertainty I saw there.

"Yes, sir, Captain," he said. "I reckon I could benefit from a little time in the saddle."

He reached into the pocket of his wool-lined Levi jacket and withdrew a set of office keys. He opened the passenger door and stepped out into the rain, squared his shoulders and nodded to me, brushed the rim of his hat brim with two fingers, and walked away.

A SUNBREAK OPENED between passing storms as I pulled in to Half Mountain Studio that afternoon and parked beside the canteen, just as I had the first time I'd been there. The smell of wet grass and freshly cut lumber spiked the air, and dozens of carpenters, line riggers, electricians, and equipment operators were at work beneath an enormous makeshift canvas tent they'd strung across the platform they were constructing. Accumulated rainwater had swelled the center of the canopy like the belly of an antediluvian beast and sluiced down from the corners into muddy puddles along the stanchions. A laborer holding a length of plastic pipe was pushing at the bulges in the canvas to relieve the weight while a cascade of sparks showered down behind him from where a welder plied his trade high in the scaffolding above the stage.

I spotted Jesse and Cricket at the far edge of the elevated drum risers, working with the documentary crew to set up a shot for the B-roll, but they didn't see me. It was difficult to imagine this venue could possibly be ready to handle ten thousand Ian Swann fans—and the facilities to accommodate them—all in just a couple more weeks.

I cut my eyes along the periphery, where a row of supply sheds sheltered stacks of lumber, bags of concrete, and stone blocks, and saw Ian Swann's manager, Mickey London, engaging in an animated conversation with three of the men I'd previously seen at the Cottonwood Blossom. As before, they appeared to be dressed for manual labor: snap-button shirts and canvas work jackets, blue jeans and roughout boots. The third man, the one who appeared to be in charge of his cadre, wore military fatigues stained with sweat and black soot from the slash pile of flaming construction debris he was tending. I could see the web of tattoos on his hands as he stripped off his leather gloves. The four of them were standing in a patch of open greensward, Mickey London at the center, waving his arms and gesticulating in the general direction of the recording complex.

The scene was exactly as Jesse had described it to me, the chaos and the buzz of power tools and frenetic activity a strikingly different environment from the creative haven Len Kaanan had portrayed the last time I had been here. A flatbed lumber hauler blew his airhorn at a knot of workmen crossing the dirt roadway, downshifted, and pulled into the baseyard as I turned away.

I moved up the pathway and poked my head inside the canteen, expecting to find someone who could direct me to Len Kaanan, but the room was empty. Rock music blared out of a portable radio in the kitchen, so I headed that direction instead. A pair of skinny kids in cutoff shorts and rubber flip-flops stood at the prep counter dicing root vegetables and tossing them into a steel pot on the burner, bobbing their heads to the music.

I had to switch off the radio to get their attention, told them I was looking for Len Kaanan and Ian Swann.

"Everybody's in the studio, dude," the taller of them told me and went back to his work. "But I wouldn't go in there," he said as an afterthought.

"Why not?"

The two glanced at each other and shrugged in unison.

"Suit yourself, man. But it's been extremely uptight around here, that's all I'm saying."

I thanked the two cooks and left, followed a narrow board-walk past the place where I'd parked, and continued in the direction of the barn that I had been told housed the recording studio. The earlier rainstorm seemed to have moved on toward the buttes, the sunbreak expanding, the sky overhead blue and devoid of clouds. I stepped between deep muddy puddles as I made my way toward the studio, the afternoon sunshine warming my back.

I slid open the barn door just wide enough to step into a windowless anteroom, where a heavyset barefooted man in a plaid shirt and overalls played solitaire at a card table in the corner. He scrunched his face and blinked at me, drawing his forearm across his wide brow as a shield from the glare of the outdoors.

"Shut the goddamn door, asshole," he said.

"I'm looking for Len Kaanan."

"*Who's* looking for him?"

"Sheriff Ty Dawson."

"You got a badge or something?" he asked, and returned his attention to the cards he'd laid out on the table, already bored by our conversation.

"I've got a badge and *every*thing, friend. You mind speeding this process up? Kaanan's expecting me."

The man leaned back on two legs of his chair, eyeballing me as he lifted the receiver from a wall phone affixed to the shiplap siding. From behind me, I heard heavy footfalls on the stairs that led down from a narrow stairwell. I turned and saw Ian Swann hustling down the steps, carrying a guitar case in each hand and being followed by a much younger male who appeared to be having a hard time keeping pace. Swann glanced distractedly in our direction, seemingly right through us, clearly irritated and preoccupied, and pushed his way outside and into the daylight.

Len Kaanan appeared on the stairwell a moment later, his silver hair as neat and precise as his clothing and his manner. To the degree that Ian Swann appeared agitated, Kaanan seemed to exude a Zenlike calm. He beckoned me to follow him upstairs, and the man at the table hung up the phone and went back to his card game.

I FOLLOWED the producer through a heavy steel door with a small window cutout at eye level. The seal was so tight to the frame there was an audible rush of air as we crossed the threshold.

The studio space occupied the entirety of the second floor, divided almost equally in thirds by thick soundproof walls paneled in some sort of exotic hardwood. The whole room smelled of Tolex, warm vacuum tubes, and new carpeting.

"Ever been inside a recording studio before?" Kaanan asked.

"Not like this one."

He smiled paternally and gestured to the area behind me, which was set up like the living room in a hotel suite, complete with a refrigerator and wet bar, beside which was a door marked with a brass plaque engraved with the words MACHINE ROOM.

"That's where we keep all the noisy gear," he said. "The quiet stuff—tape machines, console, and outboard effects racks—they're all in this room where we can reach them."

Behind Kaanan, a mixing board crowded with rows of VU meters, multicolored knobs, and lights occupied nearly the entire length of the opposite wall, looking like an apparatus that might be used to pilot the starship *Enterprise*. The mixing board was situated beneath an equally large pane of soundproof glass with a view into a third room, which, at the moment, was bustling with activity. At least half a dozen people busied themselves inside, adjusting baffle walls and pulling sound cables amid a forest of shiny chrome microphone stands and musical instruments.

"That's what we call the 'Live Room,'" Kaanan said. "Where the musicians perform the music. See that fellow in the back corner?"

He gestured toward a husky man wearing a black T-shirt and jeans, smoking a cigarette and tinkering with a pedal steel guitar. As if he'd heard Kaanan, he looked up and grinned out from a bushy black beard and nebula of dark curls. He tossed a wave at the producer and went back to his work.

"That's Jerry Garcia," Kaanan said. "He's laying down some tracks for Ian's record."

Kaanan took a seat in the executive chair at the audio console, gestured toward a matching one next to his, leaned back, and knitted his fingers behind his head. I took off my hat and hung it on an unused mic stand. I was just about to speak when one of the technicians pushed in through the door from the Live Room.

"Not now, please, Steve," Kaanan said. "I need a few minutes with Sheriff Dawson. Tell Jerry we'll be ready in ten."

The man named Steve ducked out without a further word, and Kaanan turned his attention back on me.

"Any luck finding the eagle poachers?"

"Not so far," I said.

"Ahh. That's too bad. Still makes me sick to think about."

"These things take time," I said. "It's not like TV, Mr. Kaanan. It's not all photographs, pushpins, and strings."

"Yes, well . . ." he said. "As you can see, I'm a little busy here. We're rush-releasing one of Ian's singles," Kaanan said. "Means we have to—"

"I know what a rush-release is."

"You are a man with a surprising breadth of knowledge."

"You see me wearing a cowboy hat and a pair of boots and assume I'm a yokel. I've had some life experience before you arrived in town, Mr. Kaanan."

"You keep calling me '*Mister*,'" he said. "Why do I feel as though I'm being sandbagged?"

"Funny. I was thinking the same thing myself."

Kaanan swiveled his chair and surveyed the activity on the other side of the soundproof glass. He pressed a lighted button on the console and spoke into a tiny built-in microphone.

"Hey, Steve," he said. "Set up the Neumann in the vocal booth. I want Ian to sing live with Jerry on the next take."

The smile on Kaanan's face had changed when he turned back toward me.

"Can we please cut to the chase?" he said. "I've got a live concert outside in just under two weeks, and I need to get this single out to radio by Friday."

He leaned back in his chair again, crossed his legs at the ankles, hands folded across his flat belly.

"I saw Mickey London outside by the stage," I said. "He was talking with three men who look as though they take pleasure in making bad things happen. I saw them at the Blossom the day Ian's car was vandalized."

"Mickey is taking responsibility for event security. I don't get involved with whomever he might be speaking to."

"I don't know how I feel about that, Mr. Kaanan."

"Don't trouble yourself, Sheriff. Mickey London is a prick, but he's also a pro. Between his experience and mine, we can put on this concert in our sleep. As you folks might say, 'this isn't our first rodeo.'"

"I don't abide terms like 'you people.' It implies an elitist frame of mind I find troubling," I said.

In my experience, the noisier that type of rhetoric, the more despicable the behavior, and I viewed it as a moral failing.

"My apologies," he said. "I meant no insult."

I had no real reason to doubt his sincerity, but I did anyway.

"I will not tolerate another Altamont. Not in my county," I said. "Am I making myself clear?"

"As crystal, Sheriff."

I got up to leave, and Kaanan stood to walk me out, obviously happy to see me go.

"Ian looks like he's taken a ride inside a cement mixer," I said. "Do you happen to know anything about his injuries?"

Kaanan cocked his head and studied me before he answered.

"You know," he said. "Ian took a big risk coming here. But I thought it might be cathartic for him as an artist."

"What do you mean by that?"

"You don't know his story?"

It was the first I'd heard of it, aside from the vague comment he'd made about returning to a place that's familiar not being the same as never having left at all. Even so, I failed to see Kaanan's point.

"We all carry a cross of our own making," I said.

"Are you being intentionally dismissive, Sheriff?"

"Only stating the truth as I have come to know it," I said. "But if this is intended as one of those homilies about a prophet never being loved in his hometown, you can save it for somebody else."

I plucked my Resistol off the mic stand and turned to leave.

"Please let Mr. London know I'll have some of my men here for the show," I said. "That's not a request."

He twitched a smile, but something smoldered behind his eyes.

"By the way, Sheriff," Kaanan said. "Your wife is a real pro. A real pleasure to work with."

"That reminds me," I said. "Let Mr. London know *I'll* be here, too."

CHAPTER NINE

EVEN THE PALLID AFTERNOON sunlight burned my eyes as I stepped out of the relative dark of the studio barn. I squinted my eyes and scanned the guest cabins and grass-covered knolls that surrounded the lake, hoping I'd spot Ian somewhere among them, but didn't. Failing that, I returned to the cooks in the kitchen and asked where I might find him.

"Look, I don't know, man," the skinny one said. "We're really not s'posed to say."

"That's fine," I said. "I'll just go door-to-door and pound on the windows; piss everyone off until I find him."

"No, no, no," he said. "C'mon, man. Don't do that."

"Well then?" I said, shrugging.

The two cooks shared a conflicted glance before giving in.

"See that two-story place at the far end, where the fountain is? That's where Ian's at."

"Thank you."

"Don't tell him we told you."

I described an X-motion across my heart and made for the big cabin at the outlying edge of the lake.

I heard the sound of a guitar being strummed as I stepped up to a pair of hand-hewn double doors, waited for a break in the music, and rapped hard with the ball of my fist. There was a mumble of conversation inside, and the young man I'd seen in the stairwell with Ian appeared in the entry.

He looked at me expressionlessly for a moment, then took a slow, purposeful visual inventory of me from the hat on my head all the way down to my boots. Over his shoulder I could see Ian Swann. He was seated on an upholstered divan near a window that overlooked the blue lake, plucking the steel strings of an acoustic guitar.

"Who are you?" the kid at the door asked me.

"Who are *you*?" I asked in return.

"Dowd."

I estimated Dowd to be three or four years Ian's junior. He was wearing a pair of scuffed Chukka boots, corduroy trousers, and a muslin shirt with Mexican embroidery almost exactly like the one Ian had worn when he'd come out to the Diamond D. The young man exuded an odd energy, both defensive and protective at the same time, but the look in his eyes seemed disconnected, almost vacant, and he spoke with a strange and halting cadence.

"I'm Sheriff Ty Dawson. May I come in?"

"I don't know," Dowd replied. Then he shut the door and left me alone on the landing.

A few seconds later, Ian appeared in the younger one's place. As before, he looked frazzled, and more than a little put out by the interruption. It seemed to take him a few moments to recognize who was waiting for him on his doorstep.

"Got a minute for me, Ian?" I asked.

He shook off the distraction that gripped him, almost as though he was returning from somewhere distant, back into his own body.

"I'm sorry, Sheriff Dawson," he said. "I'm a little preoccupied."

"I understand. I won't take much of your time."

"Come in," he said and led the way down a short set of stairs and into a sunken living room with encompassing view of the lake. Cathedral ceilings and a commodious layout made the inside of the place feel even larger than it appeared from outside.

Dowd watched us uneasily from a chair near the glass doors that led out to a patio separating the cabin from the rim of the waterline, a rush of wind out of the east rippling the surface and bowing the long, tapered stems of the rushes.

"This is my brother, Dowd," Ian said. "He's also my guitar tech."

I reached out to shake hands with Dowd, but he shrank from me in a way that put me in mind of a maltreated domestic animal. I took a step backward to give him some extra personal space, let my hand drop to my side.

"If you're just going to keep talking," Dowd said to Ian, "I'm gonna go read in my room."

"Yeah, sure," Ian said. "I'll come get you when I'm finished here."

Dowd stepped past us, uncomfortable and restive to the point of distress. He seemed to study me in his peripheral vision as he passed by, wary of making direct eye contact with me.

He was on his way to the staircase when Ian called out, "Bring me the D-35 when you come back, will you, Dowd?"

"Okay."

"Oh," Ian added. "And bring the Guild, too. The Jumbo."

"The blond one?"

"Yeah, and be sure to check all the strings for me."

"I always check the strings."

"I know you do, Dowd," he said. "I was just—"

Dowd glanced sideways at me, sullen.

"You don't have to tell me that," he said, mostly to himself. "I always check the strings."

"I know. I'm sorry."

"He doesn't have to tell me that," he muttered, this time to me, as he left the room.

Ian shook his head and moved to the glass doors, opened them, and stepped outside into the freshening breeze. He drew a deep breath and reached into the pocket of his shirt.

"Mind if I smoke?" he asked me.

"It depends."

"It's just a Marlboro," he said and smiled. He fired it with a chrome Zippo this time and leaned against the rail.

"How's the eye?" I asked him.

"I'll be fine. Nothing a little extra makeup won't fix. At least, that's what Len tells me."

"I'd like to help you out, Ian."

He exhaled a cloud of tobacco smoke and watched it tear away on the wind.

"I've got bigger fish to fry at the moment," he said. "I've got exactly six days to finish the new album, then film a live concert the week after for ten thousand of my closest friends."

"You don't seem excited."

"Just a little burned out, that's all."

He flicked the gray ash from his cigarette, leaned his elbows on the railing, and looked out at the lake, where swallows and blue bottleflies darted among the bayberry that grew wild along the littoral.

"Your brother idolizes you, doesn't he?" I said.

"I don't like when people say that."

"I intended no aspersion."

"It's just that I don't want to be idolized, Sheriff Dawson. It's not fair, you know. I'm just a guitar player."

"I think you might've become more than that, Ian. Whether you wanted it or not."

He drew deeply again on his cigarette and seemed to lose himself inside his own head.

"The people in the background are becoming invisible to me. Roadies and techs, production people. I'm not proud of that. That's not who I am."

I remained silent as he gathered his words, his expression almost painful to witness.

"It's just the pressure right now . . ." he said, more to himself than to me. "The album, the show . . . props, lights, stagehands, engineers . . ."

"Producers?"

He laughed, but I detected no humor in it.

"No," he said. "Definitely not producers. Len Kaanan is not easy to ignore."

He crushed out his smoke and looked at me, his tone and his countenance sincere.

"It won't be that long, and we'll be out of your hair, Sheriff."

I watched as he looked into the depths of the house through the window, something paternal buried in his expression. As a father, I thought I recognized what I saw there. It was clear that Dowd was incapable of caring for himself.

"Who looks after him when you're on the road?" I asked.

Ian knew I had seen him looking inside through the glass, knew right away what I was asking.

"I do. My brother takes care of the instruments, keeps fresh strings on them, keeps them tuned up for me during the shows."

"Looks as though he likes it."

"He loves it. Dowd loves to come out on the stage and swap out my guitars between songs. Plus, it keeps him close by."

"You've got no other family?"

Ian paused, a man familiar with lines and boundaries, especially the ones you don't cross.

"It's just been him and me since I was seventeen," Ian said after a moment. "Our mother died when we were young, and my father was killed a few years later."

I considered mentioning what Len Kaanan had said, about Ian's having taken a risk to be here, but I didn't. It felt like a bridge too far.

"I'm sorry, Ian," was all I said.

There was no imagining what he and his brother had lived through in order to arrive at this place in their lives, nor what they saw on the inside of their eyelids as they slept as a result of those experiences.

"Diamonds in the shit stream," Ian said. It was the first time I had heard him utter a vulgarity.

"I don't know if I heard you correctly," I said.

"It's something my manager used to tell me. 'You need to keep looking for those diamonds in the shit stream,' he'd say. Turns out he's been mostly right so far."

"It's a hard way to look at life, son," I said.

"It's the only way I know, Sheriff Dawson."

I had taken enough of his time, and he was clearly struggling with the deadlines he faced. He didn't want my help with the troubles he'd had—neither the damage to his vehicle, nor the assault on his person—so there was nothing further for me here.

"I'll let myself out," I said. "I just wanted to check on you, whether you'd had a change of heart about . . . things."

"Your family's been a bright spot for me," he said, following me into the living room as I made my own way to the door. "I've got something for your daughter," he added. "If you don't mind giving it to her for me."

He withdrew a cassette tape from a drawer in a sideboard and handed it to me. The label read, *Krikkit's Song (Passing Through)*. He had inscribed it, *Love, Ian. xox.*

"Wouldn't you rather give it to Cricket yourself?"

He cast his eyes toward a high window, where dust motes floated weightless on wafer-thin sunlight.

"I don't know when I'll see her next," he said. "With the album, and so little time before the show . . . They're keeping me pretty busy."

"I'll see that she gets it," I said.

He showed me a mournful, tired smile, and said, "I wouldn't trust it with anyone else."

CHAPTER TEN

JESSE AND CRICKET had already wrapped shooting for the day by the time I stepped out from Ian Swann's cabin. The studio aspens were casting long shadows of late afternoon, and I climbed into my truck and made the long drive back to the Diamond D.

Jesse was just getting out of the shower as I returned home, drying her hair with a hand towel in front of a mirror that was frosted with steam condensation. I kissed her and asked where our daughter was, and Jesse told me she'd taken a walk down to the old teahouse, told me she'd been acting sullen all day.

The teahouse was the name Cricket had given to a long-disused springhouse I had repurposed for her when she'd been a little girl. It had gone through a number of identities over the years, but *teahouse* was the one that had endured. It was about the size of a small tractor shed, constructed of pine logs and rough stone, with a roof made of shingles grown over with moss and a single glass window cut into the south-facing side. It straddled a narrow stream we called Leatherwood Creek and had been used for cold storage in the days before refrigeration.

I had been concerned Cricket might be frightened to play there alone when she was a girl, it being a distance from the main house and horse barn, but she had never been anxious or afraid about it, or much of anything else. Instead, she had decorated it in the way that little girls did back in those days, transforming along with her age from princess tea parties to books, toys, and games, and finally to posters of her favorite teen idols. Those things were mostly all gone now; the only keepsakes remaining were a collection of model horses, an antique steamer trunk, and a table and chair.

Wyatt the dog followed me down past the barn and the empty corral where the snubbing post stood. The last of the day's filtered light streamed through the tree limbs, and up high on the peaks, the timber was still dusted with snow. Wyatt ran ahead of me and found Cricket sitting on the floor in the narrow doorway of the old springhouse, swaying her bare feet back and forth across the watercourse. She whistled at Wyatt when she spotted him shambling along the trail and motioned for him to jump up on her lap. She noticed me following not far behind him a few seconds later and stood to make room for me to come inside.

I handed her one of the two frosted bottles of root beer I'd brought with me, popped the tops with the hilt of my buck knife, while Wyatt curled up on the floor.

"Are we interrupting you?" I asked. "You seem deep in thought."

"I'm okay."

She took a long draught from her soda bottle and looked past me, out through the doorway and into the denseness of the forest.

"I saw you today," I said. "Out at Half Mountain."

"You did?"

"I needed to have a word with Len Kaanan. And Ian."

She withdrew from her reverie and looked into my eyes.

"Really? Why?"

"Sheriff stuff," I said.

My daughter was very adept at silence. Not the brooding, petulant teenage brand of silence we had all learned to use as a wall or a weapon, but rather the contemplative hush of reflection. I respected that quality in her, because I'd be a hypocrite if I didn't.

"Ian gave me something he wanted you to have," I said.

I dipped into my shirt pocket, withdrew the cassette tape he had given me, and placed it gently in her hand. I watched a mist form in her eyes as she read the label, then caressed it gently in both of her hands.

The little room seemed to grow even smaller; dusty, with opaque billows of ancient cobwebs in the rafters, it smelled the way old stone and timber does when it's never been completely dried out by the sun. Beneath the floorboards, I could hear Leatherwood purring through the weir.

"I only have a few more days before I have to go back to school," she said finally.

The sorrow in her voice pained my heart. Of all the misapprehensions of youth, our reluctance to credit the wisdom of our descents is perhaps the most sad and improvident, but I forged ahead anyway.

"Ian's a grown man, Cricket," I said.

"He's twenty-five."

"It's not only about your ages. You two live in different worlds."

Indistinct light flowed through the waves in the window glass, rain-spotted and filmed by decades of weather, a rickety table and a lone child's ladderback chair arranged beneath the sill. I had built that table and two matching chairs for her when she was five or six years old, but one had been broken when I'd sat in it to join her for imaginary tea.

Cricket took a seat in the unbroken chair, and I sat on the floor with my back to the wall, cross-legged, on top of a musty horse blanket.

"Did Ian ever mention having a history here?" I asked.

"He doesn't say much about his past."

"You haven't asked him about it?"

The evening was growing colder as the last of the daylight seeped out of the sky. A killdeer called out from the depths of the thicket, and the cows and their calves milled and lowed in the distance.

"He keeps a wall around himself," Cricket said. "He can be very remote sometimes."

"Ian's life is on the road, sweetheart. I'm not sure he thinks in terms of family outside of his brother. Hard to maintain any kind of meaningful relationship at all when you're always on the move."

"You know about his brother?"

"I met him earlier today."

She placed her pop bottle on the table with exaggerated care and I saw her cheeks color.

"Why are you talking to me about this, Dad?"

"The worst things anybody ever gave me was excuses. We all have to own our own choices."

"What do you mean by that?"

"I don't want to see you get hurt, Cricket."

I could see a storm gathering behind her eyes, and then it passed, a tempest that touched down for a brief moment before it tailed away.

"I'm not stupid, Dad," she said. "I know who and what Ian is."

"I've never thought you were stupid, kiddo."

"This is only a job for spring break, that's all. Ian's cute, and he's funny and interesting. He's just a new friend."

Cricket's collection of Breyer horses was displayed on a shelf in the corner of the room; years ago, she had lovingly arranged them by breed and color. She stood now and began to reorganize them, her back to me as I spoke.

"Do me a favor?" I said.

"If I can."

"You can try to fudge the truth with me, Cricket," I said. "But you can never allow that kind of indulgence with yourself."

My daughter kept to her task, and in the near distance, I could hear a loose stone tumbling along the hillside and rolling to a stop in the talus.

"You either bear the ache of self-discipline," I said, "or you suffer the agony of disappointment. The choice will always be yours."

"I'll be okay, Dad."

She turned when she heard me rise up from my seat on the blanket and get to my feet. Wyatt did, too, stretching and rising up to follow me out.

"You going to be much longer?" I asked. "It's getting dark."

"A few more minutes, I think."

I stepped out the opening and along the short stairway to the creekbank. I could feel Cricket behind me, and I turned to find her watching Wyatt and me from the doorway.

"I love you," I said.

"I know you do, Dad."

INTERLUDE II

(1964)

THE HOMECOMING DANCE turned out to be kind of a drag, so Paul and Heather decided to join a bunch of the other kids down by the oxbow, where a party was rumored to have spontaneously arisen. Paul parked his car beside at least a dozen others in the flats behind a coppice of barberry, fernbush, and spruce.

The night had grown cool with the coming of autumn, the air sweet with pine tar and the smell of the river channeling between stones and snags. Heather's hand felt soft and warm as Paul helped her across a footbridge built from railroad ties spanning a narrow creek, the jangle of laughter growing more distinct as they neared the pulsating fireglow at the end of the path. They navigated between shallow culverts the winter runoff had carved into the soil, and just beyond, they reached a clearing where several dozen other teenagers from school had gathered around a beer keg poorly hidden at the outskirts of the firelight. Some were already laughing too loud, making out in the shadows, or dancing to music that blared from a portable radio someone had wedged into the low branches of a tree.

Something in the air made all of them feel invincible, as if time had ceased moving, all borders and boundaries dissolved, a lacuna carved out of the universe and fashioned exclusively for them. Back at home, their parents seemed shellshocked, reeling from a recent nuclear near miss in Cuba, an escalating war somewhere in the jungles of Southeast Asia, and still grieving the assassination of a US president; an entire adult population was coming to terms with its own moral inventory. But that was the establishment's burden, *their* weight to carry. Life persists, man, young lives in particular, exploring infatuations, desires, and furies as though they were the first to discover them.

Music was everywhere. The Beatles and the Beach Boys; the Supremes and Jan & Dean; Johnny Rivers and the Dave Clark Five; and Lesley Gore. The atmosphere was alive with abandon and a culture newly rejuvenated, dominated by both the joy and the narcissism of youth. So they proceeded blissfully unaware they were standing at the headwaters of a hedonistic tsunami not seen since the apex of the Roman Empire, the last of the remaining floodgates having been cobbled together from the fragile substance of tradition.

"I don't think I recognize anybody at this party," Paul said. "Do you?"

"Do you want to leave?" Heather said.

"No," Paul said, probably a little too quickly. "I'm fine."

"Want to take a walk? Get away from all . . . this?"

She looked across the width of the glade, gestured vaguely toward the beer-flushed teenagers who loitered at the fringe of a bonfire showering embers into the night sky, their glossy skins marbled with orange light. Paul didn't answer Heather's question, just stood and offered his hand to her.

"I had a nice time with you the other night at your house," he said as they walked among the damp pebbles on the bank of the river.

"You did not," she said and playfully bumped him with her shoulder, unwilling to let go of his hand. "My dad was being a jerk."

"Okay. I was just being polite. But I had a nice time being with you."

"I did with you, too," she said. "I saw you looking at the family pictures on the mantelpiece."

"You can tell a lot about people from the photos they keep."

"You think so?"

"I know so," he said.

"We used to have more, but my father's been putting them away. He thinks I don't notice."

"My dad's just the opposite. He doesn't have anything of my mom's in the house. I found an earring one time. He'd be pissed if he knew I still had it."

"Why?"

"I don't know. He doesn't talk about her."

"That's sad," Heather said. "I'm glad we still have a few things around."

"I am too."

"What can you tell about me? From the pictures, I mean."

"That you look just like your mom. She was very pretty."

They stopped walking and listened to the river, watched the glow of the moon on white water that braided the rocks.

"I don't really remember her," Heather said. "She died when I was very young."

"How?"

"Ovarian cancer."

"That's rough. I'm sorry, Heather."

"They say it's common."

"Doesn't make it any better. Or any easier."

He felt Heather looking at the side of his face, searching for something, but he didn't know what. She let go of his hand, crouched down, and scooped a flat stone from the water's edge, skimmed it across the flats.

"No, it doesn't make it any easier," she said finally. "I think my father blames me for her cancer. Do you think that's weird?"

"Why do you think he blames you?"

"The way that he looks at me sometimes. Like he wishes I was her and not . . . *me*."

She had a way of saying things, so unvarnished and sincere, that it caught Paul off guard and made him feel clumsy, inadequate and crude. Paul knew she didn't mean to make him feel that way, but life with his father had not exactly prepared him for refinement or polish, or even the basics of courteous conversation. He tilted his head upward, looking into a black sky that seemed intent on swallowing the stars. Behind the clouds, the moon appeared blue, bruised and alone, and a melancholy fell over him.

"I was only six when my mom was killed," Paul said. "I don't remember much about her at all. It's like she faded away. Images, like little movies in my head, but now they're nearly all gone."

Heather moved close to him then, slid an arm around his waist, and rested her head on his shoulder. Her hair smelled like cinnamon.

"Tell me one," she said.

"What do you mean?"

"Tell me about one of the memories you still have of her."

No one had ever asked him that before, and again he found himself unprepared. His memories were spotty, imperfect in their construction, and something about that embarrassed him. There was one, though, that had appeared in his mind without origin or chronology, no frame of reference Paul could fit into the puzzle of his early life: The day's wash was drying on a clothesline beside the house, flapping in the dirty breeze. His mother looked tired. No, maybe not tired; alone and unhappy. Paul felt himself grow sadder just thinking about her that way, looking as though she wished she could be somewhere else. Anywhere other than where she was. If she could have, she would have wanted the wind to carry her into the sky, gone and forever away.

"I'll try," Paul said finally, and he described it to Heather.

And as he did so, the image disappeared into nothing. Like the tail end of a film reel that had abruptly unspooled, vanishing into the screen, and receding into waxen darkness.

CHAPTER ELEVEN

WHEN THE BEDSIDE TELEPHONE woke me at 4:00 Monday morning, I plucked the receiver from the cradle before it could ring a second time. Through the fog of a sudden awakening and the commotion on the other end of the line, Meriwether County's volunteer fire captain informed me a blaze had broken out at the hog farm on Sahaptin Road.

Jesse turned over and reached for me in the dark as I rolled out of bed. I kissed her and whispered for her to go back to sleep. I brewed coffee in the percolator as I got dressed, poured it into a plaid thermos container, and climbed into my pickup, my breath coming out in gray clouds.

The morning was chilled, moonless and silent, and a lone katydid churred from somewhere in the brush. I pulled out of the driveway and over the wide entry lane paved with crushed rock that led out to the state road, my headlights reflecting the rubicund flicker of animal eyes staring out from the weeds growing on the embankment. As I neared the paved road, I recognized Tom Jenkins sitting horseback in the distance, pushing the better part of the Corcoran herd up the dirt track to my ranch by himself. By the time most of the folks in the county got around to eating their breakfasts, Tom Jenkins and my cowboys would be tagging the ears of those animals and hazing them out to the feedlot. I flashed my headlights to him as I passed, then turned onto the county road toward the fire.

About forty-five minutes later, I spotted the ghost of a smoke cloud in the sky, pallid and ashen against the deep blue of false dawn. Four trucks were fanned out along the periphery of the hog farm by the time that I arrived, a Type 2 and three pumpers, all painted a hideous shade of lime yellow, drowning the last of the embers that glowed at the center of a huge pile of blackened rubble. The farm was in the middle of nowhere, flanked by thick stands of fir trees and cottonwoods, its nearest neighbor a good five miles east. All that was left standing now were the rail fences surrounding the empty hog pens, the farrowing barn, and the steel posts that once supported a roof above the compost shed. The main residence, the workshop, and the hoop barn were nothing but piles of smoldering staves and plankwood with a chimney and hearth built from red brick protruding from the debris like a cenotaph.

The man who had phoned me, Fire Captain Baxter Gage, saw me arrive and climbed down from one of the pumpers, turning the controls of the deluge gun over to one of his men. He peeled the heavy gloves from his hands as he ambled in my direction, his turnout coat blackened by smoke.

"Sorry to drag you out of bed so early, Ty," he said.

"I'm a rancher," I said. "My day's already half over."

He grinned and accepted the coffee I offered from my thermos, removed his helmet, and placed it on the wheel well of my truck.

"Anyone hurt?" I asked.

"No, thank god. The place has been abandoned since the McEvoys left in . . . what, seventy-one? House still had some furniture in it."

I could recall the days when this farm had been a thriving

enterprise, back before I'd left for college and the war. Seeing it this way was not only a depressing sign of present times, but troubling as well, in that it looked intentional to me.

"Any idea how it started?" I asked.

Baxter Gage scanned his eyes across the smoldering remains of the old farm. What hadn't been incinerated by the flames had been gradually decimated by years of neglect and indifference.

"It's been clear and dry all night long. No lightning, no storms," he said.

"Arson?"

"I don't know what else it could be. That's why I called you."

"Why the hell would somebody want to burn *this* place down?"

"Who knows anymore, Ty," he said. "This world keeps getting stranger and stranger. I'm getting too old for this shit, tell you the truth."

"Mind if I have a look around?"

"Knock yourself out," he said. "I'll send you a copy of our after-action report if you'd like."

I circled the periphery of the wreckage, careful to maintain my distance from the remaining hot spots, my eyes stinging anew with every shift of the wind. I sheltered myself beneath an ancient oak that stood a short distance from where the front door of the dwelling had been, its limbs and trunk deeply scorched nearest the blaze. I could see the shattered remnants of furnishings and broken glass amid the ash, but nothing I recognized as overt evidence of arson. But Baxter Gage was right. In the absence of inclement weather, there was no other logical explanation. The place had been long abandoned, presumably with no active utilities in use or operational defects to blame. Yet the notion of arson made my skin crawl; the town of Meridian was still recovering from the emotional aftereffects of a firebomb that had cost at least one young person his life.

I thanked Gage and started back for the office, the sun as it rose from behind the Cascades burning my smoke-reddened eyes.

WHEN I HAD DRIVEN through town on my way out to the hog farm, the streets had been empty, too early for anyone except the garbage collectors emptying containers into the back of their crusher. Now, as I turned right onto Main on my way to the substation, I saw parked cars lining both sides of the street. I glanced through the window of Rowan Boyle's diner as I drove by and could tell it was packed. Across the street, I saw Lankard Downing already unlocking his front door for the day, at least an hour earlier than usual. I pulled into the small lot behind the office and noticed Jordan Powell in the park.

He looked up at me as I took a place across from him at the picnic table where he had been scooping the flesh from a mushmelon he had sliced and laid out on a section of yesterday's paper.

"Doesn't look like much of a breakfast for a cowboy," I said.

He responded with a roll of his eyes and wiped melon juice from his chin with his sleeve.

"Shasta says she don't want me looking fat for the wedding."

"Is that so? You finally set a date?"

"Looks like we're drawing a bead on one, Cap," he said. "Circling the wagons on sometime in June."

I waited for more, but that was all he chose to say about it, which was fine with me. The morning was filled with riparian smells and the susurrus of the river as it slid past the park, and we sat in companionable silence until the clock tower chimed eight o'clock.

"You smell like smoke," Powell said as he got up to dispose of his hollowed-out melon rind.

"Fire at the hog farm."

"The old Swanson place?"

"I've always known it as the McEvoy farm," I said. "Out on Sahaptin Road."

"That's the one. The McEvoys took it over and couldn't make a go of it either. Too bad, too. Some places are just plain snakebit, I guess."

I watched as he dropped his refuse in the garbage can and rinsed his hands in the drinking fountain. He shook his hands dry and returned to the table, resting one boot on the seat of the picnic table as he looked off toward the heart of Meridian. A bicentennial flag popped in the wind at the top of the flagpole, the number 76 encircled by stars inside the canton.

"Anybody get hurt in the fire?"

"No," I said. "Place has been abandoned for a few years, as far as I know."

"That's what I thought," Powell said. "Anyways, I got a couple more leads on the poachers to follow up on. I'll let you know how it goes."

"You do that, Jordan. I'm going to try to get something to eat. I'll be back in a while."

"Got it, boss," he said and ambled across the lawn to the office.

I WALKED up the street to Rowan Boyle's diner for some breakfast and found a long line of customers waiting outside the door. Inside, the dining room was filled to capacity, as was every seat at the counter. My stomach rumbled at the smell of food and I wasn't willing to wait, so I crossed the street to drop in at the Cottonwood Blossom. Ordinarily, the Blossom didn't open until ten or eleven, but Lankard Downing was not a man to squander opportunity when it showed up unexpectedly.

When I stepped inside, I was as surprised to find the place packed to the rafters with patrons as I was to see Meridian's town drunk, and the Cottonwood Blossom's near-permanent resident, Leon Quinn, working behind the counter as a barback.

"I can see the way you're looking at me, Sheriff," Quinn said. "But I'm a changed man. I'm a friend of Bill Wilson's now. Three days already, and I'm sober as a judge."

"Congratulations, Leon. Keep coming back," I said and wondered whether that was the appropriate rejoinder under the circumstances.

Lankard Downing topped off a Falstaff glass of draft and rang it up for a waiting customer before he strolled over to address me.

"We're full up, as you can see, Sheriff," he said, showing me a rare and somewhat vulpine smile. "But I can set you up with something to carry back to the office with you."

"Much appreciated, Lankard, but I'd like to have a word first."

"You smell like smoke."

"That's what I hear," I said and changed the subject. "I've never seen the Blossom opened up so early in the morning."

"Didn't want to miss a chance like this here. I guess the word's got out on some kind of rock-and-roll show somewhere up the valley soon. Look at all these people. Like Christmas and New Year's and the rodeo all rolled into one."

I knew he was already aware of exactly what and where the concert was planned to be, but playing cornpone dumb was how Downing plied his trade in idle gossip. He was correct, though, as far as his business was concerned. Every table was occupied by unfamiliar people eating plates of grits and sausage and fried eggs, or bowls of Colorado chili accompanied by tall glasses of beer. At the far end of the bar, an attractive blonde sat by herself beside the only empty barstool at the rail, sipping a salted Bloody Mary through a straw. She eyed me like a raptor for a few seconds, and then she looked away.

"I heard there was a fire out at the McEvoy place," Downing

said. "That why you smell like you've been sleeping in your smokehouse?"

There was no point in lying to him, so I confirmed I had been there.

"I'd prefer you keep it under your hat for the time being, Lankard," I said. "We're still investigating the origin."

His eyebrows arched with curiosity, but he pursed his lips and made a lock and key motion. "Mum's the word."

Like hell. But this was how things operated in Meridian.

I could see the Bloody Mary girl was still keeping tabs on me, and I watched a man approach her and sit down in the empty seat with an air of ownership that seemed somehow perverse. He hollered out an order for a stubbie of Olympia with a whiskey on the back and hooked his bootheels over the rungs of his stool. The girl whispered something in his ear, and I saw him nod, his face obscured by the wide brim of his hat.

Lankard Downing excused himself from me and went to fill the newcomer's order, and I watched a waitress and busboy work the busy room. I leaned an elbow on the countertop and kept the couple at the far end of the bar in my peripheral vision as Downing pulled a bottle of well whiskey from the bottom shelf. The Bloody Mary girl was young, midtwenties, stunning in a way that demanded the wrong kind of attention, and with mileage on her life that only revealed itself beneath the skin. She was wearing tight white pedal pushers and a cutoff T-shirt printed with a Harley Davidson skull, a tattoo of the yin-yang symbol imprinted on her shoulder. She looked beautiful and dangerous and damaged, an untamed creature who was both predator and victim at the same time. If this concert was going to draw more of this kind of crowd, I was going to require some help.

Lankard muttered something to Leon Quinn I couldn't quite make out, threw a damp bar towel across one shoulder, and returned to his place across the bar from me.

"What's up with those two?" I asked.

He didn't have to turn around to know exactly who I was referring to.

"The circus has come to town, Sheriff. That's about all I can say about what I seen so far."

I glanced at my watch and came to the point I'd come here to ask about.

"Do you remember the four men who came in here the other day? The day Ian Swann's car was defaced?"

"I believe I do."

"Have they been back?"

"Once," he said. "Couple days ago."

I watched Leon Quinn eavesdropping at Downing's elbow and motioned him to come closer.

"Did you hear anything from them, Leon?" I asked.

"One of the young ones said they were just moving through. Told me they were boomers," Leon said. "The other one said he'd been a donkey puncher for a while, but I don't know . . ."

"The ugly one, though," Lankard Downing added, "the one with the tattoos on his hands? He kept talking about the army. And the one that looked like he was half-asleep, hell, he never said a thing at all."

America had been at war almost continuously since 1950, so I assumed that any man over the age of eighteen was former military of some kind. But I'd seen that man's eyes up close and personal, and I had little doubt that he'd spent more time in the stockade than he'd ever spent downrange. That is, if he was even a veteran at all.

"Any of them mention what they were doing here?" I asked.

Lankard looked at Leon and both men shrugged, then Leon walked away along the duckboards and headed for the kitchen.

"Figured they were just passing through looking for work," Downing said. "They smelled like railroad trash."

"If they come back, I want you to give me a call."

"Sure thing, Sheriff."

Leon Quinn returned holding a cardboard box and Styrofoam container that smelled like a cheeseburger and fries. My stomach growled, and I reached into my pocket for my wallet, drew out a five, and slid it across the bar.

"Much obliged," I said and picked up the box to leave. Then I thought of one more thing.

"I heard something about Ian Swann," I said. "Heard he might have had history here once."

"Here? In Meriwether County?"

"Maybe."

"Hmm," Lankard Downing said. "News to me. I don't recognize him. 'Course who could tell with all that hair and beard and whatall . . . You sure?"

"No, I'm not sure at all. It's probably nothing," I said; then I thanked him for the food again and pushed out through the batwing doors.

Outside, the air had warmed and smelled sweetly of dogwood, the trees lining the street alive with early spring blossoms. I headed for the substation and saw Jesse and the film crew setting up to shoot more B-roll footage from the far side of the intersection, where the record store once stood and had gone up in a conflagration so intense it melted the glass lenses in the streetlamps. I waved to my wife, but as before, she was too absorbed with her work to notice.

I should have known right then it would be that kind of week for both of us.

CHAPTER TWELVE

THE NEXT SATURDAY MORNING came in hard and strong, bleaching the colors from an ephemeral sunrise. Jordan Powell arrived at the ranch almost an hour before, and I could hear Drambuie nickering inside the barn as we drew closer. The horse had heard Powell and me coming down the pathway in the predawn, excitedly pawing the packed earth and sawdust in his stall.

I saddled Boo while Powell outfitted one of his favorites, a brindle mare named Misty, that he'd drawn from the remuda. I watched him adjust his stirrups for length and take one final tug on the girth before tying it off and climbing into the saddle. An edge of anxiety showed on his face as he mounted and tested the set of the bit, and I could tell Misty sensed it as well. She threw her head and sidestepped to her offside, testing Powell, as I mounted Drambuie and led the way up the trail with Wyatt at our heels.

Caleb had informed me he suspected we had a half-dozen or so strays left behind in the North Camp, so Powell and I headed that way as the sun tipped the ridge to the east of us, casting beams of blood orange down the length of creased slopes where the grass had already begun to turn velvety green. I twisted sideways in the saddle to check on Powell, who was riding a short distance behind me. He saw me looking and nodded. Even with half his face lost in the shadow of his Stetson, I could tell he was grinning. Misty had settled, and so had her rider, and we made it to the crest of the hill to North Camp by the full flush of morning.

I thought I spotted the first pair of strays hiding deep in the brush in the lee of a rock cove. I whistled at Wyatt, and he made a wide flanking arc behind the drifters and pushed them out into the open. Instinctively, Powell rode up on the rear of them and heel-roped the leader while I threw a loop on the second. I glanced to my right and watched as Powell dallied up hard, halting the animal in its tracks. I caught Powell's eye, and he tipped his hat; it was the first rope I'd seen him throw since the day he'd been shot months ago. We moved that first pair into a makeshift holding pen constructed from timbers of deadfall and tied the gate shut with baling wire.

A few minutes later, Powell spotted another two cows at the far edge of the lea, where a fork of the Knife River cut through the flats and bent to the south. They were hiding inside a dense patch of brambles and thorny wild blackberry, and again, Wyatt flushed them out into the open where Powell and I were able to hook and drive them back to the holding pen with the others.

It took nearly another full hour before we located the last of them, an orphan calf, all alone in the bunchgrass near a half-filled water trough at the foot of a creaking windmill. A slow, halting breeze blew through the open prairie as we climbed down from our saddles. I pulled the pipe lever and released some fresh water into the trough and led Misty and Boo to it for a drink.

"Doesn't look like you've missed a step, Jordan," I said.

"Felt pretty damn good, Cap," he said. "Have to admit I was a little balled up there at first."

He shook out his reata and took a casual throw at a tree stump and caught it foursquare on the first try, as adept with a lariat as he ever had been. I watched him walk over, unhook the rope, and twist it back into a loop. He appeared to be speaking to himself under his breath as he coiled it back into place with the latigo, and he led Misty away from the trough to cool down.

IT WAS coming up on noon by the time we finished driving our small herd of strays to the stock pen and heard the welcome clatter of the chuckwagon triangle bell. Caleb and the rest of the crew were pushing a substantial mob of SoCal Purples— the breed that had made the Diamond D famous—down the alley and into the crowding pen, slamming the steel gate behind them. One by one, the men unsaddled their mounts and came over to join Powell and me where we sat at a long narrow plank table situated in the stippled sunlight beneath a stand of tamarack. The whole crew was there: Caleb, Taj Caldwell, Paul Tucker, Jaxon Stepp, and Tom Jenkins. Everyone except for Sam Griffin, who was working his shift as a deputy, running things at the substation. Even Dom Greene, the blacksmith, and Ned Streeter, the cook, stepped away from their posts to acknowledge Powell's return to the ranch.

The smoke from tri tip beef steaks and pork ribs drifted through the tree limbs from the embers of a *parrilla* grill as the cowboys took turns shaking hands with their comrade, smacking him on the shoulder and welcoming him back.

"This here's Jaxon Stepp," Caleb said, striding up last in line. "We call him 'New Guy.'"

"Howdy, New Guy."

"Heard a lot about you," Stepp said.

And the table went silent for a long, pregnant moment.

"Yeah, well . . ." Powell answered, breaking the awkward silence. Then he stood to collect a tin plate and a set of utensils off the plank table and led the way through a chow line of barbecued beef, pinto bean chili, grilled corn, coleslaw, and the cook's homemade cornbread.

I brought up the rear of the column, drew a cupful from the spigot of a steel cooler of water with a block of ice floating in it, and watched the men eating together in a manner that resembled a tintype photograph from an earlier century. I dragged an apple crate into a small clearing a short distance apart from the men, sat down beside Caleb, who was already halfway through his lunch.

"How'd the kid do out there?" Caleb asked between bites.

"Like he'd never been gone," I said.

Caleb kicked the brim of his hat back off his forehead with his knuckle and looked at me sidelong, his expression crowded with skepticism.

"You asked," I said.

At the crew table, Powell soon found himself at the center of attention, unusually reserved and uncomfortable. But he gradually warmed to the men's curiosity, answering questions about the attempt on his life and his close brush with death. I could tell Powell detected no malice or insincerity, only friendly curiosity and well-earned respect, the men eventually taking turns examining the livid bullet wound on his jawline. Nobody appreciates a good story more than a cowboy, and the stories associated with the acquisition of a new scar, flesh wound, or digital dismemberment numbered among the most popular. By the time Caleb hollered the lunch break to an end, shades of the old Jordan Powell had returned to his face, and they showed in the way that he carried himself as he observed the crew scrape their plates into the rubbish container and wander back to the remuda to resaddle their mounts.

* * *

I WALKED Jordan back to his car, the noise and dust of the boys heading out to Three Roses parcel disappearing into the stillness of early afternoon. It was clear that I had underestimated the depth of the insecurity, suspicion, and survivor's guilt left behind in the wake of the injury Powell had suffered at the hands of an FBI sniper, and I felt like a fool. I had attributed too much of his diffidence to cold feet or whatever doubts he carried regarding his incipient marriage to Shasta Blaylock, and far too little to the mental and spiritual scars he still bore.

As Jordan Powell opened the door to climb into his truck, I could sense some small part of him had been restored: a trace of the seasoned and respected cowhand, deft with a rope and quick with a joke, proficient and capable and courageous.

"You did good out there today, son," I said. "The fellas were damned happy to see you."

"Thank you, sir."

"I'm not blowing sunshine up your skirt, Jordan. There's a place for you on the crew any time you want it back."

"Roger that. Much appreciated. But for now, I think I'll just stick with police work, if you don't mind."

He looked like he was about to say something more but thought better of it and held his tongue.

"Something else you want to say?" I prompted.

He hesitated, weighing his words in his head. Then he spoke.

"You know I've still got the fire, don't you, Captain? I ain't lost my stride."

"Nobody ever doubted that for a moment, Jordan," I said. "Not a soul. Especially not me."

"I want you to know I ain't lost my nerve neither."

He looked away from me, took off his hat and laid it

crown-down on the passenger seat, then climbed in and started his truck. He rolled down the window and leaned an elbow on the opening and looked me square in the eye.

"What I mean to say, sir, is we've both seen the elephant," he said. "You know what I mean. And sometimes it just takes an extra minute or two before you're ready to see him again."

I WATCHED Powell's truck disappear down the road, then I stepped inside and phoned Captain Christopher Rose, head of the Criminal Investigation Division for the Oregon State Police, at his home. We'd been colleagues for a while, and friends for even longer, but his division's professional mandate was to provide technical support to smaller local law enforcement departments with the processing of crime scenes, emergency backup manpower, and other technical assistance.

Rose possessed the physique of a man who'd likely been an athlete at one time in his life, swift with a curse and as jaded as they come. We'd had our professional differences, but I believed him to be a straight shooter and a realist with a healthy respect for the rule of law, and we'd developed a sometimes grudging mutual respect.

It took four or five rings for him to pick up, his Texas drawl all the more pronounced, having consumed what I gathered to be at least a couple of Saturday afternoon bourbon peach coolers.

"Been wondering when I was gonna hear from you all, Dawson," he said. "I understand you boys've been huntin' down a eagle murderer. Any truth to that rumor?"

"You are correctly informed," I said. It had never ceased to amaze me how widely and rapidly certain kinds of information made the rounds, and I chose yet again not to inquire about it.

"You are aware that eagle killin' is a federal matter," Rose said.

"I am aware of that."

I heard the rattle of ice in his highball glass, followed by a short blast of a guffaw.

"I'm just pulling your leg, Dawson. You want some help with that, just say the word. I'd love nothing more than to help catch a goddamn poacher. Assholes."

"No, thank you, Chris. I appreciate the offer, but my deputy, Jordan Powell, is on top of it. Besides, he could use a win on his scoresheet."

"I hear you on that, Ty. But all bullshit aside, I wouldn't advise allowing your man to wander too far off the reservation, if you know what I mean."

"Powell's developed a whole different attitude where federal matters are concerned," I said. "He's not too concerned about their feelings."

"I suspect that he has. That boy's got balls as big as grape-fruits. I can't believe he still wants to be out on the streets after what he went through. So, if it isn't poachers, what *are* we jawboning about?"

"I could use some extra manpower for a public event that's been scheduled for next weekend. Friday and Saturday."

I heard Rose's chair squeal in protest as he stood up to pace, his footfalls landing hard on the floorboards of the card room in his house.

"You talking about that rock concert out there in the woods? Been hearing about it all week on the radio."

Which explained the crowd that had been descending on Meridian for the past several days.

"That's the one," I said. "The promoter claims to have arranged for crowd security—it's being staged on private property—but I don't want to leave anything to chance."

"I read you loud and clear. How many troopers do you need?"

"Promoter's expecting a small group on Friday from what my wife tells me. Jesse's working with a film crew out there. She says it's invited guests only the first night. Saturday's another matter entirely. Could be as many as ten thousand, maybe more."

"Shit oh Rover," he said. "Goddamn."

"I've got me and two additional deputies, but that's all I can rustle up on my end," I said. "I could use another ten or twelve of your guys. Can you swing it?"

"You better alert the hospital and an ambo crew, too, Dawson. Just in case."

"Already have."

"I'll pull something together for you," he said. "Gonna cost the county some overtime, though."

"Understood. Send the bill to my office. County Council will cover it. Eventually."

"Goddamn hippies," Rose said as a fresh set of ice cubes clinked into his tumbler. "Don't they ever do anything in small groups anymore?"

I KNEW it would be hours before Jesse and Cricket returned home, so I climbed into the Bronco and drove to Lewiston, the seat of local government in Meriwether County. Something had been nagging me about the abstruse nature of the fire at the McEvoy hog farm, and I failed to comprehend the motivation for its destruction. Jordan Powell had made an offhand remark about the property having been unlucky—snakebit—but there was nothing I could recall that resonated with me as to what he had meant.

In addition to Lewiston serving as the county seat, it was also the home of the main branch of the county library. This being a Saturday, the county clerk's office would be closed, which meant that conducting a chain of title search on the hog farm was off the table for me, so the library was my only real choice. I was curious why the McEvoy farm—or the McEvoy family themselves—would merit the attention of an arsonist. Given that official property ownership records were unavailable, the next best alternative was to have a look at archival issues from the local newspaper.

I parallel parked on an empty side street across from the courthouse and walked a half block to the library's main entrance. I ascended the broad staircase that led to a set of glass doors set in antique brass engraved with images of entwined creeping vines and gravid clusters of ripening grapes. Inside, the air was tepid, unmoving and musty, the ambience reedy and frangible.

The lone librarian behind the front desk was immersed in the pages of a thick volume whose leather cover had gone brittle and begun to crack along the spine. She acknowledged my arrival with a raised eyebrow as she removed her reading glasses and allowed them to dangle from a silver chain around her neck. She had a broad face with wide-set gray eyes, hair like spun sugar, and pursed lips, deeply lined as though she'd spent her life sucking displeasure through a paper straw.

"Can I help you find something?" she asked.

"Yes, ma'am," I said and showed her my badge. "I'd like to look through some old issues of the *Daily Post*."

"Mmm."

"Issues going back ten, fifteen years or so?"

"Which one? Ten or fifteen?"

Her voice was firm, overly loud, echoing inside the cavernous room.

"Fifteen years, please, ma'am. And if you've got issues older than that, you can bring them along, too. Do you have them on microfiche by any chance?"

She didn't answer me directly but led the way down a long

corridor and deep into the stacks. She halted abruptly and indicated a recessed area among the bookshelves that was outfitted with a small wooden desk, a reading lamp, and a microfilm reader.

"Do I need to show you how to operate the machine?" she asked.

"Thank you, but no. I am familiar with how they work."

"Fine," she said. "Wait here, and I'll bring you the films."

She returned a few minutes later, placed them on the desktop without making eye contact, then turned and departed in a fog of overtly aggressive perfume.

I scrolled through the microfilm cassettes for nearly three hours and found fewer than a half-dozen mentions of the McEvoy hog farm between the time of its founding and its abandonment. Just as Jordan Powell had intimated to me, though, each chapter of its history had ended with some sort of tragedy.

The homestead had originally operated as a poultry farm back in 1913, run by a childless couple by the name of Sanford. By all accounts, the Sanfords appeared to be well-respected in the community, successful and hardworking, until both husband and wife had fallen victim to the Spanish flu. The year was 1918, a mere five years after they'd begun. By that time, the flock numbered nearly five hundred birds, but the entire brood was destroyed by the authorities as a result of the pandemic. In the aftermath, the property lay fallow for nearly two decades.

The property was eventually purchased by an enterprising family named Wilkens at the outset of the Second World War, again boasting poultry as its primary crop. Having negotiated a successful contract with the US Army, the farm flourished for two generations, eventually expanding to include a hog and mutton operation. But in 1955, the family was beset by tragedy; the Wilkenses' young son, a toddler, accidentally drowned in a retention pond. A mere fourteen months later, the drowned boy's older brother, a child of five, was killed by the blades of a neighbor's harvester combine.

As before, the property went derelict for a number of years, eventually being acquired out of foreclosure in 1960 by a family named Swanson. This time, the story concluded with the unexplained death of a local Meridian woman, an acquaintance of the Swanson family, the subject of a case that was shrouded in mystery. The only photo of the incident was indistinct and poorly defined, as though it had been shot through a window screen. All I could make out was a blurry image of my predecessor, Sheriff Lloyd Skadden, and an unidentified man kneeling beside a sheet-covered corpse lying dead on a bed of fallen oak leaves.

According to the article, there were many in town who suspected foul play, but the property again went abandoned, and the case went unsolved and forgotten.

The final owners had been the McEvoys, who simply couldn't make a go of it, pouring every last dime of their savings into an enterprise that slowly fell victim to a mismanaged domestic economy. Mr. McEvoy slid the cold barrel of a .40-caliber revolver in his mouth and squeezed the trigger. It was said that his blood and brain tissue were still wet on the wall when his wife simply drove off and dropped the housekeys through the mail slot at the bank on her way out of town.

The only connection between any of the owners was a name I hadn't encountered in years.

Lily Firecloud.

CHAPTER THIRTEEN

GRAY CLOUDS had begun to stack up on the ridgeline as I drove the county two-lane toward the junction where the Firecloud family had built their business and homestead. I crossed the trestle bridge, the woods on the hillside already deep in shadow, but the sunlight was still glinting off the riffle and cutthroat trout lingered in the lee of the streamers of green moss. On the opposite bank, I saw three children playing near the threshold of the railbed, hunting in the ballast for old spikes and fishplates and castoff ceramic insulators from long-disused telegraph poles.

I forced my attention back to the road, felt myself slipping into old inclinations, reflecting on the years of my youth and the decades I lived in this county. Some things had been irreparably transmuted, while still others remained exactly the same as they'd been since Ewing Young traded liquor and beaver pelts on the west bank of the Willamette. But I couldn't seem to draw any meaningful recollection or significance from anything I had learned at the library. In the end, the entire ordeal struck me as a pitiful memento of local history that almost made me wish I hadn't looked into it at all. The moral disfigurement of mankind appeared boundless, and my efforts had brought me no closer to learning why an arsonist would have taken special interest in a woeful, decrepit old farmhouse, apart from the contemptible and tawdry thrill of watching someone else's past go up in flames.

A FEW MINUTES LATER, I rumbled across an iron cattle guard, pulled off the road and into a wide turnout that led to the Valley Meat Company, a low-volume slaughterhouse and locker plant that had serviced the small family-owned cow-calf operations in the county for decades. I had played high school baseball with Darrel Firecloud, whose grandfather had established the business at the turn of the century.

Just prior to my leaving for college, I attended Darrel's wedding to another classmate, Lily Bird, upon whom I had nursed a heartbreaking crush. Years later, Jesse and I had been invited to a baby shower to celebrate the birth of their only son, Charlie, and little by little, we all busied ourselves with our own growing families and gradually fell out of touch. The last time I had seen Lily, she was standing beside Darrel's grave at his funeral, her features and tears mercifully obscured underneath a black veil. I could only manage to spend a brief time at the visitation someone had arranged for Darrel afterward, at a loss for both feelings and words, numbed and worn down by the nearness of so much pointless death. That was seven years ago.

I braked to a stop at the edge of a circular drive, behind an old truck with skinned-up blue paint that was hitched to a vacated tagalong stock trailer. I climbed out of my pickup and crossed the driveway, spotting Lily. She was conversing with a man in a down vest who was waving a flag on stick, urging a handsome black Corriente steer into an enclosure with a scale on the ground. The steer gave his tipped horns a shake as he stepped forward calmly into the pen, where a young boy I took to be Charlie Firecloud clung to the steel railing and called out the animal's weight.

"Seven seventy-two," he said, and his mother turned to the man in the vest.

"You want to keep the offal?"

"Just the tongue and the cheeks," he said. "Unless you can let me have the skull and horns, too."

"I can give the whole head back to you if you want it."

"If you don't mind, Miz Firecloud. Thank you."

"You can go on back to the house, Charlie," she called out to her son. "We're almost finished here."

Lily noticed me then and showed me a familiar smile that purged the years.

"Excuse me," she said to the man in the vest. "Just for a minute."

Lily Firecloud had the same heart-shaped face I remembered so well, with eyes that were the color of topaz, her complexion and high cheekbones like those so idealized on movie screens and the covers of magazines. Her long chestnut hair was pulled up in a bun, and she wore silver earrings fashioned into the shapes of hawk feathers.

"Am I seeing a ghost?" she asked me.

"Hello, Lily."

She moved to me and embraced me gently, then leaned away without letting go.

"'Sees With His Heart,'" she whispered to me. It was the First Peoples' name that Darrel's father had given me when Darrel and I had been mere schoolboys.

Lily was wearing an oversize pullover sweater and cotton-duck work pants, a capture bolt pistol stun gun in a leather sheath on one hip, and a long-bladed knife on the other. She let go of me and took a step back.

"What brings you all the way out here, Sheriff Dawson?"

"There was a fire at the old McEvoy place. I was hoping you might be able to help me out."

"Name it," she said. "But I'm kind of in the middle of something."

"I can wait."

"Come on inside. Nothing in that slaughterhouse you haven't seen before."

Lily shook hands with the man in the vest, then waved to him as he ambled away to his truck. I followed her up a ramp and into the refrigerated confines of a small outbuilding where the Corriente steer waited calmly, gripped in the braces of a narrow chute. Lily circled around to face the creature, gently stroked his muzzle, and spoke to him in a language I did not understand. The steer's eyes showed no sign of fear or distress as she drew the bolt pistol, pressed the barrel to its forehead and depressed the trigger. His end arrived in an instant, swift and silent as his knees buckled and he folded to the floor.

Lily leaned down, proficiently employed the razor edge of the long blade on her hip, and I watched the steam rise from the steer's crimson blood as it coursed from the beast, exposed to the refrigerated air.

"We can step outside now," she said to me. "My butcher will take it from here."

I knew Lily to be as adept at dressing and processing animals as anyone I knew, but I was also well aware that she took special pride and care in the humane dispatch of the livestock she handled. Her customers were primarily small family operations—cattle, sheep, swine, and goats—processing no more than three or four animals per day; their collective livelihoods depended upon the quality and purity of their product. It was the reason the Valley Meat Company had survived nearly as long as had the Diamond D.

"Beer?" Lily asked me as I followed her along a curved gravel path toward the house she and Darrel had constructed shortly before he'd been killed.

"I still have a long drive ahead of me," I said.

"Hope you don't mind if I do."

She kicked off her boots and stepped inside the back door, took her time washing her hands and forearms, in the manner of a surgeon, at a stainless steel sink in her mudroom. She dried her hands on a terrycloth towel as she moved into the kitchen and removed a beer for herself and a bottle of soda for me.

"I'm impressed," I said, and I could tell by her reply that she knew what I meant.

"We're their caretakers, Ty," she answered. "Animals suffer enough in this life, just like we do. But we get to choose whether their last day is a good one or a bad one."

"I had an old friend who used to tell me the same thing."

"And did you take it to heart?"

"Every day."

She looked into my face for a long moment before she turned and moved into the living room, where a picture window looked out across the stillness of a slough bounded by willow trees and leafless alders whose branches were strung with Spanish moss. The atmosphere inside was fragrant with the sweet, earthy scent of palo santo, and in the distance, I could feel the vibration, the irregular rhythm of flatwheelers as the engineer windjammed the air brakes and reduced speed for the train's downward grade into the valley.

"I didn't realize your place was so close to the tracks," I said.

"For better or worse," she said. "Used to be good for business, I guess. Small ranchers could ship their livestock here by rail. At least, that's what Darrel's old man used to tell us."

"What do you mean, 'for better or worse'?"

She reached up and removed the pin that had been holding her hair in place. She shook it out as it fell across her shoulders, the narrow band of solid white still there, extending down the length from where she parted it, originating at the crown of her head. Rumor was that it had turned white overnight, but nobody knew why. And Lily never said.

"Hoboes took over the old icehouse up the road a while back. There's a whole hobo jungle up there now."

As sheriff, I had made it a practice to keep an eye on the drifters' old gathering place, several miles southeast of town beside the railroad right of way. For the most part, they kept to themselves—harmless rail tramps, sundowners, and out-of-work boomers waiting for a free ride to Sacramento or points east to seek work. What Lily was now telling me came as news.

"They ever give you any trouble?"

"I see them on foot, or thumbing rides from time to time, but nobody bothers me here. Besides, who'd want to break into a slaughterhouse?"

I watched her tip back her beer and perused the room, noticing the head of a ten-point trophy buck hanging at the center of the fireplace mantel. The taxidermy was impeccable, its umber eyes practically illuminated from within.

"Darrel did that one," Lily said. "Beautiful, isn't it?"

"Spectacular. How did he take him?"

"Traditional bow, handcrafted arrows; he even made his own fletching from turkey and duck feathers. But that's not what I was referring to."

My puzzlement must have been transparent.

"I meant that Darrel mounted that buck," she said. "He was becoming a gifted taxidermist."

"Darrel never did anything halfway," I said. "I always admired that quality in him."

"I did, too. He was a perpetual student."

She opened a glass sliding door and we stepped outside to an open deck, the air rapidly cooling as the sun slid from the sky. Between the trees at the near end of the slough, I saw that the adjoining property lay unplanted but newly harrowed. The sight of her son, Charlie, scavenging stones along the culvert and the smell of upturned earth put me back in mind of the young child who had been killed by a harvester combine so long ago and reminded me of the nature of my errand.

"I can see you have something heavy on your mind, Tyler. You mentioned a fire."

"What can you tell me about the McEvoy place?" I asked. "I understand the Fireclouds did business with a few of the owners over the years."

ON MY WAY HOME, I stopped off at Half Mountain Studio. There was no sign of Jesse and Cricket, so I assumed they were filming indoors, but I spotted the man I was looking for standing at the foot of the stage. He was talking with an older tradesman who was occupied with connecting electrical wires where the footlights and sound monitors would be linked, his two pals—I didn't see the third—absorbed with rolling extension cords and stacking them into the back of a panel truck. The tan madras shirt he was wearing was patterned with sweat, the back of his neck lined with dirt. He turned when he heard me approach, sidestepped toward the truck without letting me out of his sight.

It was clear that this man had been spawned at the bottom of the barrel, what some might refer to as white trash, his life story literally tattooed on his skin. But I did not mistake the mere fact of his upbringing would mean that he was stupid. I pushed through the protective knot the three men had formed and looked into his face in the same manner I had when I'd first seen these men at the Cottonwood Blossom. His eyeballs jittered in their sockets as if he'd just swallowed a fistful of speed.

"Tell Tweedle-Dee and Tweedle-Dipshit to take a hike for a minute," I said to the man with the tattoos. "There's something I need to say to you."

He threw a glance in their direction and the two men stepped away to share a cigarette beneath the tent canvas.

"You seem like a man who'd be familiar with certain addresses in places like Deer Lodge and Folsom," I said.

"Am I supposed to know what that means?"

"I advised you to hit the road when I saw you last. For some reason, you didn't take that to heart. So, here's the deal: if I sense one whiff of trouble out here, you're the first person I'm coming for. I will bury your nose in the dirt and drag you back to Meridian in cuffs, you read me?"

Over the man's shoulder, I saw Mickey London striding a beeline in our direction. His hands were balled into fists at his side, the skin of his throat red with rage where it showed through his unbuttoned shirt.

"Anything else, Sheriff?" the man with the tattoos said. His lips twisted into a grin, but his pupils had spun down to pinpricks, vibrating inside their sockets. "I need to get back to work."

Ian's manager arrived and stepped in between us before I could reply, moving himself into my personal space.

"Are you bothering my foreman?" London asked me. His words came out staccato, the tempo of his breathing abbreviated by the brisk walk he'd just taken and the rush of adrenaline coursing through his bloodstream.

"I certainly hope so," I said and walked slowly back to my truck.

CHAPTER FOURTEEN

THE NEXT MORNING, after church, I came home and changed into a pair of cargo pants and lightweight nylon shirt. I grabbed my creel and fishing gear and went into the kitchen to make a sandwich for later. Through the window above the sink, I saw Jesse outside filling the hummingbird feeders and the seed box for the bluebirds and their brood. Cricket came in behind me and stepped to the refrigerator to see what was inside, already changed out of her church garb and wearing a pair of cutoff shorts and men's plaid flannel Pendleton with the sleeves rolled up on her forearms.

"How's work been going?" I asked as I slid my ham and cheese into a plastic bag.

"Do you mean, 'How are things going with Ian?'"

I placed the sandwich bag on the counter and looked at her.

"No," I replied. "I meant exactly what I said."

She withdrew a bottle of orange juice and shut the refrigerator door, stood on her toes, and reached into the cupboard for a drinking glass.

"Is this some kind of test?" she asked.

"Should it be? Is there something you need to be tested about?"

She ignored my question as she poured her juice. She drank half of it in one gulp before she made eye contact with me.

"You'll always be my daughter," I said. "I'd think you'd be accustomed to that fact by now."

"I'm still working on it."

Cricket took her time putting the juice bottle back into the fridge, then turned and leaned against the counter and gazed out the window at her mom.

"I hear the flies are hatching up on the Knife," I said to Cricket. "Want to come fishing with me?"

The corners of her lips curled upward, and she moved her shimmering blue eyes to me.

"Do we have to talk?" she asked.

"Nope."

She finished the remainder of her juice and placed her empty glass into the sink, and she smiled.

"I'll get my stuff and meet you at the truck."

CHAPTER FIFTEEN

MONDAY MORNING, I drove to Lewiston to testify in court. The case involved a simple B&E that had devolved into a savage and repugnant sexual assault against an elderly deaf woman. The defendant was a peripatetic former cow buster named Jake Relfe, who by all accounts had left his eggs in the pan far too long. I finally had my chance to return the recidivist shitweasel to the Oregon State Correctional Institution for the remainder of his useless life. I wasn't about to let the opportunity slip by.

I spent the first half of the day waiting in the hallway to be called into the courtroom, seated on an uncomfortable hardwood bench that put me in mind of the pews in my grandfather's Methodist church. The long, narrow corridor was an endless procession of anguish, fear, torment, and regret, the accompanying soundtrack the echo of stiletto slingbacks and polished brogans bouncing between windowless walls and waxed linoleum. I read the daily newspaper from front to back and had made it halfway through a castoff copy of *Life* magazine when the judge called for a lunch break. The courtroom doors swung open and a convoy of weary and bored-looking people filed out, so I fit myself into the flow and moved down the staircase to the double doors that led outside.

I crossed the street and went to where I'd parked my truck behind the Lewiston substation, collected my sack lunch from the ice chest I'd left on the seat, and carried it back to enjoy it outdoors in the courthouse quadrangle. I sat by myself on a park bench in the shade of a Fuji apple tree, a gift from the Aomori Prefecture, Lewiston's sister city, according to the bronze plaque in the planter. The sunshine warmed my back as I ate a roast beef and lettuce sandwich in the coruscated light and watched a pair of gray squirrels engage in a boisterous squabble as they balanced in the branches of the tree. I pulled the tab off a can of RC Cola, took a long pull while I skimmed my attention across the forecourt. Amid the jurors smoking cigarettes and court employees enjoying their brief lunch breaks with eyes tightly squeezed and faces upturned to the sky, I recognized a man I'd hoped I wouldn't have to see again until I faced him from my seat on the witness stand.

He had the carriage and demeanor of a tennis pro, wavy blond hair swept off an unlined forehead, and a country club suntan. He wore his trademark smug expression behind his Foster Grants as he sauntered from the parking lot across the plaza with his slender leather attaché in hand.

I turned away and fed my bread crusts to the fractious squirrels, wadded my rubbish into a ball when I felt a man's shadow fall across the bench I was sitting on. I twisted in my seat and squinted into the noonday sun. He was standing close to me, intentionally too close, his profile in stark silhouette against the glare.

"Remember me?" he asked.

"How could I forget? You're Cameron Ducoyne, staunch defender of the status quo. You know very well that you shouldn't be speaking to me without the DA present."

"We're just two professionals having a casual word, Sheriff Dawson."

"Make that *one* professional and one white-shoe attorney," I corrected. "Where do you get off accosting me in public, outside the county courthouse?"

He cocked his head in mock puzzlement, shifted his briefcase from one hand to the other.

"As I said—" he began.

"I believe you are seeking to create grounds for a mistrial," I interrupted.

Cameron Ducoyne was both a media whore and malignant narcissist, locally famous for his legal representation of a disgraced Portland lawyer and politico whom I'd arrested as a part of an ongoing scheme that involved the trafficking of heroin and underage girls. I assumed Ducoyne was in town that day requesting a bail reduction for his client, an accommodation I sincerely hoped would be denied. At a minimum, his client deserved to rot in county lockup while awaiting his trial rather than in the relative luxury of house arrest.

I made a mental note to stop off at St. Stephen's to light a candle, with a prayer that my perp would be forced to live out the remainder of his miserable life looking over his shoulder in the yard at the federal supermax and having to stoop down like a chimp to retrieve fallen soap from the floor of the shower. If it was mercy and absolution the man desired, he could take it up with God. I'd done my part already.

"I would advise you to stop talking to me and walk away," I said to Cameron Ducoyne. "One more word from you, I will see that you face charges of contempt and sanctions from the bar."

The attorney shook his head and feigned insult.

"Rookie move, Sheriff," he said. "You're going to regret having spoken to me that way."

"You know, I think I got something stuck in my eardrum when I was out riding my horse," I said. "I just can't seem to hear too well today."

Ducoyne made a *tsk* with his teeth and strolled away.

I finished collecting my rubbish and threw it into the garbage can. As I was making my way back to spend the last few minutes of the lunch break with the squirrels, I spotted the new district attorney, Bridger Midland, heading my direction. He had recently replaced a man I hadn't ever had much use for, but Bridger had already earned more of my professional respect during his short tenure than his predecessor had in the whole time he had served as the DA.

"Was that who I think it was?" Bridger asked as we shook hands.

"Sure enough."

"What the hell's he doing talking to you out here in front of the angels and everyone?"

"I asked him that same question."

"That man's about as subtle as an enema."

I glanced at my wristwatch, noticed we only had about fifteen minutes before court reconvened.

"How's our trial going?" I asked.

"Like chewing on foil," Bridger said. "I'm truly sorry, Ty. I thought I woulda had you on the stand by now."

"Want me to stick around?"

"I'm afraid so. I can't tell what the defense is up to, but their strategy seems to involve boring the jury into a slow, painful death."

"I could think of better uses for my time, Bridger. I've already read today's paper twice."

"I understand," he said and shrugged.

"Tell you what," I said. "I've got some things I could be doing across the street. Call me at the station house, and I can be back here in five minutes. Fair enough?"

"Probably. Let me run it by the judge."

"I'll come with you."

* * *

AS I WAITED to offer my court testimony, I used my downtime in Lewiston to have a look at the former sherrif, Lloyd Skadden's, file archives to see what I could find regarding the McEvoy case. Between what I had learned from Lily Firecloud and the casual comment that Jordan Powell had thrown out about the place being bad luck, any tolerance I might have otherwise allowed for the existence of coincidence had all but evaporated.

AS ANYONE who has lived in a small town knows very well, you do not push against the rich or the powerful or those who wield political influence. Lloyd Skadden knew that game well. He was not a large man in conventional terms, but his carriage and brash personality created an impression of authority and prerogative that was at odds with both his physical stature and the weakness of character that I knew him to possess. Like my family, the Skaddens had helped to settle this valley and had earned themselves a modicum of respect in previous generations. But Lloyd Skadden's father had proved himself to be neither a deft landowner nor a rancher, and his deficiencies had affected the family's diminishing fortunes, though it failed to moderate young Lloyd's sense of entitlement.

As it turned out, Lloyd Skadden found his salvation in politics, rescued from his own petty designs by a friend of his father's, a man who taught Lloyd how to accumulate small pockets of influence by currying favor and exploiting the weaknesses of his peers. Lloyd won his first term as sheriff in 1955 and held on tight.

I had only encountered him after returning from my hitch in Korea, and then only in passing. Decades went by as I turned my attention to the Diamond D and my family, having only occasional social contact with the man at the annual rodeo or some other community event, always finding his manner both specious and unctuous.

Even all those years later, when Skadden had conscripted me to assist him—temporarily, he'd lied—I could still see the young man he had once been: making unwanted sexual advances in the back seats of jacked-up automobiles, swilling cheap beer and taking potshots at road signs with a .22 rifle from the bed of a speeding pickup, or shouting vulgar remarks to adolescent girls as they stood in shy knots outside the movie theater.

For nearly twenty years, Skadden had managed to hold the office of sheriff in his fist like a medieval lord before immolating himself on a bonfire of his own avarice. I had been there when he died—shot by a disgruntled business partner—was there when his eyes rolled back in his head as his life drained away, neither of us uttering a word.

I shook off the memory, unlocked the door of the office, and flicked the switch for the overheads. Errant specks of desiccation floated lazily as the fluorescent tubes fluttered to life, the stale air inside smelling of mildew and trapped heat, mingled with the remnant funk of human misery that still emanated from the disused holding cells in back.

As always, stepping into the Lewiston substation was like taking a giant stride backward in time, one that contained no fond reminiscences or sentimentality for me. This had been Lloyd Skadden's domain, and I left it that way, every stick of his furniture, every fixture, every framed photo on the wall; even Skadden's old office was exactly as he had left it on the day he'd been murdered. I moved the headquarters to Meridian when I became sheriff, leaving the Lewiston substation open only as a way station for my deputies when they patrolled this end of the valley and as a warehouse for Skadden's old case files and evidence boxes.

I made my way back to the end of the hall, unlocked the door to the evidence locker. I scanned through the file drawers first, looking for anything that might connect to the McEvoy property and the cases that Skadden would have investigated during his tenure. I sorted through case names and dates from decades past, names that meant little to me, dates that my mind only correlated with my time overseas, events for which I had no personal recollection or reference. What I found most disturbing was the absence of any meaningful filing system, as though each drawer had been emptied of its contents then put back together at random. After sorting through three separate file cabinets, I gave up the hunt, moved to the back of the room where the evidence boxes were stacked floor to ceiling on high shelves and locked inside a cage made of galvanized wire. I used the keys on my key ring to spring a pair of padlocks on the gate, located the evidence log, and took a seat at a gray Steelcase desk in the corner.

The evidence log was in order, at least, divided by year and case number. I dipped into my shirt pocket and unfolded the slip of notepaper on which I'd written the names and dates I'd found in the library microfiche. The logbook only went back as far as 1960, so I had no choice but to begin with the most recent case on my list, the McEvoy suicide in 1971. I ran my finger down a long column of handwritten entries, starting with January of 1971, flipping through page after page until I located an entry from July of that year listing a number of items that had been bagged, tagged, and packed in a box somewhere on the shelves in this room. I noted the reference number listed in the book and worked my way down the first row of shelves.

* * *

THREE HOURS LATER, I gave up the hunt. My head ached, my eyes burned, and I had discovered exactly nothing so far. I still hadn't heard from the DA, either, and likely wouldn't, but I was obliged to remain close at hand until court adjourned for the day. I stepped outside into the afternoon light, drew a deep breath, and walked to my truck. I removed the last can of soda from the cooler, peeled off the ring top, and took it back inside to Lloyd Skadden's former office.

I leaned back in the leather executive chair, rested my boots on the top of his prized desk, and massaged my temples. I nursed the lukewarm Dr Pepper as I scanned the detritus of Skadden's career: framed photos with minor political figures positioned along the sideboard and shelves, a paperweight engraved with his initials, a bronze sculpture of a predatory bird coming in for the kill, and a collection of police shoulder patches from all over the country. Two mounted stag heads hung on either side of the door, and I flashed on something Lily Firecloud had said to me.

I picked up the phone and dialed the Meridian substation. Jordan Powell answered before the third ring, but I cut him off before he could finish.

"I just thought of something . . ."

CHAPTER SIXTEEN

I COULD HEAR Jesse and Cricket in the kitchen early Friday morning, trying not to wake me as they prepared to leave to film the concert at Half Mountain. According to Jesse, the plan was for Ian Swann to perform a small private show—two or three hundred invited industry guests—to serve as both a marketing tool and as a dry run for the musicians, roadies, and film crew in advance of the main public event that was scheduled for Saturday.

I had arrived home late the night before; my testimony, finally having been called on Thursday morning, ended up taking the entire day. As the DA had predicted, the defense team slogged through a litany of minutiae so arcane and esoteric that I suspected I would still be on the stand if the trial judge hadn't intervened. As it turned out, justice was righteously dispensed, and the recidivist shitbird rapist against whom I testified was sent back to the pen.

It was still dark as I rolled out of bed and padded into the kitchen in my stocking feet and pajamas and robe, the air in the house chilled with the familiar vestiges of winter becoming spring. I looked outside as I passed through the living room, noticed the white patina dusting the potted boxwoods on the gallery and the windowpanes limned with frost.

"You're getting an early start," I said to my wife as I stepped to the pantry and took a ceramic mug off the shelf.

"Still a whole lot to do," Jesse said. "Len Kaanan wants to shoot the preshow setup, do a sound check, and there's all the backstage chaos . . ."

"Plus, Ian's throwing a breakfast barbecue this morning for the band and road crew," Cricket added as she shrugged herself into a knee-length woolen coat, her eyes bright with anticipation.

I topped off my coffee and watched the ladies gather their belongings, kissed my wife and daughter goodbye, and walked them to the door.

"I'll be an hour or two behind you," I said. "I've got a couple things to do before I drive out."

Cricket looked at me with surprise.

"Why so early? Show doesn't begin 'til dusk."

"I'm meeting Captain Rose on-site for a security walk-through," I said. "There's a lot of ground to cover out there, as I'm sure you're aware. And I need to pick up Sam Griffin from the station on the way."

"Hmm."

"Cramping your style?" I said and winked at Cricket.

I was gratified to see her cheeks flush as I opened the door.

CAPTAIN CHRIS ROSE WAS standing at the Half Mountain Studio entry gate with about a half-dozen of his uniformed troopers when Sam and I drove up. Rose had an unlit cigar tucked into the corner of his mouth and was laughing at something one of the younger men had just said. He was gesturing across the two-lane access road, where Len Kaanan had wisely set up a campground area to accommodate the crowd that had already begun to arrive for Ian Swann's show the next day.

I pulled beyond the gate and parked in a patch of dirt beside Rose's unmarked squad car, allowed the truck to idle as I climbed out.

"Didn't expect to see you here this morning," I said to Chris Rose.

"Wouldn't want to miss the freak show."

"Hope you bring more men tomorrow," I said. "I told you they're expecting ten thousand kids."

Rose grinned and strode a few paces away, where he leaned his elbows on the split rail fence and admired the tree-lined campsite across the road. He tilted his campaign hat back on his head.

"I didn't just drop in here from outer space, Dawson. I know how to rally the troops. When these fellas go back to the barracks and tell the rest of the guys about all the pretty young things prancing around out here wearing short-shorts and halter tops . . ."

"You'd better pray the weather warms up quick," I said. "Or they're likely to be wearing parkas and salopettes. You're liable to end up with a disappointed platoon."

"Take a look across the road there, buddy. I got this thing covered," he said. "'God is on the side of big battalions.'"

"Voltaire. More or less."

"Don't look so surprised, Dawson. You're not the only cop that went to college."

Rose's troopers piled into the back of my pickup, and Griffin drove them up to the amphitheater site. I watched the taillights disappear around a bend, and Rose stepped up beside me as I began to walk the property's perimeter fence line.

We moved along in companionable silence as we scanned the area that separated the road from the studio boundary, making our way through the untamed forest surrounding the site where

Kaanan had constructed the amphitheater. Even though admission to the event was free, there were obvious spatial limitations to attendance, and for security purposes, we needed to be familiar with points of ingress and egress.

The bare patches of soil between the conifers glowed red in the low morning light, the stone faces of the mountain peaks a serrated ribbon of purple marking the edge of the horizon. A while later, as the sun crested the summit, Captain Rose pulled up short and admired the view, the air sweet with pine pitch and loam and the mineral scent of underground water.

"I heard your testimony yesterday won a conviction for the DA," Rose said, breathing heavily.

"Where'd you hear that?"

"It was on the wire this morning when I got to the office. Evidently, the jury deliberated for less than three hours. That shitbird's gonna die behind the walls of a peniteniary, amigo."

"Not sure my testimony had much to do with it. Jury was so bored they would have convicted the bailiff if it meant the trial lawyers would finally stop talking."

A short while later, we ascended a short rise and passed through a copse of vine maple and arrowwood, the ground spongy beneath our boots, carpeted with fallen leaves and desiccated tree bark. The sun appeared from behind a cloud and the breeze picked up speed, bending the branches of the cedars below and carrying with it the persistent creak of rusted metal. As I shaded my eyes and scanned the slope's creases and folds, I spotted a discolored tin shed resting askew on a rectangle of crumbling concrete, its door swinging by one hinge in the wind. In the near distance, I watched a raptor angle itself into the current and hover over its prey.

"You ever work cases with Lloyd Skadden back in the day?" I asked him.

Rose eyed me oddly for a moment before he answered.

"A couple," he said. "Why? Where'd that come from?"

"I was killing time in Lewiston, so I started looking through the evidence locker and the old case files down at the sub."

"Looking for anything in particular?"

"Maybe," I said. I took off my Resistol and dried the sweat on my forehead with my sleeve. "The problem is, there was no order to anything at all. A complete shit show. Came away thinking there's a very good chance things might have gone missing."

"Yeah," he said, almost to himself.

He watched me push my hat onto my head and lean back on my heels.

"Why don't you look surprised that I said that?" I asked.

"You hear things sometimes, you know?"

He hooked his thumbs through his belt loops and gazed down the hill at the old shed.

"Like what kind of things?" I asked.

Rose sighed and tipped his face toward the sky. When he turned his eyes on me again, it looked as though he had aged in that moment.

"I really hate this kind of shit, Ty."

Over the years, I had become an expert at recognizing doubt and regret, suffering and deceit. This didn't look like deceit.

"What kind of things did you hear, Chris?"

"There were rumors that Skadden's people might have sanitized the files after he died."

"*Sanitized?* Are you saying evidence was removed from the file room? By whom?"

Rose knelt and picked up a small stone, absently rubbed its smooth surface with his thumb, then pitched it at the forsaken shack. The stone fell short and bounced once, rolled and disappeared into the weeds.

"You saw the deputies who worked with Lloyd Skadden," Rose said. "Hell, one of 'em was Skadden's own stepson. That dumb sonofabitch had a hairball for a brain, couldn't find his own dick if it had a bell tied to it. But that kid was loyal to the old man. They all were. Even the goddamn DA."

"Denton Lowell?" I said. "Useless coward."

"You know Lowell died, right?"

"I know it," I said, my patience evaporating. "If people suspected those guys were dirty, why didn't somebody do something about it?"

I regretted my tone even as I uttered the words. It wasn't Rose's fault that the county had previously been cursed with a crooked sheriff and spineless DA, but those days were over. Nevertheless, as Monsignor Turner frequently reminds me, I could use some improvement at discerning the line between forgiveness and forgetting.

"What were we supposed to do, Ty?" Rose replied. "It was a rumor. I never saw anything; never even set foot inside the Lewiston field office."

"God*damn* it."

"The corruption was a rumor," he repeated. "Nobody thought they could prove anything against Skadden. Not until you came along. Now Skadden's dead. Denton Lowell's dead, too. Hell, even the useless stepson is dead."

"Everything about that fat cocksucker is dead, Chris. I spoke out of turn, and I apologize. I've heard what I needed to hear. Now, let's get our asses back up the hill," I said and turned in the direction we had come.

A DISEMBODIED VOICE boomed out from the massive speaker stacks flanking the main stage and from the sound and light towers at the rear of the venue.

"Test. Test. Test."

I spotted Cricket near the foot of the stage, standing with Mickey London and directing two others, one of whom had a heavy film camera balanced on his shoulder, the other holding a boom microphone in London's face. Even at this distance, I could tell that the manager was clearly annoyed, stealing glances at the man testing the sound system, and I could tell by my daughter's body language that she was at least as irritated as London was.

"That's it," London bellowed, and he stormed away from my daughter, appearing again brief moments later onstage beside the roadie who was mumbling into the mic. "That's not how you test a bloody microphone, you moron," London said. "Move over."

"I'm just—"

"Shut up!" London repeated, shoving the narrow-shouldered sound tech to one side. London shaded his eyes from the overhead lights, scanned the open space before him for the team of sound engineers occupying the small tent that housed the main mixing console. "Are you idiots ready out there?"

Inside the tent, three people nodded vigorously, anxious to get this over with.

"Okay then," London began, his tone somewhere between a shout and a growl. "The small pup gnawed a hole in the sock! Two blue fish swam in the tank! The swan dive was far short of perfect!"

He was enunciating each line as if he were reciting Shakespearean dialogue, and it sounded ridiculous.

"The beauty of the view stunned the young boy!" London continued. "Are you assholes getting this?"

When I felt rather than heard Captain Rose wander up beside me, I turned and noted a bemused expression on his face.

"What in the hell is that guy doing up there?" Rose asked.

"He's helping them fine-tune the PA system," I said. "They need to get levels on a range of sound patterns. The obnoxious turd with the microphone is Ian Swann's manager, and he's reciting the old tried-and-true sound-reinforcement phrases. Sounds like gibberish, but it covers all the bases."

"Like 'The quick brown fox jumps over the lazy dog,'" Rose said.

"Exactly."

"How the hell would you know that, Dawson?"

"I spent a few years wrangling for Hollywood movies after I shipped stateside from Korea," I said. "Worked a few live events, too. It's where I met Jesse."

"How long is this guy gonna go on like this?"

I watched Mickey London, a man clearly at the end of his patience.

"Hard to tell," I said. "He seems to be enjoying himself."

"Press the pants and sew a button on the goddamn vest!" London continued, shouting from the stage. "Her purse was full of useless trash!"

"Okay," one of the engineers barked, stepping out to the front of the mixing tent. "We got it, Mickey. Thank you."

"Good," London spat. "Now, all of you assholes get back to work. Gates open up in six hours."

It looked as though he was about to stalk off the stage, but something above him caught his attention, and he turned his eyes upward to the catwalk. Whatever he saw made him furious, and he stormed back to the microphone and very publicly berated someone in the overhead scaffolding.

"You there! Yeah, *you*, asshole! Where's your goddamned tether?"

From where Rose and I were standing at the rear of the

venue, I couldn't make out the exact wording of the reply, only the murmur of a voice in supplication.

"I don't give one single shit about that," London answered, his diatribe echoing across the arena. "That's a forty-foot drop if you slip from up there, dumbass. That's as high as a four-story building, for you kids who failed math class. A fall from up there will probably kill you. So, tether up! All of you! And make sure those goddamn stage lights are secured! Some of those sonsabitches are twenty, thirty pounds each—like a fucking bomb falling out of the sky. Get your shit together, you clowns!"

Rose watched Mickey London for a moment longer before he turned to me. "This is the music business? A goddamn cultural sinkhole, more like."

The captain shook his head, smiled to himself as London's tirade concluded, and walked off toward the rear of the bowl, where his troopers had begun to gather at the catering trucks.

THE MAKESHIFT arena had been constructed in concentric half circles the shape of a cone, an earthen rainbow of fescue and pebbled walkways centered on the enormous stage structure at its vertex, rising in a gradual oblique to the rear. A small reserved seating area for two hundred people, more or less, bordered the apron of the elevated stage. This section was roped off by a cordon of stanchions and chains beyond which a pair of broad arcs of carefully manicured grass had been installed for festival lawn-seating that would accommodate another ten thousand or so. A concourse of hardpacked aggregate gravel marked the rear boundary, collared by a ring of concession booths offering food, beverages, and souvenirs, behind which was a vast complement of portable chemical toilets. In all, it appeared to be a very efficiently conceived design.

I was standing at the edge of concourse, looking down toward the stage, across the shallow bowl of seating, where a folding table had been set up to dispense weekly cash pay envelopes to the construction crew before the gates opened that evening. The smell of freshly cooked Mexican food drifted on the breeze as I watched the line form at the pay table; the scene put me in mind of a gold-rush-era mining camp at the end of a very long week.

"You didn't think I'd pull it off, did you?" Len Kaanan said as he stepped up beside me.

"I had my doubts," I admitted. "I'm a sheriff and a rancher, Mr. Kaanan, both of which have made me a skeptic. Don't take it personally."

He smiled, took in the view as he savored his moment, and it seemed as though he was waiting for something.

"It's a damn nice setting," I said and looked skyward. "And it looks like the weather's going to cooperate with you, too."

"These people—Ian's fans—they deserve it. Throw down four or five bucks for an album; seven or eight for a concert ticket; another ten bucks for a T-shirt. Gotta give them their money's worth, no?"

"I thought the concert was free of charge," I said.

"A figure of speech."

A brief altercation erupted behind us, where a small group of heavy equipment operators was overseeing the loading of their excavators, skidloaders, and other heavy steel onto a procession of big rigs hauling flatbed trailers; they were being strapped down by fortified chain with links as thick as my wrists.

"Don't mind them," Kaanan said dismissively. "An hour from now, the whole lot of 'em will be gone."

"Everybody seems wound up a little bit tight," I said.

"Opening day," Kaanan replied, as if that explained everything. "It's always like this."

"Do you always pay your employees in cash?" I asked as I watched the procession below pass before the paymaster.

Kaanan studied my face for a moment before answering.

"I don't believe I understand the implication, Sheriff Dawson. But the concert business is a largely cash enterprise. Always has been. Anyone who's been around it for very long tends to get comfortable with handling hard currency."

Beyond Kaanan's shoulder, I noticed Chris Rose wandering over from the direction of the concourse. Kaanan followed the direction my attention had taken and turned to notice him just as Rose stepped up to join us.

"This is Captain Rose," I said, introducing the two men. "He runs CID—Criminal Investigation Division—for the Oregon State Police."

"I'm Len Kaanan. I guess you could say I'm the ringmaster of this circus."

The two men shook hands and Kaanan turned to me, eyebrows arched theatrically.

"Bringing in the big guns, huh, Sheriff?"

"I told you I had concerns about security," I said.

"And I heard you loud and clear the first time, Sheriff," he said. "You'll notice I have a pair of ambulances on standby backstage."

"That's a good start," I said. "Now all we need is to move ten thousand rock music fans in and out of here tomorrow without incident, and we can call it a wrap."

Kaanan's expression went hard, about to reply to me, when Rose intervened.

"We all want the same thing, sir," Rose offered.

"I'll take your word for it," Kaanan said, and Rose and I watched the producer stalk away.

"That guy's a piece of work," Rose said once Kaanan was out of earshot. "I don't want to hurt your feelings, Dawson, but I'm not sure he likes you very much."

"I'll get over it," I said.

I POUNDED on the door of Ian Swann's cottage with the ball of my closed fist, wondering even then if he could hear it. Inside I could hear laughter and could feel the thrum of deep bass notes coming up through my boot soles. When the door flew open a few moments later, Ian Swann stood in the gap, grinning, amplified music blasting more clearly now from a stereo in the other room.

His eyes were clear, his smile genuine, and he appeared more relaxed than before. He was dressed in faded dungarees, tennis shoes, and a blue plaid flannel shirt with the sleeves rolled up to his elbows. I recognized the beaded choker he wore as one that Cricket had been crafting at our kitchen table.

Ian's brother, Dowd, stood a short distance behind Ian, giving me a once-over again, a gauzy haze of blue smoke floating near the ceiling in the other room. I touched my hat brim and tossed Dowd a wave, but he turned around and retreated into the living room once he recognized who I was.

Ian swung the door wide, swept his arm to conduct me inside.

"Come on in," Ian said. "It's just me and the band. And my brother."

I took another look beyond the threshold and remained where I was.

"I'm fairly certain you and your friends don't want me in there. But thank you just the same."

Ian shot a glance over his shoulder and took in the view from my perspective. He stepped out and joined me on the threshold, closing the front door behind him.

"I'm sorry to barge in," I said.

"You're welcome any time, Sheriff."

I looked into the sky, watched a red-tailed hawk turning slow circles in the slipstream, and I felt the meager warmth of the day slipping away.

"I expect you'll be leaving here after your show tomorrow night," I said.

"Yes, sir. I believe that's the plan."

Ian seemed relieved, or perhaps simply resigned, surrendered to the fates now that his work was completed. Either way, he appeared relaxed and ready to perform.

"I believe I owe you an apology, Mr. Swann," I said. "I made certain judgments about you when you and your entourage first arrived in town, and I may have spoken hastily."

"No apology is necessary—"

"I was right about your manager, however," I said. "Just for the record."

"I'm sure you were," Swann said and smiled knowingly.

"You've treated my family—my daughter, in particular—with respect, and I appreciate that very much. That tells me a great deal about you, Mr. Swann."

My generation of cowboys, and those who went before us, were not huggers. But that didn't stop Ian Swann from leaning in and wrapping me inside a strong two-armed embrace. When he finally let go of me, I took a step backward and shook his hand.

"I know there's a superstition about not wishing you 'good luck' tonight," I said. "So I believe the appropriate bon mot is 'break a leg.'"

"Thank you, Sheriff. When I come back this way again, I would like your permission to look you and your family up. Maybe come by for a visit."

"You have it, Ian. Take care, son."

Ian opened the door as I turned to leave. Music slid out into the gap and I heard him call out to me again.

"Hey, Sheriff," he said. "Whatever happened with that eagle? Have you caught the guy?"

"Still working on it. But we're getting closer."

"Would you do me a favor and tell me when you do?"

"May I ask why?"

He looked me in the eye from the narrow space between the door and the doorframe.

"It just made me mad, that's all," he said. "I don't want to believe people can do something like that and get away with it. Will you let me know?"

"Sure thing, Ian. I'll let you know."

IT WAS midafternoon by the time I completed my rounds and assigned Rose's state troopers and Sam Griffin to their various posts. I ambled down to the foot of the stage, the fabled "Golden Circle," the best seats in the house, where tonight's VIP audience would be treated to the best show that Len Kaanan and Ian Swann could bring to bear. I leaned an elbow on a stage riser and watched the scurry of last-minute preparations, the chaotic ballet of activity as laborers hoisted half-ton lengths of steel rigging into the girders with pull-chains and winches, and electricians hauled cable as thick as my arm across the platform. When their work was completed, that conduit would push enough voltage to light up a small village, coupled with octopus junction boxes that split the line and fed it up into the overhead rigging. It was a feat of sheer grit not entirely unlike the work being done by my men at the Diamond D.

I pulled my attention away from the stage and took in the view looking outward. A vast expanse of emerald grass angling toward the horizon, where untouched rolling hills overlooked the dwarfed stage and the piedmont beyond it stretched all the way to the skirt of the Cascades. For a moment, I wondered how it might feel to be Ian Swann, performing before a small sea of admiring faces as the timeless landscape listened in.

A small truck pulled a short flatbed trailer onto the oiled tarmac beside the stage, the trailer piled high with folding chairs, and I recognized the driver and the two men in the bed of the truck as the tattooed train jumper and his sidekicks. I watched as they off-loaded the trailer and set about arranging the seats in a pattern of prenumbered rows.

The driver noticed me as I watched them work and set down his load to eye me with an odd combination of obliviousness and complete self-assurance. I wasn't certain if I envied or pitied him. What I did know with a certainty was that I didn't want any of these men in my town.

"Last time I saw you out here, you told me you were the foreman," I said to the larger one, the one with an armful of amateur ink and janky pupils and an assertion of previous military experience. "What happened?"

He eyed me blankly, twisted a finger into his ear, and looked at what he pulled out briefly before wiping it on his pantleg. There was still nothing in his expression but for the whiff of jailhouse predation that would likely never dissipate from his nature.

"Turns out, I ain't management material," he said finally and returned to his work.

His two companions remained studiously focused on their task, neither one seeming to know what to do with their eyes. As for the man I had addressed, the whites of his eyeballs appeared clearer than the last time I'd seen him, his adrenalized speed-freak behavior subdued to a point of near normalcy that I had no valid reason to trust.

"Why do you keep harassing my men?" Mickey London shouted at me from his place on the stage behind me. I had not heard him approach, his footfalls inadvertently concealed by the noise of labor in the overhead rigging. Either that or he was a man with a guileful temperament and he had crept up on me intentionally.

"I'm beginning to question your frame of reference, Mr. London," I said to the manager. "You have a habit of mistaking simple conversations with confrontation. Are you aware of that?"

"In my experience, lawmen don't have simple conversations with men like those three."

"That observation says more about you than it says about lawmen."

"Piss off, Sheriff," London said. "Some of us have work to finish."

But the fact was, London wasn't entirely wrong. I hadn't been able to draw a bead on these three, and that fact provided me very cold comfort. In fact, it provided me no comfort at all. Amateurs were usually easy to spot, but nobody remains amateur forever. There are only two ways to move on: get out or go pro. Which category these men fell into remained uncertain.

I ignored London and the bluster he employed like a truncheon and studied the three sundowners for a few moments longer. Before I left, I stepped back toward the big man, waiting for him to make eye contact with me.

"Don't forget what I told you before," I said. "I'm going to be here tonight. Tomorrow, too, and I'm watching. One whiff of trouble, and I'm coming for you."

THE GROUND FOG seemed to roll in from nowhere, forming of its own volition from the flats near the lake, edging its way gradually toward higher ground, following the incline of the showgrounds, then cascading down into the punch bowl that Len Kaanan had painstakingly carved from the land where the audience was soon to be seated. As viewed from inside the haze, the sun seemed to liquify, ensnared in a sheet of wet cotton, the mist itself pearlescent, opaque and menacing. The atmosphere continued to fold inward, utterly still, moist and cold, and within moments, those of us on the arena grounds found ourselves absorbed within a silvery cloud, a cocoon of diaphanous vapor so impenetrable I could not distinguish the shape of my own hand at the end of my arm, so dense it dulled and obscured the transmission of sound. And the soft velvet light gave over to hushed darkness.

Someone among us should have recognized the portent.

INTERLUDE III

(1964)

"WHAT ARE YOU doing out here?" Paul said. He was filthy with hog mud and dried chicken dung from his work.

"I thought I'd surprise you," Heather said. "I asked Sarah to drop me off after practice. She's on her way up to Lewiston."

Paul cut his eyes across the feeding pens, where his father was clearing a layer of green scum from the surface of the retention pond with a long-handled net. Paul waved his arm and got his father's attention, called out when his father looked up, his expression one of consternation and disquiet at seeing Heather at his son's side.

"I'll be right back," Paul called out, waiting for a moment before his father gestured a grudging assent.

It was late afternoon, the fence that surrounded his house strung with dead leaves and brush that had been trapped by the wind. The sky overhead reflected the dim haze of slash fire smoke, and an eclipse windmill ginned noisily in the field behind the old oak near the driveway.

"Don't get too close to me," Paul said to Heather. The corners of his mouth angled upward, but his stomach was twisted in a knot. "I smell like pig crap."

Heather laughed at his sudden admission, brushed his cheek with her fingers as if she didn't care.

"I don't mind," she said. "I figured you'd probably be working. I've lived in this place for a while, I know what farms are like."

"Do yourself a favor and stay upwind, at least."

Paul led her behind the old oak, where a long time ago his father had strung a length of old fence lumber as a seat for a swing; he'd hung it with an old rope from a branch that reached out from the trunk like an old woman's knobby hand. Paul brushed the dust off the swing with a handkerchief he had tucked into his pocket and held it for Heather as she sat down. She was dressed in a pair of culottes, a loose-fitting white blouse, and the saddle shoes that cheerleaders wore as a part of their uniforms. It was clear she had hitched a ride at the last minute with one of her friends after practice, even if she hadn't admitted as much.

She swung back and forth in slow, gentle arcs as Paul sat cross-legged on the edge of an irrigation ditch, resting his wrists on his knees. She smiled and looked off into the distance, where the train tracks cut through the valley beside the riverbed, her face patterned with filtered sunlight and the shade of the oak.

"I haven't seen you around much at school," she said. "I was beginning to think you were hiding from me." Her tone suggested she was teasing him, but both of them knew there was more than a hint of truth hidden there.

"My dad said he needed me out here. Between work and tryouts for baseball, I haven't had much extra time to hang around after the bell."

Heather looked at him in that direct and unflinching way that sometimes made him so self-conscious. Even then, Paul could feel her eyes on him as he plucked a leaf off the ground and twisted the stem between his fingers—simply for something to keep his hands occupied—and he knew then that she could see straight through him and what he was thinking.

"Are you sure that's all there is to it?" Heather asked. "Just work and baseball?"

She felt something stir every time she was with Paul, but lately, things had begun to feel complicated. Her father had humiliated him at dinner at their house, and now maybe Heather herself had inadvertently done the same thing by showing up at his farm unannounced. Paul seemed distant, guarded in a way that was unlike him, like something was simmering inside him, something he was weighing in his head.

"It looks like you want to say something," she said. "Like maybe I did something to upset you."

"No. It's nothing like that. Forget it. It's stupid."

"Tell me."

He let the leaf fly away on the wind and watched as it skittered across the loose soil and fell into the gully.

"Do you remember the other night by the river?" Paul asked. His tone was soft, barely audible, his eyes glued to the leaf in the gully. "That night after the homecoming dance?"

"Of course I do."

"Do you remember how you told me you thought your dad blames you for your mother's cancer?"

It was something she had never shared with anyone before, and a part of her had regretted having done so. It had been an act of spontaneous intimacy that now felt more like perfidy to speak of it again.

"I remember," she said.

Paul grew silent again, drawn into himself. She could tell he was deciding whether to continue, and it took all her might not to get off the swing and go to him, throw her arms around him, and pull him close to her. She knew down deep he wouldn't use Heather's own words to injure her, and she wanted nothing more than to rekindle that sweet sense of tenderness and trust they'd shared that night at the river.

"What about it?" Heather prompted.

"You asked me if I thought that it was weird, weird that your dad could blame you for something like that," Paul said.

"You never answered me."

Her heart began to beat more urgently as he looked into her face.

"Can I tell you something?" Paul asked, his voice barely more than a whisper.

Heather nodded, something vaguely unsure, something hesitant growing inside her.

"Sometimes . . ." Paul began.

"Go on."

"Sometimes, ever since my mom . . . died . . . Sometimes I wonder if insanity runs in my family."

"Insanity? Why would you think that?"

Paul averted his gaze and shrugged. Heather could tell he was regretting having spoken such private thoughts aloud. She knew exactly how he felt.

"But," Heather said, "you told me it was an accident."

"What if it wasn't?"

CHAPTER SEVENTEEN

THE SUDDEN FOG lingered for nearly an hour that evening, motionless, cold, and enveloping, then slid away, dissipating as suddenly as it had arrived. By the time I ordered the troopers to unbolt the main gate for the VIPs, it was as though it had never been there at all. The guests took their time filing inside, exploring every corner of the new concert venue and locating their assigned seats, ushered all the while by their host, Len Kaanan himself. Overhead, a slender crescent of ivory moon floated on a skyscape the color of lilac and laced with brush-strokes of clouds in shades of tropical coral.

Captain Rose and I stationed ourselves at the rear of the vale, between the unoccupied stretch of lawn meant for tomorrow's general admission crowd and the concession concourse behind us. From this vantage point, we could make eye contact with nearly all the security personnel, including the handful of thugs that Mickey London had conscripted for the job.

As we had been led to expect, the evening's guests were a conglomeration of industry people, pundits, and promoters—anyone in possession of the wherewithal to bang the drum for Ian Swann and his new album. There were record producers, movie directors, radio station owners, disc jockeys, entertainment press, and a cadre of significant others and hangers-on whose behavior and attire could only be described as eclectic.

I had worked the studio back lots for a while, understood that business was business, and I held no enmity in that regard. My contempt was reserved for the individuals who viewed performers as singular tools, created solely to be manipulated for their own power and prestige. Having come to know Ian Swann, that conviction had come even more sharply into focus, though I would have recognized some of these people anywhere, by the sheer nakedness of their mercenary nature, but the expression on Captain Rose's face seemed bemused.

I tell myself I'm still a tolerant and youthful man, forbearing of humanity and all its shortcomings, but that is not the truth; at least, it's not the truth in full. My interfaces with people and their odious impulses and motivations have complicated my redemption, so for the time being, I rely on divine grace. And a gun.

ODD SNIPPETS of conversation floated over the low-frequency purr of the crowd, and Rose and I looked on as a small group of a half-dozen guests spread a plaid picnic blanket across the grass a short distance away and set up an elaborate spread of charcuterie and champagne that they drew out of an oversize wicker basket. One of the men wore a polo pullover and khaki slacks and no socks with his tasseled loafers, while the others appeared dressed to perform some sort of manual labor on a seedy walk-up in El Segundo. We watched as they popped champagne and distributed it into flutes of cut crystal, taking turns uttering snide, pithy remarks regarding the venue, Len Kaanan, and Ian Swann.

"I swear to Christ I don't understand some of these people," Rose said to me.

"They occupy a different planet than you and I do."

"Maybe so," he said. "But how about a little freaking gratitude?"

I didn't disagree. The pervasive reek of entitlement was practically palpable out here. Sarcasm and irony were the lifeblood of their conversations, but the language they used betrayed the emptiness of their indulgences, the pathos of the lonely and lost.

"Seventy-six is turning into a mean year, Chris," I said. "And we're not even halfway through it yet."

CHAPTER EIGHTEEN

THE RUMBLE OF recorded thunder accompanied a simulated flash of lightning as Ian Swann and his band took the stage. A heavy blanket of man-made haze drifted across the length and width of the entire platform just as a single spotlight caught Ian standing at its center, arms spread like a cruciform, as though floating knee-deep in a cloud. Overhead, a bright beam from a camera chopper vectored down out of the sky, and I wondered whether Jesse was inside.

The small crowd roared in approval at the unexpected eruption of light and sound, and the band launched into Swann's signature hit, a song I recognized as "Horns, Thorns & Wings."

IAN SWANN performed for nearly two full hours without a break, winning over a crowd equally divided between cynics and supporters with his charm and charisma as much as with his music. I caught a couple glimpses of Cricket working in the wings, directing a pair of cameramen as the star of the show remained in constant motion, working from one edge of the dais to the other. My daughter appeared composed and confident, a woman fully in her element, and I realized I was seeing her through a different set of eyes for the first time in my life.

The stage lights in the scaffolding high above the band began to dim, receding like colored beacons in a blackened sky, and I watched Cricket line up another angle as Swann stepped to the microphone at center stage, thanked the audience, and waited as the band exited the stage.

A single spot caught him alone inside an oblique cone of light, and three shadows emerged from different corners of the stage. I recognized one of them as Ian's brother, Dowd. He was carrying an acoustic guitar he'd selected from a row of instruments lined up like soldiers on chrome stands, waiting at the edges of the spotlight while the other two members of the crew approached Ian before it was Dowd's turn. The other men wore dark-colored nylon jackets with the word STAFF stenciled in yellow lettering across the back; one brought a four-legged shop stool and placed it in the center of the stage, the other carried a pair of microphone stands—one for Ian Swann's guitar, the other for his voice. Dowd took his turn, delivering Ian's instrument into his hands, then waiting in anxious silence as Ian settled himself behind the microphones, in anticipation of the nod that would be his signal for the crew to depart the stage.

The drama was as palpable as it was calculated; three people on a mostly darkened set, one seated inside the circle of a spotlight, three others hovering beside him in the dark while the audience waited in spellbound expectation.

What happened next happened fast. No warning, no presentiment, no nothing.

SOMETHING STARTLED Ian Swann, and I noticed him look upward, into the rafters, in the direction of the suspended catwalk high above his head. The framing of the stage structure obscured my view, but it was clear that Ian was alarmed by what he saw. Without warning, he dropped his guitar to the floor and took a half step toward his brother, shoving Dowd backward just as a fifteen-foot section of light rigging plummeted to the floor, tailing a length of live electrical cable as thick as a python, spewing sparks of deadly fire as it whipped back and forth.

The falling light cans and cable raceway connecting them must have weighed five hundred pounds, the assembly's leading edge catching Ian Swann across the shoulders and trapping him beneath its weight. The thrashing electric cable wrapped itself around the microphone stand Dowd had instinctively clutched onto when his brother had attempted to push him to safety out of the crash zone. But the live filament connected with the chrome shaft Dowd gripped so tightly in his fist and shot fifteen thousand volts of electricity through Dowd's frail body. The boy's musculature constricted involuntarily, rendering him unable to release his grasp, and the force began to rip the ligaments and tissues of his body to shreds as the surge of electricity charred his flesh down to the bone.

The steel scaffolding and battens skidded sideways when the light rig hit the stage, propelled by the imbalanced weight and charged with deadly voltage by the slithering live cable. The film cameras were still rolling, stunned disbelief affording no time for their operators to react. The lenses captured the entire scene, caught the rogue section of tension grid as it spun sideways, mauling the two nylon-jacketed roadies underneath its bulk.

Somehow, it appeared that Ian Swann was still moving, unable to extricate himself, but reaching vainly for his younger brother, the boy's expression frozen as his tendons seized and convulsed from the unrelenting stream of electrical current that was at that very moment burning him from the inside outward, disabling his internal organs one by one.

Ian Swann continued inching forward, clawing at the floorboards, dragging himself and the quarter ton of steel that held him captive for one final surge of effort that allowed his fingers to reach out and touch his little brother. Ian didn't stand a chance when he finally made contact with Dowd, grasping his brother's wrist and closing the circuit; and Ian's body, too, began to convulse grotesquely from electrical shock.

EVERYTHING WENT black when someone backstage killed the power, and an odd and encompassing silence passed over the crowd. It lasted only for a moment before the stillness degenerated into pandemonium, the atmosphere roped with greasy smoke that bore the stomach-turning stench of incinerated flesh.

I sprinted through the blackness, elbowing my way through the crowd of horrified witnesses, fighting forward to the stage and to the ambulances whose flashing light bars flickered deathly shadows across panicked and bewildered faces. For a moment, I imagined I could hear incoming choppers and APCs, the sound of steel helmets and leather straps, the flash of incoming artillery rounds, the percussion of their impact carving a rutted path along a dark and crowded road.

I felt the rotor wash, and a dust cloud pushed down on me as I looked skyward and saw the camera helicopter making slow passes over the bedlam, strafing the turmoil in which I stood with a thin white spotlight fixed to its doorframe. The chopper's noise and presence was escalating the hysteria into all-encompassing panic, and I waved the pilot away as I continued to fight my way forward to the dais.

I finally found Sam Griffin near the rear of the stage, where he and another stagehand had finally been able to kill the main breaker panel and were trying to isolate a circuit that wouldn't place the paramedics in danger as they hunched over the supine bodies of Ian Swann, Dowd, and the two roadies stretched prone beside them on the boards. I could only make out passing images as the med techs passed their flashlight beams across the victims, assessing their vitals and status in triage.

"We gotta get some lights on that crowd," I shouted to Sam through the continuous wail of the screaming spectators and the throbbing moan of the ambulance's howler sirens. "They're gonna trample one another."

"We're on it," Sam said, and as he did so, the man who stood beside him threw open a subpanel breaker that controlled the fixtures at the tops of the sound towers, and bathed the frenzied throng in pale yellow illumination.

The light helped calm the chaos, and a number of Captain Rose's state troopers began to herd the onlookers to the rear of the amphitheater where they could collect names and contact information for witness statements. I leaped onto the stage as a separate group of troopers conducted a cursory search of the stage apron and curtilage. All appearances suggested this disaster had been an accident, but there were protocols that had to be observed.

One small section at a time, the darkened venue began to rise out of the darkness, but the stage remained a black cavern, all power cut off. Two pairs of medical technicians examined the four victims, and from where I stood, I could see that Dowd's clothing was still smoldering, the air putrid with the odor of singed hair and human flesh.

I squinted into the darkness of the stage set. When I had last spotted my daughter, she and her camera crew had been positioned in the wings adjacent to the monitor mixing board, and I half expected to find her pressed into a corner, curled into a ball and suffering hysterics. But when I finally found her, she was icily calm, her eyes reflecting myriad unspoken and unspeakable contemplations, a nylon jacket draped across her shoulders as she watched the attendants work on Ian Swann. I came up beside her and we stood together as we saw him lying helpless at center stage, pinned beneath five hundred pounds of steel girders and lighting, the skin of his forearms and wrists blackened, already dead or dying from severe electrical shock.

She turned and looked at me, her expression a mask about to shatter, and she reached out for my hand. Cricket had always been self-sufficient, strong and sensitive, a rare blend of a romantic and a realist, qualities I always associated with Cricket's mother, but she wasn't bulletproof, even though sometimes she believed herself to be. I wrapped her in my arms and felt her breathing on my chest, then I felt her lean her weight on me and finally allow herself to sob.

I STOOD beside Cricket as we watched the paramedics load Ian's gurney into the back of the ambulance, an old Cadillac Meteor model that smelled of antiseptic and engine exhaust. The driver threw an arm out to bar Cricket from climbing in the back with Ian and reached in an attempt to shut the door.

"She's going with you," I said to the driver. "This woman is a friend of Mr. Swann's."

"I'm sorry, but—"

"Please don't make me repeat myself," I said and helped my daughter climb into the back of the vehicle.

"If she's not family, sir—"

"The two of us are all the family he's got at the moment," I said. "Now, get going. That young man's hanging by a thread."

I watched the red lights of the ambulance fade away along the curved road through the forest, and I turned around just as the medics pulled white sheets over the faces of the two roadies and Ian's brother, then slid them, one by one, into the maw of the remaining ambo.

"We're not supposed to transport DBs," the driver said as he pulled up the screen on the rear window.

"You say that like you're doing me some kind of favor," I said.

"No, sir, just saying—"

"Do yourself a favor and stop saying everything that pops into your head. This is your job, and everyone here expects you to do it with dignity. Are you hearing me?"

"Yes, sir. I hear you."

"Take these three people to the morgue. Use your flashers if you want, but no siren. They're not in a hurry to get where they're going, and I'm sure they'd appreciate a little peace along the way. I'll meet you there shortly."

"Okay, Sheriff," the driver said. "Roger that."

"Much obliged," I said.

I HAD told the sundowner with the tattoos that I would look for him if anything went sideways out here, and I meant it. And things had most assuredly done that.

I found the man standing alone in a dark corner of the back-stage enclosure, hands thrust to the wrists inside his trouser pockets, rocking back and forth on the heels of his steel-toed work boots. His eyes were glazed, the skin of his face as pale as a fish belly, staring into a void in the trees where the last of the ambulances had disappeared around a corner, a sudden silence enveloping the woods behind it.

"What the hell happened here?" I asked him.

He turned his head slowly and stared at me as though searching his memory to recall how he knew me. I recognized shock when I saw it, so I waited for him to collect himself.

"I don't know . . ." he said, as if speaking to himself. "It just came undone and fell."

"Where were you?"

He shook his head, drew his lips into a seam, and breathed through his nose.

"Stage right," he said. "In the wings near the rail. I was supposed to keep an eye on the crew while they brought out the instruments for the acoustic set . . ."

"So what the hell happened?" I repeated.

I watched him as he evaluated my question again, saw him begin to shiver.

"Those were my friends," he whispered hoarsely, and he looked like he was about to pass out.

"Have you got a car?" I asked.

"No. I hitch if I have anywhere to go."

"I'm headed to the hospital," I said. "Care to ride along?"

CHAPTER NINETEEN

IT WAS A twenty-minute drive to the hospital from Half Mountain, deadly quiet as I drove, only the road hum and the intermittent tick of stray raindrops striking the windshield, each one provoking an involuntary flinch from my passenger.

We didn't say a word to each other as we walked across the darkened parking lot into a rear entrance to the hospital. The door was down a short and narrow stairwell, unlocked and marked with a simple plastic sign that read CORONER.

He followed me inside, into an empty corridor dimly lit by flickering fluorescent lights. Industrial-grade floor tiles ran the length and breadth in squares of chalky beige and a somber shade of mossy green that had no analogue in nature. The atmosphere inside the building reeked of disinfectant, cleaning solvent, and human waste, the air untouched and fetid in the stillness of the hall. I tried the door handle that led into the coroner's workspace and found that it was locked, the lights behind the wire glass dimmed to near darkness.

"What's with the colors in these places?" he asked me, the walls a similar unnatural hue as that on the floor tiles, casting both of us in a shade that looked like death. "Looks just like the VA clinic in Clarksburg."

"As I recall, the public buildings in Korea used a shade of pink that might be even worse than this," I said.

I left him to wait in the hallway outside the coroner's office, pacing beside a stretch of molded plastic chairs that had been bolted to the floor.

"Wait here," I said. "I'll be back in a few minutes."

"Where are you going?"

"My daughter's in this building somewhere. She came here in the ambulance with Ian Swann. I want to find her, and I want to locate somebody who can tell us where to find your colleagues."

"I'll come with you."

Where I was headed next did not include spectators.

"No," I said. "Wait here. I won't be long."

He began to say something more and moved to follow me, but I halted him with my expression.

"Don't move away from here," I said. "Don't poke around or look through any windows in this place. I'm doing you a favor telling you that. There's nothing down here that you want or need to see, trust me. That is a stone fact."

I RECOGNIZED the charge nurse, Cathie Fields, as I stepped off the elevator and onto the third-floor burn unit. I had seen enough of battle trauma to know that this would be the floor they'd bring Ian to.

"You were present at the event?" Nurse Fields said as I stepped up to match her rushed pace as she moved down the passageway.

"Yes, ma'am, I was."

She paused when we reached the double doors that led into the ward and the operating rooms beyond.

"You can't come any farther," she said. "Not that you'd want to."

"My daughter was in the ambulance that delivered Ian Swann."

"Room three oh four," she said. "I'll come in and update you as soon as I can."

Nurse Fields disappeared into the depths of the burn unit, and I navigated through the maze of intersecting corridors until I found room 304.

Cricket was standing near the window of a dimly illuminated room divided by transparent partitions made of heavy plastic and crowded with sophisticated electronic equipment laden with cathode screens and catheters and cables. Despite the closeness in the room, she was still wearing the sweatshirt she'd been wearing for her work and the nylon jacket around her shoulders, gazing through the glass into the dimness of the night and the scattering of streetlights that traced the river's course. She had tied her hair back in a knot behind her head, unaware the skin along her cheeks and neck had been left smudged and blackened in the chaos, or perhaps the outreached hands of Ian Swann.

She turned when she heard me enter the room, the angles of her face severe, fierce and ardent in a way I knew had stripped away the final vestiges I was likely to have ever recognized of my daughter's youth. She came to me and held me, more out of habit than privation, and I could smell the smoke and ambulance odors in her hair.

"He's in the OR," she said. "Don't know how long they'll be."

"Was Ian conscious?"

"I don't think so. He moaned a little when they moved him, but that was all. I never even saw him open his eyes."

She gently pulled away from me, her own expression washed in pain and confusion, and I could feel we both had the same foreboding as to how this was to end. I noticed a stain of blood on the sleeve of her jacket had already turned to rusty brown, and a small section of seared skin that had sloughed from Ian's body and fixed itself onto it. I stepped up behind Cricket and slipped the jacket off her shoulders before she discovered that shocking artifact herself, folded it over the back of a chair.

Cricket was about to say something to me when a scuffle broke out in the hall outside, and I heard Mickey London verbally abusing a young nurse as she unsuccessfully attempted to bar him from Ian's door.

"I was assured that this room would be assigned to Ian Swann exclusively," London shouted. "I was told it was to be a *private* room."

"I assure you, sir—" the young nurse began, but Swann's manager was having none of it.

"If this is a private room, then what in the *hell* are *they* doing in here?" he interrupted.

"Keep your voice down, Mr. London," I said. I nodded to the nurse, and I watched her as she backed out of the room into the corridor, her expression washed with gratitude.

"I want you out of here this minute," London said, jabbing a stubby finger first at me and then at Cricket. "Both of you. You people and your Mayberry, aw-shucks bullshit. Get the hell out of this room, out of my sight. Get the bloody hell out of our lives."

To her credit, my daughter did not respond or react in any way to the man's histrionics, having either grown immune to them through recent association, or from simple disinterest. I searched London's face for something I might use to decode this burst of hostility and found only the same predatory carnality I had always seen behind his eyes. I've known men like Mickey London on the field of battle and on the open range, their solipsism and narcissistic motivations practically lacertian in nature, possessed of a hardwired instinct for self-preservation that defied description in human terms and placed everyone around them in grave danger.

"You are lucky to be standing in a hospital, Mr. London," I said to him. "Might come in handy for you, depending on what you do next."

He cocked his head and tried to peel the skin off my face with his gray eyes.

"Apologize to my daughter, Mr. London," I said, "and I will let you leave."

Mickey London clicked his eyes from me to Cricket.

"This little twat—" London began, gesturing with his stubby finger in her direction again.

"If you say one more word," I said, "I will cram that entire sentence back down your throat with my bootheel, together with pieces of your shattered teeth. Go ahead and do it; see if I am joking."

London took a step backward, a sheen of perspiration forming on his upper lip. He smoothed his braided ponytail with one hand and showed me what was supposed to be a condescending smile.

"This is not finished," London said to me.

"Oh, I'm fairly certain that it is. Good night, Mr. London. Someone will contact you when you have permission to return to this hospital. Until then, you may come no closer to this building than the entrance to the parking lot."

I watched Mickey London stomp down the hallway to the elevator. When I looked back at Cricket, she had the suggestion of a smile touching her lips.

"Sorry about that," I said.

"Don't be sorry," she said. "I only wish I had it on film."

I lifted the nylon jacket off the chair where I had placed it and folded it carefully over my arm so she wouldn't see the stains.

"They're liable to take a while with Ian, sweetheart," I said. "Want to come with me and get a cup of coffee from the refectory? Stretch your legs?"

"I think I'd rather stay right here," she said. "Just in case."

"I can bring something back for you."

She declined with a tiny shake of her head, any trace of the former smile vanished. I turned to leave, and she touched me on the sleeve.

"It's bad, isn't it?" she asked. "Ian, I mean. He's in bad shape, isn't he?"

I didn't like to lie to the people who placed their trust in me; never have.

"I'm afraid so, Cricket."

I RODE the elevator to the subbasement and stepped out into the dimness, the beige and green floor tiles, and the sour stink of sorrow and mortality that hovered in the air. The man I'd left down here had finally stopped pacing and was seated in one of the uncomfortable molded plastic chairs anchored to the ugly floor outside the coroner's office door.

"Anybody come by to see you yet?" I asked him.

He looked at me blankly, gestured a wordless *no* in my direction, and shrunk inside himself again. I couldn't tell with certainty in the pale light, but it looked as though he had begun to shiver again, though it was far from cold inside these walls.

"When's the last time you had something to eat?" I asked.

"I don't remember."

"Come with me."

I PEELED off several bills and passed them to the cashier as I watched the man select a table near the window, balancing a plastic commissary tray piled high with steaming plates of food he'd gathered from the server behind the hot entrée line. By the time the attendant counted out my change and I topped off my

Styrofoam coffee cup, my companion was halfway through his Salisbury steak and mashed potatoes, the thick brown gravy dripping from one corner of his mouth.

"You can slow down, pardner," I said as I took a seat across from him, placing my hat crown-down on the empty seat beside me. "You're not in the joint. Nobody's going to take that grub away from you."

He looked up at me, his dripping spoon halted in midair, inches from his lips. I watched him scan the mostly empty dining room, occupied by surgeons in white lab coats, orderlies, and nurses wearing colored scrubs. A private thought passed behind his eyes before he shoveled the laden spoon into his mouth and he watched me as he chewed. He wiped his mouth with a paper napkin and took a gulp of water, leaned back into his chair, and glanced out the window into the dark, our reflections rippling on the glass like apparitions.

"You know, you've never asked my name," he said. "Not once. Why do you suppose that is?"

From the first time I had laid eyes upon the man and his cohorts at the Cottonwood Blossom, everything about his behavior and attire had placed me on high alert. His speech and mannerisms, and the body art he carried like a permanent biography, told me this man carried calamity and misfortune with him everywhere he went. But something had gone out of him tonight, hunched and bent and smaller than before, and I almost felt sorry for him.

"You never thanked me for your dinner, either," I said. "Why do you suppose *that* is?"

He tipped his head to one side and studied me. Then he dipped his spoon into his mound of mashed potatoes and scooped it into his mouth without a word. Whether either one of us had been aware of it before or not, I now realized he had ceased to be an individual and had become a *type* to me. I watched as he devoured his dinner with all the efficiency and haste of a man too well acquainted with the penitentiary system. It was then that I experienced an epiphany of a sort that caught me unawares: I had failed to internalize that this man's life had likely been an unending cycle of loss and heartache, defeat and deficiency a foregone conclusion of any given day. As a churchgoing man myself, I felt a twinge of shame that I had not discerned those facts before, then engaged in a form of self-absolution by acknowledging that I'm a sheriff not a priest.

"What's your name?" I asked.

He threw back another gulp of water and wiped his wet mouth with the backside of his hand.

"Dewayne," he answered.

"Dewayne *what*?"

"Dewayne Gomer. Don't laugh."

"I'm not laughing."

He placed his utensils on the tray and leaned in closer, his elbows on the table.

"No, I can see you're not," he said. "Most people do. It's 'cause of that stupid TV show. People laugh at me because of my name. My name ain't a joke."

That final utterance was one I had no doubt had led to bloodshed in his past.

"Everybody's got a name, Dewayne," I said.

"Amen to that," he said, then he glanced at his own reflection in the window and resumed his meal.

"You say that like a man who's been submerged."

"I was baptized in a church that had a water tank inside it, like a little swimming pool," he said between bites. "The preacher had a plastic bottle, and he said it contained water from the river Jordan. He poured some of it into the tank before he dunked me in it. Far as I'm concerned, I been river baptized in the same water where Crazy John baptized his cousin."

Motion in the wide hall outside the cafeteria caught my eye, and I recognized the charge nurse, Cathie Fields, a clipboard tucked into the crook of her arm and making her way in my direction. Dewayne looked up from his plate and followed the direction of my gaze, and finding nothing there of interest to him, he returned his attention to a slice of warm peach pie.

"I'm not gonna tell you I saw Jesus on a piece of toast," Dewayne said. "Or the Blessed Mother's face on a moldy plaster wall, but I'm also not the man you think I am, Sheriff. Jesus found *me* in the yard at Huntsville, and I got myself immersed as soon as I got paroled. You want to believe me, that's fine; if not, well, that's fine, too."

Nurse Fields stopped short of the doors to the commissary, waited in the alcove, and gestured for my attention. I plucked my hat off the empty chair, put it on my head as I excused myself, stepped over to speak with her in a too-small waiting area adjacent to the elevators.

"Your daughter told me I might find you here," she said. "I hope you don't mind my calling you away, but I don't recognize the man you're sitting with."

"I appreciate your discretion, ma'am," I said. "How is Mr. Swann doing?"

"May I be candid?"

"Please."

"As I explained to your daughter, Sheriff Dawson, Mr. Swann suffered not only a devastating set of injuries from the scaffolding that fell on him, but the trauma he sustained from the subsequent electrical shock burned him rather severely; what's worse is that it's threatening internal organ failure. Heart. Liver. Kidneys."

"You told my daughter all this? The same way you just told me?"

Her expression remained neutral, but something softened in her eyes.

"She is a remarkable young woman, Sheriff. The truth is, the prognosis for Mr. Swann and the other gentleman is questionable at best."

"I beg your pardon? What other gentleman? I was under the impression Mr. Swann was the only survivor."

I had watched the ambulance attendant slide white sheets across the faces of Ian's younger brother as well as the two men in matching nylon jackets.

"One of the stagehands still had a pulse when the ambulance arrived. They're working on him now."

I cast a glance over my shoulder at Dewayne Gomer, still hunched across our table like a carrion bird.

"The man I'm sitting with is an acquaintance of the stagehand you just mentioned. Would you mind speaking with him? I'm not certain whether he knows if his friends are alive or dead."

Her hesitation and the momentary aversion of her eyes made my blood run cold. She had just described the two survivors' prognosis as "questionable," but it now appeared that might have been a prevarication of compassion.

"He's in an extremely serious condition, Sheriff Dawson. Both of them are. The doctors are doing everything they can."

I led her to our table, where Dewayne Gomer listened to Nurse Fields with rapt attention. She confirmed that only one of his colleagues had survived the accident and went on to describe the nature of the man's condition and the uncertain outlook as to his recovery with a dignity and equanimity I found to be extremely admirable and sincere. When she had finished, Dewayne stood and thanked her, shaking her hand in both of his.

The sad smile she offered him was one familiar to professions whose main currency was grief, an expression well practiced by doctors, priests, and morticians.

"I take it you don't live here in Meridian, sir," she said. "Do you have a place to stay while your friend is in the surgical ward?"

"No, ma'am," he said. "I got nowhere to be."

She caught my eye and the tiny nod I gave her, and she touched Dewayne gently on the arm.

"That's no problem," she said softly. "I'm sure I can find an empty room for you where you can get some sleep. It's likely to be several hours before we know anything further."

"Thank you very kindly," he said. "I would appreciate that."

"You may also want to show him where the chapel is located," I said.

She motioned for Dewayne to come along with her as she turned to leave, and I began to bus our table, stacking the dirty plates and napkins on the plastic tray. When I looked up, the two of them were halfway to the door, and Dewayne pulled up short and turned.

"Hey, Sheriff," Dewayne Gomer called out.

"You forget something?" I asked.

"Just that I never thanked you for dinner."

I tipped the remnants from the service tray into a rubbish can, stacked it with the others, and touched the brim of my Resistol.

"You're welcome, Dewayne."

CHAPTER TWENTY

I DIDN'T SLEEP that night, keeping one ear open for Jesse's arrival home, which never came. The house felt lonesome, cold and empty, each of its three occupants consigned to our own personal disquiets: my daughter to sit her private vigil at County Hospital; my wife to complete her film work at the studio; and me to continue tugging on the threads of other people's lives, threads that led to either restoration or destruction.

By the time morning arrived, it came so softly that it felt like a eulogy, the underlayment of the clouds glowing like coal embers for only the briefest of moments, soon swallowed by a still and steely sky that stole all but the ambient glow of sunrise. I brewed some coffee and, as I watched the bluebirds taking turns feeding their brood inside the bird box, glanced down toward the horse barn and saw one of my full-time wranglers, Taj Caldwell, smoking a cigarette alone beside the creek. A little farther along the escarpment, the windows of Caleb Wheeler's cabin reflected a blush of copper light, and a single strand of woodsmoke floated from his chimney, not even a breath of wind that morning to disturb it. I poured black coffee into a speckled cup and briefly considered hiking down to visit with Taj or Caleb, but it already didn't feel like that kind of day.

* * *

I PHONED Half Mountain Studio and, when I asked for Jesse, was told she had been given one of the guest accommodations for the night, and she hadn't yet arisen for breakfast. I had no doubt she was exhausted and was operating on little more than adrenaline, willpower, and grit to complete the assignment she had been hired to do, having now been made all the more horrific for its tragic outcome. I considered reaching out to Cricket at the hospital, but thought better of that, too, not wishing to wake her on the off chance that she might have finally drifted off to sleep.

I made one final call to Captain Rose at the state police barracks. He picked up his line on the second ring, already agitated by a nine-car pileup on the interstate that had closed all but one of the northbound lanes; he had engaged a small cadre of troopers, EMTs, and fire personnel to sort out the mess.

"The shit never ends," Rose said. "Of course, it only happens when I've gotten about two hours of sleep."

Rose brought me up to speed on the follow-up from the concert venue after I'd left for the hospital. He and his troopers had collected names and contact information from the VIP attendees while my deputy, Sam Griffin, did the same with the musicians and stage crew, sorting out any useful witnesses and initiating the interview processes. The event intended as a cele-bration of the ascendency of a young star had now become a deathwatch.

"Did you hear anything from any of the witnesses to suggest it might not have been an accident?"

"Not outright," he said. "For the most part, the crowd was understandably shook up. Sitting there watching a show, and a thousand pounds of lights and electrical rigging fall out of the sky and fry a bunch of guys. Yeah, I'd say they were in shock. Why? You thinking something else?"

"I don't know," I admitted. "It just seemed too . . ."

"Orchestrated?"

"The entire stage is empty except for Ian Swann and three poor bastards just doing their jobs. A job that should that have taken thirty seconds at the most. But when the scaffolding fails, it happens to be the only section that would land on top of all of them? Center stage, in the spotlight. You know how I love coincidence."

"I'll keep my ears open," he said. "And I'm sure Griffin will let you know if he heard anything."

"Copy that," I said. "I'll be in touch."

"One last thing, Ty: I sent some of my guys down there to disperse the flower children who were camping out for Saturday's show, but only a handful of them departed," Rose told me. "I'm leaving a couple troopers behind in case the Swann kid doesn't make it and their little fireside singalong turns into a Norse funeral. Or worse."

I DROVE to Meridian and stopped off at Rowan Boyle's diner to pick up a fried-egg-and-bacon sandwich and a doughnut to take to Cricket at the hospital. The sky pressed down like crenellated steel as I turned off the county road, where a road gang worked clearing the shoulder of debris and tails of smoke rose up from stump fires on the valley floor. I tossed a wave to the gang boss as I passed; after pushing along the twisting two-lane in silence for another fifteen minutes, I pulled into the lot at the hospital.

It was still early, and the reception desk was empty, so I made my way up to the burn ward and the room that had been assigned to Ian. The hiss and sigh of medical equipment filled the room, my daughter curled up and sleeping on a reclining chair at the foot of Ian's bed, a thin blanket tucked under her chin. Ian Swann was lying on his back, eyes closed, heavily bandaged and heavily sedated, inside a bedsize prison cell whose walls were made of clear plastic sheeting.

Cricket's eyes flickered open as I stepped into the room, and I knelt beside where she'd been sleeping and kissed her on the cheek. I showed her the bag I'd brought from the diner, and she followed me out of the room into the central nurses' station. One of the duty nurses brought Cricket a fresh cup of hot tea while I set out her breakfast on a napkin on the counter.

"How long has Ian been out of surgery?" I whispered to Cricket.

Her face was drawn, color leached out from her skin from stress and dread and exhaustion. The look she showed me nearly broke my heart.

"They brought him in around one o'clock this morning, I think," she said. "Five hours of surgery for his burns. The doctor said they're keeping an eye on his heart and kidney function because of the electrical shock. He said they'd probably have to take him back to surgery again today, depending."

I didn't want to make her explain to me what "depending" meant, so I asked her if she'd been able to speak with Ian instead.

Cricket took a sip out of the paper cup of tea, her index finger looped into the flimsy paper handle. She grimaced at either the temperature or the flavor of her beverage and placed it on a corner of the napkin I'd laid out on the Formica.

"Ian's been unconscious—sedated—since he arrived here. I haven't been able to speak with him at all."

"I'm sorry, Cricket," I said. "Would you like me to drive you home, so you can maybe take a shower, put on some fresh clothes?"

She appeared grateful for my offer, but I could tell she had no intention of leaving Ian's side. I asked her if there was anything she wanted me to bring to her from home, and she wrote out a short list of sundries that I promised to bring back to her when I returned. I waited with her as she girded herself at the threshold of the door to Ian's room, watching as she looked into his nearly lifeless face, as well as at the tubes and wires that snaked across his cheeks to help him breathe and those that trailed beneath his bloodstained bandages and soiled gown to monitor his organs. I felt her draw a deep breath as she stepped across the doorsill, turning to whisper a soft "Thank you, Dad" into my ear before she moved inside.

THE RECEPTIONIST was settling at her desk as the elevator doors opened up before me on the ground floor. I inquired as to whether either the coroner or the charge nurse had arrived yet for the day as the young woman, gazing into a handheld compact mirror, finished applying pink lipstick.

"I'm sorry, Sheriff Dawson," the receptionist told me. "But I do have a message for you, I think."

She reached into a numbered mail slot and withdrew an envelope with my name printed on it. I tore it open and stepped into the light beside the glass doors and read the note that Nurse Fields had written out for me in the small dark hours of the morning.

Dear Sheriff Dawson,

I wanted you to know that Mr. Gomer's friend's surgery was unsuccessful, and he passed away on the operating table at about 2:00 this morning. Mr. Gomer was very upset, but I was able to give him something to help him sleep. I set him up in room 199B, so you should find him there. I am terribly sorry. Please let me know if there is anything I can do.

"Is everything okay?" the receptionist asked me as I folded the note into my shirt pocket, and I wondered at the vacuity of such a question in such a place and circumstance as this.

"Can you please direct me to room 199B?" I asked her.

The entire hospital seemed to be in the process of waking at this hour, so I treaded lightly down the dimly lit corridors until I found the number I was looking for. I opened the door as quietly as I could and peeked my head around the doorframe and into the darkened room.

And when I moved inside, I discovered that the room was empty, the bed pillow had been wadded in a ball, and the covers tossed aside. Dewayne Gomer was gone.

CHAPTER TWENTY-ONE

THERE ARE DRINKING establishments where the customers possess no memory of names or faces, places where the time of day is irrelevant and conversation consists of monosyllabic utterances inside clouds of smoke from cigarettes lighted from cardboard matchbooks or from a butt left smoldering in a cheap glass ashtray. The passage of time is measured differently there, as are the value and the relevance of life and loss and death.

I stepped through the door of just such a place, located at the western edge of Meriwether County, just outside of town boundaries and across the street from the Cayuse Motel, itself a seedy relic of the postwar automobile travel boom. It didn't even have a name, only a hand-painted signboard screwed into the cinder blocks that read simply BAR. There were no windows in the place, save for the small diamond of wire glass embedded at eye level in the front door, the only other illumination emanating from lighted neon beer signs and a half-dozen mismatched fixtures dangling from the ceiling at uneven lengths from knots of electrical wire.

I stood in the vestibule as the heavy door swung shut behind me, waiting a moment as my eyes adjusted to the hazy gloom inside. I scanned the room and counted thirteen souls, not including the bartender, the clientele a collection of day drinkers that represented every strata of desolation, from the miserable and the lost to the wicked and morally disfigured. Half of them glanced at me with genuine disinterest as I walked in, while the other half examined me with hooded eyes that strayed toward the cowboy hat I wore, the Colt Peacemaker on my hip, and the badge clipped to my tooled gun belt. I spotted Dewayne Gomer at the end of the bar, seated alone and staring vacantly into a barback mirror that reflected a row of liquor bottles, their images rippled along the smudged and dusty glass that had begun to desilver at the edges.

"How'd you find me?" Dewayne Gomer asked me as I pulled up a stool beside him. He was hunched over the scarred wooden rail behind an empty double-shot glass, peeling the label off a sweating longneck with his thumbnail, and I could smell a stale and musty odor rising from the wrinkles of his clothes.

"Lucky guess," I said.

The bartender moved down the duckboards and pulled up in front of me, his belly like an overfilled hot water bottle, his hair dyed raven black and slicked along his pate like melted wax. He didn't speak to me, but his expression was a clear inquiry as to how long I intended to remain inside. I answered his unspoken question by ordering a cup of black coffee.

"I'm sorry about your friends," I said to Dewayne after the bartender waddled away.

"They were the only friends I have," he said. "Had."

His face was still unshaven from the day before, his skin a sallow greenish shade inside the cloudy light, tiny threads of red and purple veins spidering his nose and cheeks.

"How did you come to know them?" I asked.

"What do you want, Sheriff?"

"Just wanted to talk to you."

The bartender brought me a steaming mug of coffee and slid it across the counter. I peered into the cup and saw the surface was speckled with loose grounds, picked it up and sipped it anyway, ordered another round for Dewayne Gomer as a gesture of goodwill, and waited until it had been delivered and the fat barman moved out of earshot before I spoke again. I watched as Gomer knocked back half his whiskey and chased it with a slug of beer. He stifled a belch and turned to look at me with eyes misted by fatigue, grief, and alcohol.

Gomer coughed up his life story like a hairball, a man born to believe he was an unwanted accident and a failed abortion. Two years spent in juvie as a teen and two hitches in the military helped him shrug off the curse. But once he received his honorable discharge, he fell in with a bad crowd again; ended up in Ely, Nevada, deeply in debt to moneylenders who possessed neither mercy nor compassion. Dewayne Gomer caught a boxcar headed southeast and ended up in Texas, where he learned the ways of the itinerant freight hopper, a bindle stiff and flat-rail boomer, an American nomad.

"Once you start down that path," he said as he wrapped up his story, "it gets harder and harder to convince folks you ain't either dangerous or crazy."

He looked at that moment like one of the saddest human beings I had ever seen.

"From the first time I saw you at the Cottonwood Blossom— you and your three pals—I had you marked," I said. "I could tell that you've had trouble following you like a stink all your life. And the accident that just killed your friends, well, that's a damn bad stroke of luck. Problem is, I've never believed in coincidence, pard, and this one troubles me."

"You saw where I was standing that night, in the peristyle," he said. "I was nowhere near that stage."

"I didn't say I thought you were guilty of anything, Dewayne. But if you know something I need to hear, you have to talk to me."

"Like what?"

"Let's start with how you came to know your three companions."

"I only really know the two of 'em. The two of 'em that's dead now. The ones you called Tweedle-Dee and Tweedle-Dipshit."

"I suspect they have real names," I said.

Gomer slugged back the remainder of his shot and watched a cockroach the size of my thumb crawl up the paneling behind the bar.

"I don't think I even heard their real names, just the nick-names we all use out there along the tracks. One of them was called Bongwater; the other one was Fuzzy Sam. You probably don't want to know how they came to acquire those handles."

"You are correct," I said. "But go on with your story."

"I don't know, but I think them two might have been related, cousins maybe. I ain't completely sure. One of 'em was mostly deaf, not all the way, but the other one made signs with his fingers and sort of translated for him anyway. Strong as bulls though, both of 'em. Clever, too. Probably shouldn't tell you this, but them two could strip the shelves off a Quickie Mart in thirty seconds flat. Kept us fed when we couldn't land fair wages. Like I said before, not everybody's willing to take a chance on rail-road bums."

"Who's the third man you were with?" I asked.

"Calls himself Esau, but everybody I know calls him Bigfoot on account he likes to tell stories about how he's seen Sasquatch. Me and Fuzzy and Bongwater first met up with him in Tulsa, in a hobo jungle near the railyards. The weather was starting to turn bad down there, so all four of us caught out for someplace warmer, someplace out west. We stayed in Arizona for a bit, then moved on to California for a while longer; then Bigfoot said he knew a place up in the timber country where we could prob'ly find daywork in the lumber mills or maybe cutting trees out in the forest with the 'jack crews. Once we got here to Oregon, ol' Bigfoot seemed to know his way around, and somehow he landed us a gig with that music producer guy, but I don't know how he did it."

"You don't know how you landed the jobs out at the studio?"

Dewayne Gomer smiled at a private recollection and shook his head; as he took a long pull from his longneck beer, a strange expression crossed his face and disappeared.

"That Bigfoot is a talker," he said. "He can talk himself up his own asshole, that's no lie. But he's handy to have around sometimes. Man can be vicious mean, too, if he's got the notion."

That comment got my attention.

"Why is viciousness a 'handy' trait?" I asked.

"There's a gang out there on the tracks—they're everywhere—they're called the Freight Train Riders of America. Sounds like a club or one of them animal lodges, don't it? Like the Elks or Mooses, or what have you. Well, they ain't like that atall. These FTRA guys don't fool around. Bad, bad, scary dudes. But they didn't seem to hassle Bigfoot any."

I knew the hobo jungle could be a savage and inhuman place, where insanity and violence were not only prevalent but often rewarded, part of a social order that rivaled the complexity of the Levant.

"Maybe he's one of them," I said.

"Maybe he is. I never asked."

"Why not?"

"You never been out there living on the ground, have you, Sheriff? It don't pay to ask too many questions about other people and where they been and what they done. It's one of the unspoken rules."

I had been studying Dewayne Gomer's body language, his features and his tells, the whole time he'd been speaking to me. I have always been adept at spotting liars and dissimilators, and I didn't feel like I was looking at one now, but I needed to be certain.

"You got something bothering you?" Gomer asked.

I decided to prod him one last time.

"You're telling me you're just little ol' Charlie Hodge, huh?" I said.

He cocked his head sideways.

"Who's the hell's Charlie Hodge?"

"Exactly," I said.

"I'm serious. Who's Charlie Hodge?"

"He's a guy who picks up Elvis's sweaty capes off the stage floor in Vegas."

"And you're saying Bigfoot is Elvis? I'm just some kind of lackey?"

"No, I don't believe you're anybody's lackey, Dewayne," I said. "But I don't think you're Elvis, either, and he's obviously not one of your two late companions. My deputy interviewed everybody from the crew last night, so I assume he's talked with your friend Bigfoot. But if this guy has already lit out from Half Mountain, I need to know where you think I might find him. I'd like to have a word."

Dewayne Gomer cocked his head sideways and looked at me, then spanned an appraising glance across the room. At the far end of the rail, a tall man wearing overalls and a red-and-black hunting jacket sucked on an unfiltered cigarette; he looked at me with eyes as round and vacant as a pigeon's, flicked his ashes into an upturned bottle cap, and turned away.

"You mind if we wrap this up, Sheriff?" Dewayne Gomer said. "You're not winning me any friends in here, and I might want to come back some day."

* * *

WE STEPPED OUTSIDE into midmorning dappled light. Even in the broken overcast, it took a moment for our eyes to readjust. Dewayne Gomer followed as I took a few strides across the unpaved parking lot and leaned against the fender of my truck. There were pockmarks in the soil where a band of deer had wandered through not long before.

"There's something you're not telling me, Dewayne," I said.

"I ain't lied to you. Not once."

"I didn't say you lied straight-out to me. I said there's something you're holding back. Something you're not telling me. I can see it on your face. Now you and I both know that's pretty much the same thing as a lie, don't we?"

He cut his eyes across the street, in the direction of the Cayuse Motel and the readerboard sign out front that was shaped like an Indian headdress. The plastic letters from the marquee had all been blown away or stolen, and a brick thrown by a teenaged vandal or a drunk had left a ragged hole that exposed its internal lighting mechanisms.

"I'm trying to help you here, Dewayne," I said. "I need for you to appreciate where we stand, you and me, and the nature of this situation. I feel bad about your friends. I truly do. But it's my job to find out if it was just an accident or if it was something else."

He puffed his cheek into a pocket of air and sighed.

"Look, Sheriff, I don't know about what happened last night. I was there just like you were. It all happened so fast . . ."

"But?"

"But maybe there's something else I know about."

I looked at my watch.

"That house," he said, his voice barely above a whisper. "The one that burned."

"What about that house?"

"It ain't been burned on purpose. It was just a place to sleep, somewhere away from the jungle. Bigfoot said he knew about it, so we went there—"

"*Who* went there?"

"Me and Bigfoot, Bongwater and Sam. Maybe one other guy, I don't exactly remember."

"What happened?"

Dewayne's mouth was drawn tight, eyes darting, landing everywhere except on my face.

"It was really cold that night," he said. "We stuffed newspapers and sticks and tree branches inside the fireplace . . . but when we lit it up, the chimney caught. It was like an explosion. That's all. We were just trying to stay warm and dry, and we barely got out of there alive."

"You said Bigfoot knew about the house? How?"

"I don't know."

"You said he's the one who brought you all up here to Oregon. You said he seemed to know his way around. Why?"

"I already told you, I don't ask questions. I. Don't. Know."

"Okay," I said, and I stepped away to give him some distance.

I waited while a compact car pulled in and parked at the far end of the lot. At one time, that car had been showroom-new and painted the same shade as a ripe tangerine. Time and disregard and misadventure had since faded it the color of stomach bile, dropped a quarter panel off the front, and powdered it with road dust. Dewayne and I waited in silence as the car's two occupants disappeared into the bar.

"There's a difference between a hobo and a tramp and a criminal, Sheriff," Gomer said once they'd gone inside. "And I ain't no tramp or criminal."

A gust of wind bent the tree branches overhead, carrying the distant wail of a locomotive's airhorn and the heavy rumble of steel wheels along the rusted tracks.

"What's your plan, Dewayne?" I asked. "What's next?"

He shrugged.

"You gonna arrest me?" he asked.

"For what?"

"For what I just told you. About the fire."

"I swear," I said. "Sometimes, this time of year, my ears clog up something fierce. Must be allergies."

Dewayne Gomer showed me a slow smile and looked down at the scuffed work boots he was wearing.

"I was thinking on waiting around until my friends go in the ground," he said. "Seems like the Christian thing to do. I'll likely catch out after that."

"Where do you plan on staying?"

"I'll find someplace. I always do."

"Follow me," I said.

THE MOTEL MANAGER opened the office door and immediately went pale. My presence here had never boded well for him or his establishment in the past.

"Hello, Sheriff," he said. His eyes were small and hard, and he bore a scar on his forehead from the last time I had saved him from his clientele.

"This man needs a room," I said. "For a week."

"In advance?"

"Send the bill to the sheriff's office."

He eyed Dewayne Gomer from head to foot, and I could see the predatory calculus operating behind his eyes.

"Standard weekly rate and not a penny more," I said and

peeled off a pair of one-dollar notes from my billfold. "And he'll need two dollars change for the laundry machines."

The manager stepped into his office to make change and I moved into the shade beneath the overhang. I peeled off another twenty and a ten and handed them to Gomer.

"For incidentals," I said.

"That's very kind of you, Sheriff," Dewayne Gomer said.

I began to walk back to my truck and thought of one last thing.

"Tell me something," I said. "Were your two friends men of faith like you?"

A look of puzzlement crowded his expression.

"I honestly don't know," he said.

"I get it. You don't ask questions," I said and began to walk away. I was nearly there when I turned around again and called out to Dewayne. "Tell you what. I'll light a candle for the both of 'em, just in case."

I climbed into my truck and looked out across the pebbled parking lot into the dense woodland. A larch tree teemed with chickadees, and beside it, I saw an oriole perched all alone inside the upper branches of a buckthorn as I pulled out and drove away.

CHAPTER TWENTY-TWO

THE WARMER WEATHER had begun to swell the rivers with snowmelt, white water rushing over cataracts and roiling across boulders that had wedged themselves between steep banks lined with fragrant spruce and cedar. I could hear the grumble of the rapids in the narrows a short distance away, smell the fresh scent of piñon in the air as I unlocked the back door to the substation and went inside.

Jordan Powell was seated at his desk, wearing a khaki uniform shirt that appeared freshly pressed, his boots clean and polished, and his cowboy hat hanging from a hook along the wall beside him. He acknowledged me with a toss of his head as he listened with great interest to the telephone receiver he had wedged between his shoulder and ear.

I stepped into the coffee room and found Sam Griffin sipping coffee at one of the circular tables, several stacks of file folders spread out before him. He looked up from the file he was reading when he saw me come in, put down his mug, and placed the file on the top of the heap.

"Interesting reading?" I asked.

"Interview notes from the other night."

"Captain Rose tells me you drew the band and the crew?"

"Roger that."

The whites of Griffin's eyes had gone red at the corners, dark half-moons of exhaustion underneath. Unlike Jordan Powell, Griffin was wearing a snap-button western shirt that looked as though he had slept in it.

"You had any shut-eye, Griffin?"

"A little," he said. "I know we've got to clear these witnesses ASAP, sir. I can sleep after I'm done with that."

Griffin was right. It was one of the odd contradictions of law enforcement, but in a case such as this one, if it turned out that it had *not* been an accident—and we had failed to properly vet the witnesses—then the suspect's defense lawyer would use that failure against us, claiming that there were literally dozens of viable potential suspects among the attendees. That argument alone had the capacity to create enough reasonable doubt to tank a case.

"What've you found out so far?" I asked.

"The musicians, the chopper pilot, the film crews—your wife and daughter included, of course—have all come up clean. Still working through the production people, sound, lights, and stage."

"Have you run across a man who goes by the handles 'Bigfoot' or 'Esau'?"

"Esau? Like in the Bible? I think I'd remember that."

"How about 'Bigfoot'?"

"I haven't gotten all the way through the pile yet, sir, but I'll keep my eyes open."

"Good work," I said.

"One thing you should know, though, Sheriff," he said. "When I matched up the statements I collected from the crew against the payroll list, there's five people unaccounted for."

"I thought the payroll was handled in cash."

"Yeah, it is, but they still kept a list of who got paid so they wouldn't accidentally pay somebody twice."

"Who's missing?"

Griffin pulled a folder from the bottom of one of the stacks, rifled through the pages until he found what he was looking for.

"Three stage crew, you know, roadies; plus two production guys."

"These people have names?"

The tired smile he showed me was an admixture of humor and futility.

"Let me read them to you: Fuzzy Sam, Gomer, and—you'll love this one—Bongwater. Those are the three roadies."

"Two of those men are among the victims," I told him. "Both deceased. The one named Gomer is a rail hobo. He's at the Cayuse."

Griffin's eyebrows drifted upward.

"I set him up with a room. I wanted to encourage the man to stick around just in case."

"In case of what?"

"I don't know, Sam," I said. "That's what 'just in case' means."

"What's to keep the guy from taking off anyway?"

"He says he wants to see his friends receive a proper burial. That, and a soft bed and hot shower's an upgrade from the jungle, I suspect. I don't think he's going anywhere. At least, not for the next week or so."

"You trust the guy?"

"Not even a little bit," I said. "But I believe what he told me."

Griffin showed me his palms in surrender and went back to the list he'd been reading from.

"Last two names are—here it is—Sasquatch. That's the same thing as Bigfoot, right? What do you know? And the last one on the list is called Tiger."

I stepped into the pattern of sunlight that shone in from the fixed window high on the breakroom wall, felt the warmth on my back, and looked over Griffin's shoulder at the list he held.

"That's it?" I asked. "Everybody else is accounted for?"

"Except Ian Swann's brother. He's not on anybody's list. But we know where he is, don't we?"

"Two crewmen missing. What kind of work did they do?"

Griffin thumbed through the loose papers in the file and pulled out a lined yellow sheet that had been torn out of a legal pad and passed it to me. I scanned down the list and found where Griffin had placed stars beside the two names I was seeking.

"Production? That's it?"

"'Fraid so. These folks weren't real sticklers about record-keeping, sir."

"Do you even know what 'production' entails?"

"From what they told me, it could be anything from pulling cables to operating the soundboard or lights or rigging . . . It's a broad category."

"You said 'lights'?"

"Yes, sir."

"Like the lights that dropped out of the rigging, that crushed and electrocuted three people?"

"Could be."

"Shit."

"What?"

"Nothing," I said. "For now, finish with those witness statements. Make sure they're tight."

"Will do," he said as I returned the list he'd handed me.

A bouquet of red and peach-colored roses was arranged in an antique glass vase and had been placed on the counter in the coffee room.

"Where'd these come from?" I asked as I was about to leave.

"Ask Jordan," Griffin said without looking up from his reading.

I picked up the vase and carried it into the main office, waiting until Powell finished his phone call.

"What's up with the roses?" I asked him.

"Shasta picked them from her garden and brought them over this morning."

"Cut flowers, pressed shirt and jeans, greeting card with hearts on it sitting on your desk," I said. "You know the saying: happy wife, happy life. You're living it firsthand."

"We ain't married yet, Cap."

"In a few weeks you will be, and it's never too early to gather matrimonial wisdom from those of us in the know. You're gonna need it. By the way, Powell, that happy wife thing? It's God's honest truth, I'm not joking. Write that one down."

I could see I'd embarrassed him, and he cut his eyes to the vase I was carrying.

"I can get rid of those if you want me to," Jordan said.

"I like them. In fact, I've got a better place for them." I pushed aside a few stacks of papers and made room for the roses on a long table beneath a pinboard crowded with Magnafaxed copies of police wanted posters and the eight-by-ten photo I'd framed of Meridian's disgraced County Council chairman, Nolan Brody, who'd been run out of town on a rail. I considered Brody's arrest and subsequent incarceration to be one of my greatest civic accomplishments so far.

"Draws the eye, don't you think?" I asked.

"I think I might have a lead on the eagle poacher," Powell said, eager to change the subject.

"Well done," I said. "Care to tell me about it?"

"Still too early yet. But I can tell you it grew out of the idea you came up with when you met with Lily Firecloud. Which reminds me . . . She left you a note."

"What's Lily doing all the way down here? When was this?"

"About half an hour before you came in. She said she'd be over at Boyle's diner for lunch before she heads back to her place. She's probably still there."

I read the message she'd written on a piece of notepaper that had the logo of the local hardware store printed across the top. It was written in pencil, essentially repeated what Jordan Powell had already told me, and was signed with a feminine flourish. I checked my watch.

"I'll be at the diner," I said and walked out the front door.

THE NOONTIME STREETS were teeming with visitors and tourists, most of them young and outfitted in clothing that looked like it had last been worn at Woodstock. The morning's overcast had been mostly burned away, the temperature warming up nicely. Overall, it was becoming a perfect day for the rock concert that should have been.

I threaded my way among the window-shoppers who were milling along the oldest block in Meridian, flip-flops, huarache sandals, and bootheels all snapping and clattering the deeply scarred surface of an elevated wooden sidewalk still embedded with steel rings meant for the tethering of horses. Though the visitors seemed to be enjoying a sunny Saturday, the locals and shopkeepers seemed on edge, something brittle in the atmosphere, an indefinable simmering quality to the outward idyll.

I slipped past the line that had formed outside of Rowan Boyle's diner with all the civility that I could muster and found Lily Firecloud standing near the front door settling her check at the register. She counted off one or two extra bills from the change she'd been handed, eased her way between the packed tables to deliver the tip to her waitress, leaned in for a whispered remark and a friendly shared smile.

Lily followed me outside onto the sidewalk where we found a patch of shade underneath the overhang. Her long, dark hair was cut square at the ends and fell past her shoulders, as straight as if she had ironed it. She was wearing a goose down vest over a long-sleeved men's flannel shirt and a silver necklace with an agate pendant that was the color of her eyes.

"Am I allowed to hug you in public?" she joked.

"You can hug me anywhere you'd like," I said.

"It's a small town, you know."

"Not today, it isn't. Want to take a walk and get out of the crowd?"

"How about the park? I'd like that."

We crossed the street so we could walk in the sunshine, reaching the park just as the clock tower tolled one o'clock and chimed the Westminster Quarters. The grassy open space was dotted with dozens of couples and groups occupying shared blankets and eating deli sandwiches wrapped in wax paper they'd bought from a shop once operated by a hippie commune. A trio of young men wearing Rastafarian T-shirts, each with hair down to the center of his back, played hacky sack beneath the leafy branches of an ancient ash tree.

"Good god," Lily said. "These people are everywhere."

"Do you smell that?"

She tilted her face to the wind, sniffed once, and pursed her lips, stifling a familiar grin.

"I'll be right back," I told her.

I left Lily standing beside a stone monument topped by a bronze statue depicting an unidentified pioneer in the throes of some manner of valiant anguish and jogged the short block to the substation. Powell and Griffin were both exactly as I had left them as I pulled the door open and stepped inside.

"Powell," I said. "Put on your hat and gun belt and go take a stroll through the park for me, will you?"

"Something wrong?"

"Nothing that a little law enforcement visibility can't fix. Just wander through the park and make eye contact with people and smile."

"Those tourist kids smoking reefer out there, Cap'n?"

I couldn't tell if Powell was razzing me or not.

"I don't care what they do in the privacy of their homes, but I can't have it on the streets of my town, you read me?"

"I read you, Sheriff."

"Don't cause any trouble," I said. "No need to arrest anybody. Just fly the flag a little, make sure you're seen, then you can get back to your work."

I could hear Powell and Griffin muttering something to each other as the door swung shut on its hinges behind me, and the resonance of guitar and flute music grew louder as I returned to the park.

I led Lily to a place I knew that wasn't likely to have been discovered by the tourists, on the far side of the old church graveyard where many of Meridian's original founders had been interred. The clapboard church house was long gone, but the ancestors of some of Meridian's first citizens still rested here, visited less and less frequently with the passage of years. As Lily and I pressed deeper into the park, the tourist crowd thinned out, and we walked slowly beside the cemetery enclosure in deferential silence, the stone grave markers blackened with age, immortelles and flower bouquets mostly dead, the Ball jars that contained them crusted and opaque with algae. I shouldered my way between the branches of a copse of laurel bushes that had all grown together, held them open for Lily Firecloud to follow me, and stepped out onto a secluded promontory overlooking the river.

"This is a picnic spot Jesse and I favor in the summertime," I said. "It's quiet here, and I figured you had something on your mind."

Lily looked at me strangely for a moment, tilted her head to one side, and seemed to mull a thought before she responded.

"You really love her, don't you?" Lily asked. "Your wife."

"Jesse," I answered. "Yes, ma'am, I do. Sometimes she packs a basket with a picnic lunch for the two of us, and I'll slip out of the office and we'll share it out here."

"You always were a one-woman man."

"That's a fact," I said. "Not that you would know. You never went out with me."

She smiled gently and turned her face to me again, something distant in her almond eyes.

"I'm a keen observer of human behavior," Lily said. A swollen moment hung between us like warm rain, and her expression, usually so stoic, took on a sorrowful cast. "I keep thinking people will change. I guess I keep clinging to the old days."

Lily took a seat on a flat stone and gazed down at the swiftly moving river, and I sat on a tree stump beside her.

"Same rodeo, different clowns," I said. "What's on your mind, Lily?"

"I had a dream that I should come here to see you. To speak to you."

"I understand," I said, though I'm sure she could discern my puzzlement.

"When you came out to talk to me the other day, I wasn't completely honest with you."

"Honest about what?"

"You asked me about the fire at the McEvoy place. You asked if I knew anything about the history of the place. I left a few things out."

"What things?"

Down below us, a McKenzie boat carrying two fishermen floated quietly between the banks. The oarsman dodged a boulder and slid into a slough, then allowed the craft to drift across the flats. The lid of a wicker creel lay open on the deck between the two men, revealing a morning's catch of walleye and panfish.

"Did you ever think you'd leave here, Tyler?"

"I did leave," I said. "For a while. I tend to think in terms of 'before' and 'after,' these days."

She pulled her eyes away from the McKenzie boat, leaned over, and plucked a dandelion flower from the grass between her feet.

"I do, too," she said. "But the dividing lines are very different for the two of us, I think."

"I truly hope so, Lily."

"I heard about the accident out at the concert last night. That was terrible."

"Three people died. Ian Swann is still in the hospital and hasn't regained consciousness. I've seen injuries like Ian's before. In the war. In all honesty, it doesn't look good."

"I think I know him," Lily said and looked at me as though to gauge my reaction to her statement.

"Ian Swann? Millions of people know him, Lily."

"That's not what I meant," she said. "I meant, I think I know him from *before*."

INTERLUDE IV

(1964)

"WHAT DO YOU MEAN, '*What if it wasn't an accident?*'" Heather said.

She was still seated on the tree swing, but she had stopped swaying beneath the branches, her expression indistinguishable between puzzlement and distress.

"Nothing," Paul said. "Never mind."

"No, no, no. Not a chance, Buster Brown. You can't say something like that and back away."

Paul cut his eyes across the length of the farm, beyond the house and into the shade beneath the feedlot canopy. His dad was still mucking moss off the retention pond, but Paul could see that his father was keeping a close eye on them, and Paul was beginning to feel pressed to return to his chores.

"It's just something I think about sometimes," Paul said. "I was only a kid at the time, probably six years old at the most. What would I know?"

Heather remained motionless on the swing, studying him, her eyes moist with emotion.

"Can I come over there and sit with you?" she asked.

"Sure. I guess." He would easily endure his father's wrath to feel her close to him. "Just remember, I warned you I smell like pigs."

She settled in next to him, not caring that she was sitting in the dirt, not caring that he carried the odors of agrarian living in his clothes and in his pores. She looked at Paul and saw something inside of him—some internal barrier—collapse, and the story he had kept to himself for a teenage lifetime came out in a torrent, coughed up like shards of glass.

PAUL'S MOTHER had been killed in a single-car crash on a disused and deserted county road nearly a decade ago. It had been twilight at the time, that particular evening like so many others: stagnant, unexceptional, and drab, just like her expression when Paul had spied her pinning laundry to the clothesline behind the house. Her car had been moving fast, far too fast, striking a poplar with such force that it sheared off the tree trunk and launched the car over a levee where it landed upside down in the stagnant rainwater runoff of a six-foot-deep agricultural reservoir.

Icy water spilled in through the cracks in the driver's-side window and flooded through a fist-size void the impact of his mother's skull had cleaved through the windscreen. Not even the rush of near-freezing green water could rouse her from oblivion; unconscious and profusely bleeding from the wounds she'd sustained, her lungs distended, swelling with murky fluid.

But Paul's mother had not been driving by herself that night.

The three-year-old boy whom she had belted in to the passenger seat beside her had also been trapped inside the car, ensnared for so long he lost consciousness just as his mother had, actually drowning before being rescued and revived by the inexplicable appearance of another motorist. Thanks to the ministrations of that Samaritan, the little boy survived. But not before he sustained severe oxygen deprivation to his brain, a condition the emergency doctors termed hypoxic-anoxic injury, though the clinical terminology would never disguise the damage that had been inflicted on him.

In the absence of air to breathe, human brain cells begin to die after two or three minutes, the first cells to perish being those which reside in the temporal lobe, where all of life's memories dwell. In the aftermath of the accident, the little boy spent three days in a coma, and the injury that had already been inflicted on him from his near brush with death left him with severe memory challenges, periodic spasticity, disorientation, and measurable cognitive impairment. The doctors said the child would be lucky if he were ever to attain the intellectual and emotional development of an adolescent.

But the boy *had* survived, and his mother had not. It was the simple calculus that would come to define Paul's life, and the lives of his father and young brother, Shane, and would continue to do so for all the days that were to follow.

PAUL AND HEATHER sat in silence for a long while after Paul had finished his telling of it. Overhead, the redwings and tanagers were settling into the spurs of the old oak, and the atmosphere took on a smell of water that had gone green in a trough.

"What are you two doing over here?"

Paul's father's voice startled both him and Heather. Paul watched his father step out of the shadows on the far side of the tree, his expression dark and unreadable.

"Time for you to get back to work," he said to Paul. "Dusk is coming soon."

"I need to give Heather a ride home," Paul said. "Her friend dropped her off here. I didn't know she was coming."

Heather sensed she had crossed some sort of invisible line, though unsure of how or what it might have been. Families were complicated—she knew that as well as anybody. But it was clear that Paul's father was angry, even though his eyes were shaded from her view, his features obfuscated by the failing light. Heather felt guilty that she had goaded Paul into telling his story, and now she wondered how much of their conversation Paul's father had overheard.

"You got your work to get to, son," he said. "I'll drive the girl home. I reckon I know where she lives. I used to know her daddy."

CHAPTER TWENTY-THREE

I WATCHED as the McKenzie boat carrying the two fishermen disappeared around a sharp bend in the river, where a young doe and her fawn emerged out of a thicket of rhododendron growing from the edge of the cliff bank, sniffed at the air, and trotted off into the woods. The water was running fast and clear, the leaves the current pushed along the sandy bottom clearly visible in the sunlight.

"How do you know it was Ian Swann that you knew from before?"

"Have you seen his eyes?" Lily asked. "They're the color of a turquoise gemstone, and his complexion's just like mine. Some folks used to say that his mama was Cajun, but that could be just another rumor. She was long gone before that poor boy even lost his first tooth. If I'm right, he didn't go by Ian back then, though. I don't really remember. He was a lot younger than we were, so I didn't pay that much attention."

"Why don't I recall any of this?" I asked.

"You had already left for the army, Ty. There's no reason you would have remembered this stuff. The Fireclouds did business with the boy's dad, Jake Swanson. They butchered his hogs for him. I was practically living with the Fireclouds by then. I was out at their place all the time. You remember what my home life was like."

"I remember," I said and saw a certain darkness pass behind her eyes and vanish. "Why are you telling me this, Lily?"

She studied the dandelion blossom in her hand and brushed the tiny floret with the ball of her thumb.

"I don't know," she said, looking into my face. "It seems dumb hearing myself tell it to you now. Thing is, I don't know what I know. Maybe it's nothing. I was an in-between in age back in those days; younger than the grown-ups and older than the kids. I just remember that the whole thing felt strange and sad, and I felt sorry for the whole bunch of them. Felt sorry for the kids, anyway. They all seemed so hopeless."

Columns of yellow sunlight spiked through the canopy of trees, and it felt as though winter had finally surrendered and let go. The day had grown warm enough for me to remove my jacket, so I folded it across my lap and rolled my shirtsleeves up my forearms.

"I saw a newspaper clipping at the library," I said. "It was the only one I could find. From '64 or '65. It mentioned the death of a girl, said it was 'unexplained,' but no victim's name was given. I assumed it was because she was a minor."

"People said that house was cursed. I'm starting to believe it's true."

"Do you remember anything about the girl?"

"They said they found her hanging from the oak outside the house, but that could be a rumor, too. The Swansons moved away right afterward. So did the girl's father. Nobody ever talked about it after that. Like it was Meridian's big dirty secret."

THE CLOCK TOWER was chiming again as I parted the laurel branches and Lily Firecloud and I emerged into the park and garden. As we crossed the wide expanse of lawn, I noticed that Jordan Powell had moved one of the black-and-white police cruisers from behind the substation and parked it in conspicuous view along the curb at the park's entrance. The sweet smell of marijuana I had detected earlier was long gone, as were the majority of the sunbathers and picnickers who had been there when Lily and I had begun our conversation.

"Thank you for listening to me, Tyler," she said as she unlocked her car. "I hope you don't think I'm crazy."

"I don't think you're crazy. Truth is, there's precious little information about what happened at that house. One photo in an old newspaper, and the whole incident seemed to disappear."

I didn't mention that the case files I should have found in the Lewiston substation had gone missing as well, and a sound filled my ears like the wind blowing across a vast and uninhabited savannah.

Lily reached her arm out of her car window and waved goodbye to me as she pulled out onto the street and drove away. Halfway up the block, I spotted Lankard Downing taking down the VISITORS WELCOME sign he'd hung up in the Cottonwood Blossom's front window. I caught up with him as he was about to go back in, held the door for him, and followed him inside.

Downing seemed distracted and more irascible than usual, and the crowd inside his bar had thinned to nearly normal levels. I leaned an elbow on the edge of the rail and waited for Downing to stash his hand-painted banner in the storeroom and return to his usual station behind the stick.

"These folks were drinking like it was an Irish wake," he said.

"I would've thought you'd be grateful for the business," I said.

"Tourism is overrated."

"You heard what happened last night?" I asked.

He nodded and appeared unexpectedly sorrowful. Aside

from booze and burgers, gossip was Downing's mainstay, and his delight in sharing bad news was usually in direct proportion to how depraved the scandal was.

"It's all anybody's talking about," he said. "A damned shame. A genuine damned shame."

"Have you seen Lankard Downing around here?" I asked him. "You look exactly like him, but you don't sound like him at all."

"Very funny, Dawson. Thing is, I kinda liked that kid. I was damn sorry to hear he got hurt. He ain't likely to make it, is he?"

"Hard to say," I said.

Downing plucked a damp rag off the sink and began to work slow circles with it along the polished wooden surface of the bar. Leon Quinn stepped out of the back room, took one look at Lankard Downing, and disappeared inside again.

"Tell me something," I said to Lankard. "You've been around here for a while. You remember a family named Swanson? Had a hog farm out there by the old ice house."

He stopped wiping the countertop and eyed me with something resembling suspicion.

"What about 'em?"

"Do you recall anything about a dead teenaged girl? Would have been ten or twelve years ago, 1964 or thereabouts."

He shook his head and somehow managed to appear even sadder than he had before.

"I don't remember much about that, Sheriff. Ugly business. Wasn't something folks wanted to talk too much about. Plus . . ." His reply trailed off into silence as he picked up the rag again and resumed polishing.

"'Plus' what?" I asked.

Lankard Downing sidled down toward me, studied the floorboards for a few moments before he answered.

"I drank a little more than I should have back in those days," he said. "My recollections ain't what they should be."

"What happened to the girl?"

"I heard they found her hanging from a rope," he said. His whisper took on a tone somewhere between reverential fear and superstitious dread.

"Suicide?"

"I don't know. Sheriff Skadden couldn't get her in the ground fast enough, though, I can tell you that. Nobody said nothing about it after that."

"Why do you suppose that was?"

"I don't know about that, neither. But it did some heavy damage to my peace of mind. Didn't do much good for nobody hereabouts, especially a man like me back then who was prone to swallowing his troubles with a chaser."

"Nothing ever came of it? No investigation?"

"Oh, I s'pose old Lloyd Skadden did some poking around, but it's like I said: I never heard another word about it. Some people moved away after that, other people died or went crazy, I heard. I can't say for sure. I drank them memories away."

He stepped away from me and shivered involuntarily, like a dog who'd been caught in a downpour. Lankard Downing had been a fixture in Meridian for as long as I could remember and was considered a connoisseur—if not embellisher—of the odd salacious tale, so his response to our town's most recent misfortune troubled me for reasons I had yet to define. Nevertheless, it was clear that Downing was reaching the end of his tether on the subject and my pushing him much further would get me nowhere.

"One last thing before I go," I said. "Do you recognize Ian Swann as having been around here before?"

"Here? In Meridian?"

"Yes. I'm asking if he looks familiar to you."

"Hell, Sheriff," Downing demurred. "I look at these kids, all I see is a faceful of hair. I don't know how they recognize *each other*, let alone me trying to do it."

"Is that a no, Lankard? You don't recognize him?"

"That's affirmative, Sheriff," he said. "I never seen that boy before. But he had good manners, and I liked him. Damn sorry to hear he got hurt. Now, can we talk about something else, please?"

IAN SWANN'S ROOM was dark when I arrived, the drapes drawn tight across the windows, the only light cast from the electronic displays of medical machinery keeping Ian alive; the only sound the rhythmic hiss of the respirator and the soft rumble of Cricket's snoring. My daughter was curled up in an uncomfortable-looking ball on a reclining chair, and Jesse looked up at me in surprise from an old dog-eared copy of *Look* magazine as I came in.

"I wasn't expecting you," she whispered.

"Has she been sleeping long?" I asked.

"Half an hour, maybe."

I looked at Ian Swann behind his shield of clear plastic curtains. He was lying as he had been when I'd last seen him, bandaged nearly head to foot, only one-quarter of his face exposed. He resembled a mummy strung with wires, tubes, and leads, his chest expanding mechanically every few seconds.

"He's still not breathing on his own, and he hasn't regained consciousness," Jesse said. "They came in to change his dressings an hour ago or so. My god, Ty, he looks horrible."

Jesse looked to be unwell herself, pale and drawn, as drained and worn-out as I had ever seen her, and even so, I knew the source of her concern was more for Cricket and Ian Swann than for herself.

"Have you heard any prognosis from the doctors?"

"No. But their expressions seem more dire every time they come in to check on him."

I tipped my head in the direction of the nurses' station, gestured for Jesse to follow me. I had some things I needed to talk to her about and I didn't want to risk waking our daughter.

I touched my hat brim in silent acknowledgment of the attending nurse, then leaned an elbow on the counter as I waited for my wife to come out from the room. A castoff copy of this morning's *Daily Post* sat on the counter, a photo of Ian Swann and the accompanying story about Friday night's debacle splashed across the front page, above the fold. I flipped it over so neither my wife nor daughter would have to look at it, then thought again and tossed it in the waste bin.

"I hate to do this, but I have to ask you a couple things," I said to Jesse as she joined me, her eyes pressed into narrow slits, adjusting to the harsh light of the corridor.

"I understand."

"Do you have any footage of the stage from Friday night?"

She looked at me curiously before she answered.

"I was in the chopper getting aerials of the crowd. I might have some flybys of the stage. Why?"

"I just want to be thorough," I said, but even I could hear the thread of prevarication in my tone as I spoke the words. I lowered my voice and leaned closer to Jesse and added, "Three people lost their lives, Jesse. Every death is suspicious until they're proven otherwise. You know the job."

Her focus drifted back into Ian's darkened room, to the young man wrapped in bandages and gauze, stained pink and yellow from the slow leakage of bodily fluids. When she turned back to me, there was something different in her eyes.

"If someone hurt these kids, Ty, I hope you burn them to the ground."

"I need to have a look at that footage."

Jesse crossed her arms across her chest.

"Cricket and her crew were backstage last night. She shot the footage you want to see."

"Where is it now?"

"Len Kaanan sends the film stock up to Portland at the end of every day. A photo lab up there processes it overnight and sends it back. We watch the dailies from the day before every afternoon. Costs Kaanan a fortune, but that's the way he operates."

"I'll call Kaanan and have a look."

"There was a second-unit crew roaming around as well, but Cricket's team was the only one shooting from onstage."

"She saw the whole thing, Jesse."

"I know. It breaks my heart."

"I offered to take her home to get some sleep and a change of clothes, but she wouldn't leave that room."

Jesse touched me on the sleeve and stood on her toes to kiss me.

"I'll bring her home with me tonight," she said.

I watched my wife move back toward Ian's room, and I turned to leave, but I didn't make it very far.

"Hey, Tyler," she called out softly as I strode down the hall.

When I turned back around, she was standing in the corridor, hands on her hips, her eyes like ice and fire.

"If it turns out that this was not an accident," she said, "I will help you build the gallows, Sheriff Dawson."

If there is a downside to being married to a strong, beautiful, and independent woman, I have not yet discovered what it might be.

* * *

IT WAS well after five o'clock by the time I left the hospital, the stores along Meridian's main drag closing their doors for the night as I drove through town. The spring days had begun to grow longer, as had the shadows that marked the ridges in the distance, and a bank of low clouds softened the edge of the horizon. The two-lane highway was nearly deserted as I pushed through the pass, the Catherine glass in the spire of St. Stephen's basilica glowing like an opal in the light of the retreating sun.

I had been reared in a time when much had been spoken from pulpits with respect to tolerance and grace, though I don't recall witnessing much of it in practice firsthand. My grandmother had been raised Catholic, a brand of worship looked upon suspiciously by her Protestant neighbors and friends, and a faith she quietly stepped away from when she got married to my grandfather, largely out of deference to an unyielding mother-in-law.

Every now and then, when I was a boy, she would sneak me to St. Stephen's for a mass, or sometimes merely to light a candle and sit quietly inside, surrounded by ornate colored windows and mystical aromas. There was always something of a twinkle in her eye when we would depart the chapel, and she would wink and remind me, "This will be our little secret, Tyler." Then she would take me for an ice cream at the dime store and she'd tell me stories about when she was a young girl.

The day always felt different to me inside those stone walls, the priest and his minions attired differently than the minister across the street at the church my father took us to; the basilica seemed mysterious and hallowed, hushed and solemn and devout. I never claimed to understand too much of what was happening inside that imposing hall, much less what was being confessed in the tiny wooden booths in the back where the congregants lined up to speak with the parish priest, wearing expressions of shame or contrition, sometimes trepidation and dread, on their faces. My grandmother would smile and squeeze my hand as we departed, and I never uttered a word about those outings to anyone. It was Grandma's and my secret.

Paradoxically, it was during those irregular visits that I discovered anything I ever learned with regard to forbearance, and I felt little wonder at my compulsion to stop by now on my way home to the ranch, carrying the burden that I had misjudged my fellow man in the form of Dewayne Gomer and had treated him poorly as a result of my preconception. For that matter, I had misjudged Ian Swann as well. In truth, I embraced a genuine belief in man's capacity for honor and nobility but had personally witnessed too much of his aptitude for atrocity. Even as I seek the one and deplore the other, I always seem to find myself besieged by both.

I removed my hat as I stepped inside the narthex. The stone walls reflected a soft glow with flickering light, the air sweet with incense and melted beeswax.

I was about to seat myself in the last row of the nave when I heard the sacristy door swinging open on its rusted hinges; I turned and saw Monsignor Turner twist his key in the lock as he exited and crossed between the pews to come greet me. He was dressed in black slacks and clerical collar, with a purple silk stole draped across his shoulders. His pewter eyes appeared to be freighted with disquiet and reflected the fragmented slivers of colored light that shone in the stained glass behind me.

"It's been a while, Sheriff Dawson," he said. "Always a pleasure to see you."

"Lying is still a sin, isn't it, Monsignor?"

He smiled and some of the distress he carried seemed to fall away.

"You may bring trepidation to others whom you encounter in your professional life, Sheriff," he said, "but I always take comfort in seeing you here."

"Likewise, Monsignor," I said, and he chuckled aloud.

"I was sorry to hear of the recent misfortune out in the woods. I understand it was a fatal malfunction of some kind. Is that what brings you here?"

"I promised someone I'd light a candle for the deceased."

"I've always appreciated that you are a man of your word," he said and gestured toward the transept. "As you know, the votive stand is just over there. You'll find the oratory in the small space next to it."

I slid a few bills into the offering box and lit three candles contained in pebbled glass vessels of deep crimson. I lit a fourth one for Ian Swann, then stood silently, watching the wick take the flame. In the distance, I could hear the faint echoes of the choir rehearsing the upcoming Easter mass, and I moved through the nave toward the door.

"Go in peace, Sheriff," Monsignor Turner called out as I reached for the cold iron handhold.

"Thank you, Monsignor, I intend to," I said. "But it doesn't always work out that way."

INTERLUDE V

(1964)

THE AFTERNOON was rapidly fading, and Shane Swanson had begun to feel the familiar press of anxiety that arose when he was left alone too long. It used to be a rare occasion when neither his brother nor father were home to keep him company, but it was happening more and more now that Paul had made the high school baseball team and his father had been taking on odd jobs and pickup work as a handyman for extra money.

It wasn't all bad, though, to have the house all to himself. He could pretty much do what he wanted, like play a record on the hi-fi, or take a drink of milk right out of the bottle. He just didn't like it when it started to get dark.

Shane tried to distract himself by watching television, but the picture was all crumpled up. He tried to adjust the rabbit ear antenna but only seemed to make the Portland stations even more fuzzy than they were before. He switched it off, watched the tiny blue dot at the center of the picture tube fade away. When Shane was little, his brother Paul told him to gently rub the dot with his forefinger to erase it. Now that he was older, he knew that Paul was just making a joke. But Shane still remembered it.

He had to get his mind off the thoughts that were starting to swirl inside his head. The train sounds and the car sounds, all the scary noises from outside. Shane wandered to his father's room, where he had recently discovered a small collection of men's magazines underneath his bed. He slid one from the pile and thumbed through the pictures inside; soon, he started to feel light-headed and an uncertain heat rose up his neck. Shane didn't know very many girls in real life. He really didn't know *any* girls. Except for Paul's girlfriend, Heather. She was pretty. And only a bike ride away. A long ride, but worth it.

Shane replaced the magazine where he'd found it, thought about playing the radio and singing along with it, like his brother did sometimes. But then he got a better idea.

Half an hour later, he was crouching in the low shrubs, his bicycle stashed inside the shadows thrown by the low ebb of the sun as it began to slide behind the mountains.

THE WINDOWS of her house were warm and yellow, woodsmoke streaming from the chimney. The nights were getting longer now, and it dawned on him that soon it would be too cold and rainy to do much of this kind of thing for a while. At least, not until it was summertime again.

Shane knew which room was Heather's, which window to watch and wait for. Sometimes he would see her there, talking on the phone, or dancing by herself in front of her record player, or sometimes, if he was lucky, changing her clothes. Once he had even seen her stepping out from the shower and brushing her wet hair before the full-length mirror on her wall.

Shane felt that weird feeling down there again, the heat in his stomach, and the dryness in his mouth. There was so much he didn't understand, so many changes happening and the thoughts that crossed his mind, thinking different things now than he used to. But tonight it seemed like there was something else. She wore a strange expression on her face, and he could see her exposed breasts between the open buttons of her blouse. And that weird feeling again down there. She looked so unhappy, though. Scared, even. Shane couldn't be sure.

He stepped closer to Heather's window, knowing better than to stand so close that the light wash from indoors would reveal his presence. He couldn't help it, but the feelings in his loins grew more intense as he watched, blood rushing through his veins and making his skin feel warm and clammy like it had the last time.

Then all at once, the heat in his stomach turned to ice and his scalp constricted as if a length of bale wire had been torqued tight across his head. Someone else was inside the room with her. Someone he thought he recognized.

Shane's own astonishment and curiosity drew him closer to the glass, and he couldn't help himself, even though he risked being revealed in the glow. But it all happened so fast after that.

The window sash was suddenly thrown open, squealing in protest as it was thrust beyond the checkrail, and Shane recoiled backward into the trees, too late.

Shane retrieved his bike and began to push it through the undergrowth, vines and creepers tangling the forest floor as he made his escape through the woods, and an angry voice called out from Heather's open window.

"I saw you out there, you little sonofabitch! If you say one goddamn word about this, I will gut you like a pig. I swear to god, I will gut you like a goddamn pig!"

CHAPTER TWENTY-FOUR

I GAVE UP PACING back and forth across the living room floor at about four o'clock that morning, quietly got dressed, and took Wyatt the dog with me down the path to Caleb's cabin. The predawn air was chilled, my breath clouding in the dark, the atmosphere dead silent but for a pair of owls calling to each other out of the depths of the old-growth forest. Overhead, the moonless sky was so clear I could see the Milky Way. I switched on my flashlight, cut it back and forth across the path, and let Wyatt take the lead along the incline that led up to Caleb's porch.

The light fixture beside the door flicked on as soon as my boot soles touched the top step, and I heard the throw of the deadbolt from inside. The door cracked open slightly, with Caleb standing in the narrow breach gripping a Winchester .30-.30 in his right hand, its barrel poking out into the cold, aimed squarely at my chest. He lowered the Winchester when he recognized it was only Wyatt and me standing in the yellow wash of light.

"Well, look who drifted back to his own ranch," Caleb said, his vocal cords rusty with sleep.

He had two days of gray stubble on his chin, was wearing a

heavy wool bathrobe over his nightshirt and had stepped into deerskin slippers, his battered gray Stetson hat screwed onto his head. Caleb pulled the door just wide enough to let us pass inside, then shut it tight against the nearly freezing morning. He leaned the Winchester against the wall and I followed him as he ambled into his kitchen, watched him scoop coffee out of a tin can and into the percolator.

"I see you dropped by empty-handed," Caleb said as he filled the pitcher with tap water and plugged it in.

"The ladies were still sleeping, and I didn't want to wake them."

"*Everybody's* still sleeping," he said and cocked an unruly eyebrow at me. "You may not have noticed that while you and your dog were taking your hike out there in the dark."

I started to speak, but he cut me off before I had uttered my first word.

"Hold on for a minute," he said. "My brain's still wearing its pajamas, and I ain't had my coffee yet."

Caleb moved into the living room, then knelt and swung open the door of the woodstove. He struck a lucifer match on the stone hearth, blew on the kindling, and adjusted the air vent as he warmed his palms against the growing flames before shutting the door.

"Coffee ought to be ready by now," he said. "How 'bout you go pour us a couple of mugs and bring 'em in here. It's hard to get motivated to move too far away from this fireplace."

I did as he asked and came back and took a seat on the hearth, the riverstone already warmed by the blaze.

"Lily Firecloud came to see me yesterday," I said.

"Is that so? I always liked that girl—she's got backbone," Caleb said. "How's she doing? How's her little boy? What's his name again?"

"Charlie. They both seem good. Little Charlie isn't so little anymore; he's ten or eleven years old now."

"Goddamn, but time moves along, don't it?"

"That's why I came down to see you this morning."

"Can't help you stop time, son. Wish'd I could."

"Lily said she had a dream that she needed to see me about. Said she needed to tell me she thought maybe the accident the other night had something to do with what happened all those years ago at the McEvoy farm."

"The place that just burned down?"

"Yep."

He closed his eyes, but only for a moment. The traces of a personal thought crossed his features, then he looked up at me and shook his head.

"I assume Ms. Firecloud was referring to the girl they found dead there, back in the sixties?"

I nodded.

"Thing is, I don't remember anything about it," I said. It was becoming an increasing source of frustration to me that I had no recollection of an incident as perverse and gruesome as this was proving itself to be.

"No reason you should remember," Caleb said. "You and Jesse had just got married and were raising a little girl. On top of that, you'd just come back here, taking the reins of the ranch from your daddy after he died. I think you had your hands full, Ty. Besides, there wasn't nobody too excited to dwell on the matter anyhow. If you didn't study the newspaper or drink in the bars every day, you wouldn't have heard much about it. This country had just had a president murdered by some idiot in Dallas, and we were all watching the Vietnam body count on the news every goddamn night of the week; we didn't need to go looking for more misery."

Caleb's reminder contained the ring of truth. I had turned

away from gossip back then, my sleep already burdened by nightmares I'd brought home from overseas, and I had never been one to borrow trouble in the first place. I appreciated the absolution Caleb was offering me now, but I was still troubled by a vague sense that those years of my absence from this place had taken something irreplaceable from me.

"From what I understand," I said. "The victim was just a kid, a teenager. Seems like somebody should have done something about that."

"People make choices," Caleb said simply.

"Not everybody gets to choose from good options."

"That's a fact," he said. "Still, everybody knew that girl's death wasn't a blister that came up after a short walk, I can tell you that much."

"What's that supposed to mean?"

"A lot of the scuttlebutt around town was just that: nothing more than rumor and speculation. But in my experience, that young girl's daddy, Gavin Lomax, was a belligerent hothead; and that Jacob Swanson was simple white trash. Nobody liked either of 'em overly much, and them two men didn't like each other. When it was all said and done, nobody in town really cared about them either way. Sure it was sad, but after they found that girl in the tree, the sheriff could hardly wait for the whole thing to go away. I figure most of the town agreed with him for one reason or another."

"I saw a photo of the scene in an old copy of the *Post*. Lloyd Skadden was in it, together with somebody else, but I couldn't tell who the other man was."

"Probably Doc Brawley," Caleb said. "He was the only doctor around here back then. Also served as the coroner at the time; chief cook and bottle washer, too, most likely."

"Nobody in town thought it was strange there was no follow-up on the case?"

"Expectations regarding law enforcement was pretty low in those days, Ty. Lloyd Skadden wasn't a lawman, he was a two-bit politician. He wouldn't know to pour piss out of a boot if it had instructions wrote right there on the heel. He only got the sheriff's job as a favor to his daddy."

What Caleb was describing was just as Lily Firecloud had told it to me: a rural population with a negligible expectation of investigation, or even a simple explanation of what happened, neither of which had ever been delivered. And as is the tendency in small towns, legends grow larger with time, facts get lost and metastasize to rumor, innuendo, and outright fabrication. It came as no surprise to hear that both the Swanson and Lomax families moved away in the wake of the tragedy, and I had little doubt that both households expected the entire county to come after one or the other of them with pitchforks and torches if they'd stuck around.

"What was the pronouncement as to the cause of death?" I asked.

"Pronouncement?" Caleb said, his tone freighted with irony. "Wasn't no pronouncement. But I do recall the fancy language from the newspaper. Doc said it was death by 'external pressure on the neck.' Why in the hell do they have to talk like that? Why not just say *hanging*?"

"Those words don't mean the poor girl hung herself," I said. "Somebody else could have done it to her. Or could have strangled her beforehand and obscured it with a rope. Still, they labeled it a suicide? And that was the end of it? Simple as that?"

"They said there wasn't no way to know for sure, there being no note or nothing like that left behind. Ruled it a 'death by misadventure.' Ain't that something? *Misadventure.*" Caleb sipped at his coffee and his attention wandered out beyond the darkened window for several seconds before he continued. "When Sheriff Skadden cleared everybody involved of wrongdoing, they all skedaddled out of here right damn quick."

"Where to?"

Wyatt sidled up beside me and curled up at my feet, and Caleb's train of thought appeared to glide away again.

"Where'd they go, Caleb?" I repeated.

Caleb shrugged and gazed into the firebox as he opened the door and fed a branch of cut cedar into the flames and watched them sputter to life.

"Hell, I don't know," he said. "I didn't pay attention to it anymore. The whole episode was so sad and pointless. I was glad to see an end to it. I suspect everybody else around here was, too."

Caleb set down his coffee cup, stretched his arms, and yawned. He combed his mustache with his fingers and looked into my face.

"Why's this thing got you fussed up so much, Ty? That happened a long time ago."

"I don't know for sure. Lily Firecloud thinks she recognizes the musician, Ian Swann, from years ago. Thinks she saw him here in Meridian back in the day. Swann, Swanson. Wouldn't be much of a stretch. Performers use stage names all the time."

"Anybody else think the same thing as you?"

"I talked to Lankard Downing."

Caleb chuffed and took another gulp of his coffee.

"What'd that old bastard have to say about it?" Caleb asked.

"Said he was a drunk back then and didn't remember too many details about it."

"He ain't lying about that, that's for damn sure."

"Downing said he didn't recognize the kid, but he didn't want to talk about it, either."

I reached down and scratched Wyatt behind the ears. He groaned and wagged his tail once and sprawled out on his side.

"You might want to try and speak with ol' Doc Brawley's widow," Caleb said. "Assuming you ain't done it already. Ruth was his nurse, you remember."

"I was thinking I might do that," I said.

Outside the window, the purple luminosity of false dawn paled the sky, the winking constellations disappearing one by one. The horned owls continued hooting to each other as the silhouettes of towering sequoias revealed themselves against a background of speckled velvet.

"You know," Caleb said, "somebody told me once that horses' brains are wired differently from you and me. Something about the way they see things allows them to see two completely different images of their surroundings at the same time. Can you imagine that?"

"That's got to be a might confusing, but I'm beginning to feel a little bit that way myself."

"You'd think it would be, wouldn't you? Sit down and I'll fix you some breakfast, son. You're looking peaked, and by the expression on your face, I strongly suspect you're fixing to have another long day ahead of you."

CALEB AND I finished a breakfast of fried eggs, biscuits, and bacon; then we washed the pots, pans, and plates and left them to air-dry in the sink. By the time we had finished, it was full light outside, the sounds of horses and hired hands already busying themselves at the snubbing pen.

Morning had broken across the valley at once, a sudden incursion of daybreak, golden sunlight and white clouds floating low on the blue sky as we stepped outside. Off to the west, a layer of brown dust hung in the air above the North Pasture, where

Taj Caldwell was disking the soil behind the Massey Ferguson, turning under the red clover we'd planted as a crop rotation, the breeze redolent with the smell of damp earth and cut grass.

"Let's hobble on over and see what them boys are up to," Caleb said. "Whatever you've got on your list can wait a few more minutes."

Caleb and I wandered down to the corral, where three of my men were saddling an unwilling and unsettled mustang. I leaned my elbows on the fence and watched New Guy fit a hackamore over the horse's recalcitrant head. I wondered again at the singular life of a cowboy, their culture and customs utterly unique to this life, this world of cattle and horses and wide open country, viewing their world from between the ears of a horse. These are men who work hard at a difficult, demanding, and dangerous job. Their hours are long, their wages are low, but their lifestyle is one that none of us would ever trade for anything else in the world.

The proof of that statement was directly in front of me. The entire team of my Diamond D wranglers was spending their only day off breaking rough stock and busting sod, doing for fun the same things they'd be doing tomorrow for pay, and doing it together, like a team, like a platoon, like a family. I admired these men; they rode for my brand and reminded me of the depth of my obligation to them in return.

It put me in mind of the parable that my father had told me—repeatedly as I had grown up on this ranch, the third generation of Dawsons to have the privilege to do so, a privilege that was worth shedding blood for. He told me a story of a man who was new to the territory—presumably my grandfather, though I knew it to be more allegory than history. This newcomer encounters another man out in the open valley, building a cabin and stock corral with his own hands. The newcomer asks the man, "Whose land is this?" and the other man answers, "It's mine." The newcomer says, "How did you come to own it?" and the other man says, "I fought for it." As the story has it, the newcomer takes stock of the settler, looks out across a rolling green pasture ringed by tall pines with a river of fresh water running right through the middle. "You say you fought for it?" the newcomer asks. And the other man says, "That's what I said." With that, the newcomer takes a step forward and says, "Then, how about I fight *you* for it?"

"Where'd you slip off to?" Caleb said, a quizzical look on his face.

"I was just thinking about my old man," I said. "I still miss him."

"Yup. Your old man was a good'n, one of the best. Tough sonofabitch, and I still miss him, too."

We watched New Guy climb into the saddle and give Tom Jenkins a nod, the sign to slip loose the knot. Young Tom hopped back between the fence rails just as the mustang threw his head and crow-hopped to the center of the pen.

That horse snuffed and sunfished, corkscrewed, and went berserk, but the rider miraculously remained in the saddle until the animal eventually ran out of steam. Tom Jenkins and Paul Tucker were seated on the top rail at the opposite end of the split fence, hooting the whole time as if they'd been watching a buckle event.

"Takes a sticky cowboy to stay on a horse like that'n," Caleb said, grinning.

"New Guy knows how to set a mean horse."

"Ain't bad, is he? He's turned out to be as good a rough stock handler as we've had around here since you were a tadpole."

Tom and Paul Tucker helped rack the mustang to the hitch rail, and the rider swung down from the saddle. He retrieved his hat out of the dust and brushed it off on his pant leg.

"C'mon over here for a minute," I called out to him and watched him amble over, bandy-legged and sore, with a grin he couldn't seem to wipe off his face.

"Yes, sir?"

"Tell me your name again, son," I said.

"They call me 'New Guy,' sir."

"I'll let the trail boss keep calling you that if he wants to," I said. "I think I'd prefer to call you by the name your folks gave to you. That was some fine riding I just watched."

His face colored as he turned his eyes to the ground, then he gathered himself and looked at me square-on.

"Jaxon Stepp is my name, sir."

I offered him my hand and he shook it, his grip firm and dry, his palms calloused as thick as a boot shank.

"Nice work, Jaxon Stepp. Glad to have you on the ranch."

"Thank you, sir," he said. "I'm glad to be here."

My father had been right. This ranch and this life are worth fighting for, worth every drop of sweat and blood that it takes to hold on. And I wouldn't trade it for anything.

CHAPTER TWENTY-FIVE

I CHECKED IN on Jesse and Cricket when I got back to the house and found both of them still sleeping soundly. It was clear we were going to miss church, so I stepped into the kitchen and quietly made a sack lunch for myself. I put a ham-and-cheese sandwich in a brown paper sack together with an apple and a small bag of chips, poured some fresh coffee into a thermos, and scribbled a note to tell Jesse I'd gone to the office.

The morning was young, so the shops along Main were still closed, the sidewalks still serene, but for the bustling business I witnessed through the shop window at Boyle's diner and the shadows passing behind the saloon doors at the Cottonwood Blossom. I pulled into the parking lot behind the substation and saw Leon Quinn pacing back and forth near the back door. He was wearing an oversize down jacket, a knitted toboggan cap, and a pair of ski gloves, and exhaling silvery clouds into the air.

"You okay, Leon?" I asked as I unlocked the door. "How long have you been waiting out here?"

I held open the door and Leon stepped inside. He flipped on the light switch for me while I headed over to adjust the thermostat.

"I don't know," Leon said, peeling off his gloves and rubbing his raw-looking palms together. "I wasn't keeping track. Half an hour, maybe."

Leon Quinn was the stuff of legend in Meriwether County, or had been at one time, and had remained in town long enough to become one of its oldest residents. Short, stout, and wizened, with a bushy beard shot through with gray, he resembled an old tintype of a California gold rush prospector. While the details of his life remained elusive, the rumors of his brushes with good fortune and failure lingered on. It was said he had experienced more than his share of triumphs and calamity, the latter defining his later years to the point that the mere mention of his name had become a cautionary expression.

Leon's exact age was unclear as well—I guessed him to be nearing eighty—but his standing in local society had diminished to that of a town character, a relatively harmless drunk who could most often be found napping at a table in a dark corner of the Cottonwood, a caricature of himself, though the kindness of his true nature still dwelled inside him. I had long harbored a private regret that I had not known the man during his prime, but his recent run of honest work as a barback for Lankard Downing—and Leon's attendant and unexpected sobriety—was a welcome development for everyone involved.

I went to the break room, checked on the lockup room upstairs, and when I came back out into the office area, Leon was dragging a wooden chair across the floor, positioning it in front of the heating vent. He lowered himself into his seat, warmed his palms beside the flue, his features patinaed with something approximating distress.

"What's the problem, Leon?" I asked. "The Cottonwood is open for breakfast by now. You and Lankard have some kind of falling-out?"

He looked up at me and pursed his lips, weighing his words inside his head before he spoke.

"No, Sheriff, nothing like that."

I returned to the kitchen and poured a couple of hot mugs, came back and handed one to him. He cradled his in both hands for a protracted moment and set it on the bench beneath the framed photo of the disgraced city councilman I'd arrested. The vase of flowers I'd placed there the day before now sat at the corner of Jordan Powell's desk.

"I don't want to drink, Ty," Leon said finally. "I'm afraid if I go in that place this morning, I believe I'll fall off the wagon for sure. In fact, I know I will. I can feel it."

"Something in particular troubling you?"

"It's not any one single thing. It just feels weird around here is all. Too damn many strangers, for one thing."

I pulled up my office chair and rolled it close to him, looked him in the face until he met my eyes.

"How long has it been since you went this many days without a drink, Leon?"

He glanced at the toes of his scuffed Sorel boots and, to his credit, lifted his head and regarded me openly again.

"I can't recall the last time I went a whole week without waking up somewhere that took me a few minutes to identify."

"That's a hell of an accomplishment, don't you think?"

"Don't seem like much, Sheriff."

"I think it takes a lot of backbone to try and do something like that, don't you?"

"I s'pose."

"Listen, I'm pretty sure I've got a checkers board in this office somewhere," I said. "Care for a game or two?"

A look of gratitude washed through his eyes as he reached for his coffee.

"You're busy, Sheriff," he said. "You ain't got time for that."

"Oh, hell, Leon," I said and got up to retrieve the game board. "I only come to the office to get out of the house. Truth is, I'd appreciate the distraction. So are you in or are you out?"

LEON AND I were halfway through our third game when Sam Griffin strode in through the door holding a paper bag tucked into the crook of his arm. He was dressed in a pearl-button shirt and blue jeans, a black Justin hat low on his brow, which was noteworthy only because my deputies tended to wear their tan uniform shirts while on duty, a practice I leave to them.

"Hey, Leon," Griffin said, then turned to me. "What are you doing here, Sheriff?"

"I work here."

"It's Sunday."

"I'm aware of that. What are *you* doing here?"

"Powell's got some kind of G-2 operation going," he said with a smile. "Wanted me to join him on recon."

"Anything I need to know about?"

Griffin shrugged.

"It can't be too serious," he said. "Powell asked me to bring along a six-pack."

I was about to continue my line of questioning when the phone rang. I picked it up and announced myself.

"Oh, good. I'm glad it's you, Sheriff. This is Cathie Fields. Charge nurse from the hospital?"

"Everything okay, Ms. Fields?"

The muted sounds of an announcement over the hospital public address system spun down the line behind her as she spoke.

"It may be nothing," she said. "But I thought I should call you anyway."

The hair on the back of my neck stood on end as I waited for her to drop the other shoe.

"When I came in this morning, the security desk informed me that an orderly caught somebody trying to get into Mr. Swann's room late last night."

"What happened? Who was it? Everyone all right?"

"Nothing happened," she said. "Nobody's hurt. They stopped the man before he got to the room. Problem is, he got away. I just thought it was something that you'd want to know."

Odds were it was an overzealous fan, or perhaps even a tabloid photographer. But the way that this whole situation was beginning to unfold, I felt it unwise to take anything for granted.

"I'll send somebody up there, Ms. Fields," I said. "I appreciate your telling me. How's Ian doing?"

The pause before she answered was perceptible.

"He's still the same, Sheriff," was all she said.

I placed the receiver back into the cradle and looked at Sam Griffin.

"Sorry to bust up your picnic," I said. "But I need you to run up to the hospital. I'm told somebody tried to get into Ian Swann's room late last night. See if anybody got a look at the guy."

"Roger that," Griffin said and carried his brown paper bag to the kitchen, where I heard him place it in the icebox.

"One other thing," I said to him before he reached the exit door. "Take a fingerprint kit with you. I want you to roll Ian Swann's prints."

"Don't we need a warrant for something like that?"

"Who are you now? Perry Mason?"

"I'm only asking."

"Do me a favor and roll the prints, okay?"

"Sure thing, Sheriff," he said and made a move to hightail it outside to his vehicle.

"One more thing," I said. "When you're finished, I want you to run the print cards over to Captain Rose at the state police barracks. Make sure they get to him personally. And tell him to start the search in California. Ian Swann's car has Cali tags, so he's probably got a driver's license there."

"Got it," Griffin said and slipped out the door before I could add to his list of things to do.

Leon grinned and I stood up to refresh our coffees. He had grown noticeably calmer than he'd been when he'd arrived, though I could see his leg was bobbing like a jackhammer, his fingers tapping an irregular cadence on the surface of my desk. We finished our third game and Leon was setting up the board for our fourth when Jordan Powell pushed in from the parking lot. He was uncharacteristically hatless and dressed as though he was preparing to go hunting for ducks.

"Hey, Leon," Powell said. "Hey, Cap. What're you doing here?"

"Why does everybody keep asking me that?"

"It's Sunday."

"So I hear."

"Where's Sam? He was supposed to help me out with something."

"I had to send him on a job," I said. "How about if I back you up?"

He considered my offer momentarily and then dismissed it.

"You'd better not," he said. "I'm afraid they might recognize you."

"Who?"

"I've got a little undercover thing going. Nothing fancy, but I might be closing in on this eagle business."

"You sure you don't want someone to watch your six?"

Powell smiled at me and shook his head, looked at Leon, and gave the old man a thumbs-up.

"Naw," Powell said. "I'm not expecting any danger. Just a little intelligence-gathering mission is all."

"A G-2 mission that requires a six-pack?"

"It's all about authenticity, Cap," he said. "You know how it goes."

A HALF HOUR later, I packed up the checkers board.

"You going somewhere, Sheriff?" Leon asked.

I judged that Leon had finally settled himself enough to go back out and face the world. Either that, or at least return to his own home without incident. But there was an urgency in his tone that told me I'd been mistaken. For a moment, I had entertained the idea of asking Leon what he remembered about the Swanson case and whether he had any recollection of them from all those years ago. Now I was glad that I hadn't. It was clear Leon Quinn was still busy battling his demons.

"There are a couple of people I need to talk to today, Leon."

"I understand," he told me, but he made no effort to put on his coat, cap, or gloves. "Can I ask you a favor, Sheriff?"

"What is it, Leon?"

"Do you mind if I stay here? In one of the cells upstairs?"

God knows he'd spent plenty of time in there before, but this particular request was heartbreaking.

"You still worried you're going to drink?" I asked.

He nodded and averted his eyes, blinked and looked outside into the street.

"I don't want to go out there, Sheriff," he said softly. "And I don't want to be alone at home."

"C'mon with me, Leon," I said. "I'll get you set up."

I gathered a couple of clean blankets and pillows from the

supply locker and handed them to Leon, plucked a used copy of Friday's local newspaper and a couple of magazines off the break-room table, and retrieved the portable radio from the counter beside the sink. I led him upstairs, where three small holding cells occupied the length of the room against one wall, each with its own cot, water basin, and latrine. Of privacy, there was none, but that morning, Leon Quinn was the room's sole occupant.

"You know the drill, Leon," I said and started for the stairwell. "Turn off the lights and make sure the office door's locked behind you when you decide to leave."

He placed the pillows and blankets on the cot and left the reading material at the foot of the rack. When he called out to me, the expression he wore was one I could not define.

"Sheriff?"

"What is it, Leon?"

"One more favor? Would you mind shutting the door?"

"To the cell? You want me to lock you in there?"

"I'd be obliged if you would. Maybe leave a note for one of the boys to let me out later on? I'd consider it a kindness, Sheriff."

I studied the man who stood before me, pictured him as a young boy. There had been a day when he had contemplated his own future, made plans to see the world, maybe even fall in love. I cannot imagine what kinds of memories lived in his head these days, or the images he revisited when he fell asleep.

"I'll be right back," I said, but Leon didn't budge from his place in the steel cage.

He was seated on the cot when I returned, his back pressed to the wall, the magazines and radio set up neatly beside him. When I handed him the sack lunch and thermos I'd brought from home, he took it and smiled.

"I'll let the boys know you're in here, okay, Leon? You just tell them when you want to go home."

I shut the cell door and twisted the old-fashioned key inside the lock and left the key ring on the empty desk in the corner of the room.

"Thank you, Sheriff."

I threw him a wave and turned away without speaking another word, for fear my voice or the damp heat forming in my eyes might betray me.

CHAPTER TWENTY-SIX

I HEARD THE RADIO upstairs echoing down the stairwell from Leon's cell as I came back down. The Oakland A's were leading the Angels in the third. I sat down at my desk and dialed the main number for Half Mountain Studio, asked the girl who answered to put Len Kaanan on the line.

"How's our boy?" Kaanan asked me when he came on.

"Not good," I told him. I elected not to share with him that someone had tried to sneak into Ian's room. Or perhaps Kaanan already knew and wasn't telling me, either.

"Mickey London's gnawing on the carpet over here," Kaanan said. "He's pissed you had him banned from the hospital."

"When he stops acting like a rude, entitled asshole maybe I'll change my mind. In the meantime, tell him to hold his goddamn water just like everybody else. Or better yet, put him on the line and let me tell him myself."

"What can I do for you, Sheriff?"

"I understand you receive viewable copies of the daily film footage you've been shooting. I want to see the film you shot on Friday."

It took so long for Kaanan to respond, I thought I'd lost the call.

"The film stock didn't get to the processor in Portland until Saturday," he said finally. "Takes them a couple days to turn it around. Today is Sunday, Sheriff. Even people in showbiz take a Sunday off now and then."

"I'm well aware what day it is."

"I should have the film back here tomorrow by noon. You can come out and have a look at it then. Call first."

When I next spoke, I found that I was talking to a dial tone.

I NEEDED some fresh air, so I took my time and walked two long blocks to the bakery, the sun in my face and the sough of the river wafting up from the rift. The doughnut selection had been fairly well picked over by this hour of the morning, but I was able to assemble a dozen decent ones and had the owner pack them inside a pink cardboard box tied with a crosshatch of twine. I placed them on the passenger seat of my pickup and made the short drive out of town toward Doc and Ruth Brawley's house.

I turned left on Clark Street and headed southwest, following the gently curving tracery of the river. Iridescent rainbows of spray from the wheel lines in the beanfields banded the sunlight, the freshly ploughed furrows dotted with early season Canada geese. A short distance beyond, I entered a quiet neighborhood whose tree-lined streets had been named for spring flowers. I drove slowly through the cluster of houses with wide porches and green lawns, many decorated with American flags fixed to porch columns or jigsaw-cut bargeboards, their windowsills lined with disused lard cans planted with tulips and daffodils. I spotted the Brawley house at the end of the block and pulled to a stop at the curb out front.

I picked up the bakery box by the string and carried it to the base of the driveway, where Ruth Brawley was preparing to dig a hole for a rosebush in a front garden already blooming with azalea and blue hyacinth. She turned when she heard my footfalls on the concrete, smiled, and brushed her cheek with a gloved hand, leaving a faint trail of wet dirt on her face.

"Well, hello, Tyler," she said. "This is a pleasant surprise."

"I brought some fresh doughnuts from the bakery for you, Miss Ruth."

She leaned the shovel against the stoop rail and came over to give me a hug. At nearly eighty years of age, she felt even smaller and more birdlike than the last time I had seen her, the blue of her eyes even more pale.

The Brawleys had been fixtures in the county for as long as I could remember, operating a medical practice out of a second-story walk-up brick building across from the park, their doors open six days a week for forty-eight years without a misstep or complaint. Ruth was not only the doctor's wife and life partner but had performed as his nurse, accountant, and receptionist all the while. It had been less than a year since the senseless and brutal murder of Ruth's husband, Abel "Doc" Brawley, and by all rights, she could have easily retreated to some distant emotional abyss reserved for the survivors of violence, but instead she was weathering her grief with a dignity and strength I could only admire and respect.

"Come inside, Tyler. Let me fix you some tea. Or some fresh lemonade, if you'd prefer."

"Tea would be fine," I said. "But only if you let me take over for you with that rosebush, ma'am."

She pulled at the fingers of her gardening gloves, plucked them off, and laid them across the rim of a tin bucket she'd left at the foot of the perron. Soft sunlight shone between the branches of a flowering fruit tree she'd strung with a collection of empty glass bottles, and I listened to the music they made in the slow breath of breeze. She stepped over to me and I placed the pink bakery box in her tiny hands, her complexion latticed with fine wrinkles that resembled the obverse of an autumn leaf.

Ruth Brawley went indoors and I finished digging the hole for her rosebush; then I untied the canvas from the root ball and tucked in the new planting with loam and topsoil. I used the backfill to form a shallow basin and filled it with water from the hose at the side of her house, washed the dirt from my hands, and made my way up the porch stairs.

I rapped on the doorframe and announced myself as I pushed open the screen door and entered Ruth Brawley's house. She was standing at her kitchen counter wearing a sweater embroidered with white daisies, steeping tea for the teapot and arranging the doughnuts on a porcelain serving platter decorated with designs of pinecones and holly boughs.

"I miss having a man around," she said. "I am reminded of that every time I have to operate a shovel or rake."

"I'm sure you miss Dr. Brawley very much, ma'am. I believe we all do."

I carried the tea set from the kitchen to the low table in front of the couch, took a seat in the chair she offered me, and looked around the room as she filled our Devon cups. It was almost exactly as it had been the last time I'd been there, an elegiac diorama forever sequestered in amber, everything as it always had been when two people shared this household. Outdoors, it was springtime in the year of our nation's bicentennial, but inside this home, it would forever remain the summer of 1975.

"So, what brings you by, Tyler?" Ruth asked. "I'm sure it wasn't to deliver baked goods and help me gussy up my garden."

"I hate to do this, Miz Brawley, but I wanted to ask you about something that happened a long time ago. Something you might be able to help me with."

She sipped from her teacup and placed it gently on its saucer, knitted her fingers together, and rested her hands in her lap.

"If old people can't draw from our deep well of memories and share them, what use are we, anyway?"

"That's not exactly what I meant," I said. "I intended no disrespect."

She laughed aloud, and it sounded like birdsong in crystal.

"I'm only teasing you, Tyler. You don't have to handle me. I may be small-boned, but deep down I'm actually a pretty tough old broad. I was a medical nurse for more than five decades. There's not much I haven't seen or heard in my time."

Her remark caught me off guard, and I could see it tickled her to have done so.

"I wanted to know what you remember about the Swansons," I said. "The family who ran the hog farm back in the early sixties."

"Oh my. That is going back. A lot has changed around here since then."

And a lot of things have remained the same, I thought but did not say. While she accessed her memory, I chose an old-fashioned frosted doughnut from the serving tray, broke it in half, and took a bite as I waited in silence. What she ended up relating to me turned out to be a tragic cesspool of a story.

"Jacob Swanson was a simple man," Ruth Brawley began. "He worked odd jobs, did some handyman work, raised his hogs and sheep. A few chickens, too. I used to buy fresh eggs from him once in a while. I remember he did a good deal of the butchering himself, had the meat rendered and packaged by the Fireclouds. You knew Lily Firecloud when you were in school, didn't you?"

"Yes, ma'am, I did. Can you tell me anything more about the Swansons? And whatever you might recall about the Lomax family?"

"Jacob Swanson worked for Gavin Lomax for a while—Mr. Lomax had a contracting business—but something went wrong between those two, I don't know what it was."

I noticed a sour expression crossed her face as she uttered Gavin Lomax's name. I was about to ask why, but it turned out I didn't need to.

"Pardon my saying so," she said, "but Mr. Lomax could be a very difficult man, had a rather nasty disposition. So I suppose I shouldn't be surprised those two men had a falling-out. It always troubled me, even though it was none of my business. The two of them had a lot more in common than they might have believed. Both were widowers, both raising teenagers all by themselves. Anyway, once Jake Swanson got fired by Mr. Lomax, the Swansons fell on hard times. Jacob started writing bad checks around town and began drinking rather heavily, I think. A pity, really. Jacob's older son was a good boy. Tragic, though, about the younger one."

"Do you recall their names?"

"Let me see . . . Started with a 'P' I think. Peter? No. I'll think of it. The younger one was called Shane. I remember because of the movie. Doctor took me to see it at the movie house up in Lewiston."

I found it curious that she had always referred to her late husband in that manner, but it was Ruth's way. She lifted her cup and saucer and tilted the cup to her lips, the glass shades of the torchiere on the side table marbling her face in hues of bronze and apricot.

"Paul. That was the elder Swanson boy's name. Paul Swanson," she said as she replaced her teacup on the table and shook her head sadly. "He was dating the Lomax girl. She was an only child. She's the one who . . . passed away. Pretty little thing. So young. They made such a cute couple."

"I saw an old newspaper photo of Sheriff Skadden at the . . . scene," I said. "There was another man in the picture, too. Was that your husband, Miss Ruth?"

"You were going to say 'crime scene,' weren't you?"

"Yes, ma'am, I was."

"What stopped you?"

"I'm not completely certain it *was* a crime. There's a saying that it's not about what you believe to be true; it's about what you can prove to a jury in a court of law."

Ruth Brawley's expression grew wistful.

"Doctor used to repeat that very same adage," she said. "Yes, that was Doctor in that photograph you saw. He disliked being put in the newspaper that way. He loved his profession, but he hated doing the things he did that day."

The castoff comment caught my attention, and I couldn't allow it to pass me by.

"What things did he do that day?" I asked.

"He didn't think very highly of Lloyd Skadden to begin with. But the sheriff's attitude about that poor girl, and the fact they found her hanging in the tree like that . . . Well, Doctor couldn't bear the thought that prosecuting somebody for her death was going to be a practical and legal impossibility. Nearly broke his spirit."

"Your husband didn't believe she killed herself?"

"That was the problem. He couldn't say with any certainty, but something about it always bothered him. It was obvious she died from suffocation, but whether it was suicide or not, well, that was something else entirely."

She tugged a wad of tissue from the sleeve of her sweater, dabbed it at the corner of her eyes. Her attention wandered the room as she composed herself, its focal point eventually finding purchase on a worn leather portmanteau, an alabastrine vase balanced on top and bursting with flowers from her garden.

"Do you recall her name, Miss Ruth?" I asked softly. "The Lomax girl?"

"You're really putting my memory to the test today, Tyler," she said and tried to smile.

"It would be a great help to me."

Ruth tilted her head and lapsed again into a glazed state of abstraction, placing her hand over her lips; then something lit inside her eyes. She breathed a muted gasp and turned to me again.

"They came to see Doctor, not long before she died. Heather was her name. Heather Lomax. Such a darling girl So frightened. So upset."

"They?"

"Heather and the Swanson boy."

INTERLUDE VI

(1964)

IT WAS NEARLY five o'clock when Paul pulled into the parking lot at Duke's, a drive-in burger place at the southern edge of town, favored by lumberjacks, off-duty state troopers, long-haul truckers, bikers, teenagers, and the occasional tourist. The air was heavy with the smell of grilled onions and burger grease that billowed from the roof vent, the atmosphere already aglow in pink and blue neon from the tubes that scrolled along the edge of a wide eave overhanging a mismatched collection of scarred picnic tables, protecting them from the elements.

Paul didn't bother locking the door to his beat-up Chevy, but immediately crossed the parking lot and paid for two bottles of orange soda at the counter. Heather was seated by herself at a small table near the pickup window, reading a paperback novel, a sweater draped across her shoulders over the cheerleader's uniform she'd worn to school.

As Paul sat down with Heather, he slid a paper straw into one of the soda bottles, sat it on a napkin for her, and leaned back and took a pull from the neck of his. She glanced up from her book, showed him the twitch of a smile, her expression indecipherable.

"Just a second," she said, and he watched her as she read, waiting while she found a good place to stop.

At the far end of the parking lot, kids from Meridian High had begun to gather in factions, assembling near the open doors of shoebox lead sleds, hot rods, and project cars, and the dropped tailgates of pickups whose radios spilled Hank Williams tunes into the dwindling light. Paul recognized a few of the teens, faces gone shiny with hormones and perspiration, speaking and laughing too loud, seeking attention inside the illusion of immortality that animated their worldview.

"Why are you looking at me like that?" Heather asked, sliding a bookmark in between the yellow pages and slipping the book into her purse.

"I wish I could freeze time."

"Not me," she said, but immediately regretted her tone when she saw Paul's expression. "I just mean I can't wait to get out of here. Sometimes I feel like I'll never be able to leave this place."

"What's not to like about Meridian?"

"It's not the same for you," Heather said. She looked away from him for a moment, eyes focused on something in the middle distance, and sighed. "I shouldn't have said anything. Forget it."

The twilight had an unfamiliar lime-colored tint, and Paul felt a change coming in the weather. A cold gust of wind plucked loose pieces of rubbish from the bin, sent them tumbling between the tables, and a flicker of dry lightning pulsed in the clouds.

"I brought you something," Paul said.

He showed her a bag with the name of a record shop printed on it, placed it on the table between them. Heather reached inside and withdrew a 45 rpm single, examining the label in the wash of the pink and blue neon overhead.

"Simon and Garfunkel," she said.

"'The Sounds of Silence,' it's called," Paul said. "It's new. I heard it on the radio and I thought of you."

She slipped the record from the paper sleeve, examined it as if there was something hidden between the grooves, then carefully replaced it in the bag. When she lifted her eyes, there was an emptiness he had never seen in them before.

Paul slid to sit closer to her, and she scooted sideways to make room on the bench. Her sweater fell away from her shoulders and onto the ground as she moved, and Paul bent to retrieve it.

When he went to drape it across her shoulders again, he noticed a pattern of bruises on the soft skin of her arm, like fingerprints, and another the color and size of a ripening fig on the inside of her thigh. She followed the course of his focus, the expression that fleetingly passed over his face. She adjusted the fall of her sweater, pulled at the hem of her skirt, but it was too late, and not nearly enough to conceal what Paul had seen.

"Are you okay, Heather?"

"I'm fine."

"Come on. I'm not an idiot."

"I don't want to talk about it," she said without looking at him.

Paul didn't know what he'd done to upset her and found himself desperate to reclaim what he had somehow spoiled.

"Maybe we could run away together," Paul said, his tone half joking, in case he had blundered again. "We could go somewhere neither of us has ever been before."

Heather remained silent, her eyes fixed on the tallest of the serrated peaks at the fringe of the valley, purple in the waning twilight. Horsetails of rain drifted from gray clouds slowly cloaking the mountaintops, but she sustained that one distant summit in her sightline before it was lost inside the weather.

Paul watched her wordlessly, until it appeared as if she had stopped breathing.

"Heather?"

She came back into herself at the sound of her name, drew a deep breath, and took a drink from her orange soda.

"I don't think I feel like talking anymore," Heather said. "Can we do something else? Maybe go for a walk by the creek?"

"I didn't mean to upset you."

She stood and the wind caught a lock of her hair. He watched her gathering the silhouette of the mountains again as though she was memorizing the view.

Heather was different the next day at school, never quite seemed the same after that night, or for that matter, ever again.

"YOU'D BETTER SHUT that goddamn dog up before I put a bullet in his head!"

Paul had spent the past three sleepless nights lying in bed, staring at the ceiling and wondering what he had done to make things go wrong with Heather, so lost in his own miserable contemplations that he hadn't even noticed that Rufus was barking like crazy outside. Now, Paul's dad was pounding the wall with his fist and cursing the dog, and Paul knew that he ought to go out and get control of Rufus before his father took over.

Paul threw the blankets aside, put his Pendleton jacket over his pajamas, and slid on his slippers. Where was Shane? Why wasn't he out there seeing after the dog? It was frustrating sometimes, and he felt vaguely guilty for feeling that way, but Paul already had enough on his mind.

"I'm counting to ten, and that dog had better shut the hell up by the time I finish counting," his dad hollered from the next room. "Don't test me, I'm not kidding you."

Paul rushed down the narrow hall, grumbling to himself, making his way toward the front door, where it sounded like Rufus was making his protective stand. Shane was only three years younger than Paul, but the accident that had taken their mother all those years ago had left Shane with the mental and emotional capacities of a six-year-old.

Paul's brother could be mercurial and prone to grand fits of petulance, but he loved his dog, Rufus—all animals, really—and loved his family with everything he had. The trouble was that as Shane's body continued to grow, so did the natural urges that accompanied the changes, and his retrograde curiosity and childlike inability to filter his utterances and emotions had become a source of frequent embarrassment to Paul, feelings for which Paul wished he had more patience.

Shane's bedroom door opened a crack as Paul passed down the hall, and Paul felt newly remorseful for thinking unkindly about his younger brother. It was clear that Shane was frightened by the commotion and had been waiting for Paul to take the lead.

Rufus was barking the same way he would bark at a stranger or a stray animal that had wandered too close from the woods. Paul had rarely heard the dog this fiercely protective before, and his stomach clenched tight as he switched on the porch light in hopes of scaring off the intruder. But the light only served to make Rufus much more unruly, and Paul's dad had just reached number seven in his countdown to death. Almost out of time, Paul grabbed the baseball bat from the umbrella stand, made eye contact with Shane, and tugged the door open, ready to swing if necessary.

Rufus stopped barking at the sight of the two boys, made a mewling sound, and nestled himself between them. Paul glanced at his brother, and the expression on his face was neither shock nor revulsion; rather, it was an expression of blind terror.

In the silence, Paul could hear his father's footfalls stalking down the hall toward them, red-eyed and angry, but Shane couldn't pull his gaze away from what he now saw.

It was one of Shane's prized shoats, one he'd raised up from a piglet for 4-H. The animal had been splayed open from throat to anus, left to bleed out on the blistered landing, its entrails steaming in the cold, its tiny heart pumping its last as the two boys stood speechless.

The dog backed away as Paul's dad reached the doorway, smelling of stale cigarettes, squinting at the bright light and the bloody mess that had been left for them to find. It was clear that a human being had done it; this was no accident or animal attack—this was intentional, savage, and unnecessarily cruel. Paul could hear his brother begin to sob, and he pulled Shane close, where the younger boy buried his face in his elder brother's chest.

Shane was mumbling something to himself, but Paul couldn't make out the words that were lost in his brother's grief and repulsion.

"Get that mess cleaned up before the coyotes come after it," Paul's father said, then he turned and shambled back down the hallway to his bed. "And make sure that damn dog stays inside the house."

A HALF HOUR LATER, Paul had finished cleaning up. He had disposed of the carcass and entrails, hosed off the blood from the stairs and porch rails, and gone to the kitchen to wash up. He found Shane sitting cross-legged on the floor underneath the kitchen table, the room lit by a single naked bulb over the sink. Rufus rested his head in Shane's lap as the boy stroked the dog's ears, rocking back and forth, repeating the same phrase over and over as tears continued to stream down his face.

"Gut you like a pig . . . Gut you like a pig . . . Gut you like a pig . . ."

CHAPTER TWENTY-SEVEN

JESSE AND CRICKET resumed their vigil at the hospital Monday morning at first light, and I drove northward through the clear blue morning, past the blossoming pear and cherry trees that marked the gateway to Meridian's main street, where the tourist crowds had thinned down to a trickle. The grama in the fields along the highway were growing faster now that spring was taking hold in earnest, some already standing so tall as to obscure all but the eyes and ears of the white-tailed does that roved the rim of the ravine.

I followed an empty stinger truck that had a bumper sticker reading AMERICA, LOVE IT OR LEAVE IT for several miles, until I lost him in a cloud of greige exhaust as he downshifted and turned onto a logging road where a roadside barbecue and fruit stand was preparing to open for the season.

A few minutes later, I pulled up to the intercom box at the entrance to Len Kaanan's place, pressed the button, and announced myself. I could hear a commotion in the background as Kaanan himself wrested the phone away from whoever had answered it.

"I asked you to call first," he barked.

"How would you define the activity that's taking place right now?" I asked. "How 'bout you open up this gate and let me in so I can do my work."

Ten minutes later, Kaanan and I were seated in the screening room upstairs at Half Mountain Studio, where three rows of finely upholstered leather club chairs had been arranged before a commercial-grade theater screen, replete with heavy velvet curtains the color of claret wine. The room appeared to have been newly cleaned, fresh vacuum marks still in evidence on the deep pile Karastan, but the odor of stale cigarettes, pine solvent, and something else I couldn't identify lingered in the air. The walls were papered in some kind of exotic animal print, lined with both framed photos of Len Kaanan posing with the artists he'd produced and gold records with plaques engraved with sales statistics.

Mickey London was hollering at someone over the telephone as he paced a flattened footpath in the carpet that abutted the projection room in back, chewing on an unlit Montecristo. I looked to Len Kaanan, who had seated himself in the row ahead of me and one chair to the right; I noticed a surrealistic painting by Joan Miró on the wall that looked entirely out of place.

"Everyone seems a little tense this morning," I said to Kaanan.

"My artist is lying in a coma and I have a film project that is likely to remain unfinished. The record label and the movie studio have millions invested here, and both are climbing the walls, and frankly, so are we."

"Care to come clean with me?"

"Excuse me, Sheriff?" Kaanan said. "Can you please repeat yourself?"

His complexion flushed, and the expression on his face was one of rage and puzzlement.

"You said something to me before," I said. "You asked me whether I was familiar with Ian Swann's story. The implication was that it had something to do with Meriwether County. I've been trying to figure out what you meant by that, but recollections in this town seem to be a little spotty. So I'm asking you straight out: What's Ian Swann's story?"

Len Kaanan stood and faced me, slipped his hands into the pockets of his pleated slacks, his lips drawn tight as he scanned the rows of photos on the wall.

"I don't know," he said finally. "He never told me."

"You said it took courage for Ian to come here."

"It was the whole point of the movie, Sheriff. You've probably noticed we've been shooting B-roll all over town. Once the concert was finished, Ian wanted to do a sit-down; he had some kind of dramatic reveal in mind."

"But he never told you what it was? I find that difficult to swallow."

Len Kaanan moved deliberately along the periphery of the room, stopping from time to time to study one of the gold records on the wall. He halted in front of Ian Swann's first album, pursed his lips, and sighed before he spoke to me.

"Ian Swann is an artist, Sheriff. Creative people have a unique mindset and temperament, and I've learned not to push them when they don't want to be pushed."

"It didn't strike you as odd that his car gets vandalized when he comes to town, and he gets himself assaulted two days later? Now *this*?"

"Some projects are cursed. It's an accepted fact in the film business. Look at *Rosemary's Baby*, or *The Exorcist*, or even *The Wizard of Oz*."

"And you figured that's all this was? Just a run of unfortunate luck?"

"What was I supposed to think? This was Ian's story, and he was going to tell it the way he wanted to. Period. And it didn't involve cluing me in beforehand."

"And what about his manager?"

"He knows even less than I do."

"Are you prepared to help me out, Mr. Kaanan?"

"Seems like we have a one-sided relationship."

Mickey London was still pacing at the back of the room, the phone pressed to his ear, his face so red it looked like he might burst a blood vessel. These people were exhausting to be around.

"If you don't like the nature of our association so far," I said, "you really won't like the direction it takes if you're not more forthcoming from this point onward."

Kaanan studied me, obviously unaccustomed to being challenged.

"What can I do to help you, Sheriff?" he asked.

"I'd like to begin with the footage Cricket and her crew shot from the wings of the stage and go from there," I said.

He stood and strode to the projection room, opened the door, and transmitted my request to the projectionist, then gestured to Mickey London to finish his call. By the time Kaanan returned to his seat, the lights had dimmed and my daughter's raw footage from that terrible night began to flicker on the screen.

ONE FILM CAN at a time, we watched the backstage preparations for the Friday evening concert as they unfolded: the staging of the set decor, sound reinforcement tests, the musicians and their roadies tuning and prepping instruments, mugging for the cameras, and the installation of myriad cords and cables that would drive the light and sound across the stage and open amphitheater.

Midway through the fourth reel, the fog I recalled from that day began to fill the seating basin beyond the rostrum, then rolled slowly across the stage itself. I remembered well the premonition I'd felt when I had seen it for myself, the cold, damp embrace and claustrophobic envelopment of the mist.

At first, the crew working on-screen appeared oblivious or simply unmindful of it, focused on their tasks as time before the show rapidly wound down. However, as the stage was swiftly overtaken, the work there turned to pandemonium. I focused my attention on the catwalk that hovered over center stage, paying particular attention to the lighting rig that was soon destined to spectacularly fail. I watched the man who was working on that section, noticed him eyeing the incoming vapor, hands working furiously as he tested electrical connections before drawing a long, steel-handled tool out of the tool belt he wore around his waist. He was bareheaded and wore a green plaid shirt with a black bandanna tied around his neck, slipping in and out of the frame. Something about his body language seemed familiar as he worked the wrench on several bolts along the tension grid, his head seemingly on a swivel, taking inventory of the other workers' positions on the skywalk as he worked the anchor pins.

All at once, the man in the green shirt on the high scaffolding disappeared in the miasma, and the entire screen went smoky gray as the site was consumed within a cloud. It was impossible to tell how much time passed before Cricket and her crew were able to resume shooting, but my recollection was that it had been nearly fifteen minutes until the haze had cleared enough to see again. When the film resumed, the angle was the same as it had been before the fog had interrupted filming, but I could see that the man in the rigging was no longer there.

"Who was that man in the rigging above center stage?" I asked. "The one in the green shirt?"

Len Kaanan shot a glance to Mickey London, who was

standing in the rear of the room, leaning his back on the wall. London shrugged and chewed his cigar stub with disinterest and returned his attention to picking a hangnail off his thumb.

"I guess we don't know," Kaanan said.

I recognized the man on film was not one of those killed later that night, but I could not get a decent angle on his face. I twisted in my chair to make eye contact with London, who returned my gaze with bored contempt.

"Does the name 'Sasquatch' or 'Bigfoot' mean anything to you?"

London took his time before he shook his head.

"Nope."

"Can we move ahead chronologically and pull the reels from the time leading up to the accident?" I asked Kaanan. It was clear that Mickey London had zero interest in assisting my investigation in any way whatsoever. Kaanan went back to speak with the projectionist again, and I waited as the film was threaded and the lights went down again.

This time, the image unspooled on a scene from several hours later in the day; the day had faded into early evening, the first few rows of guests and invitees visible in the illumination that bled from the footlights and spots, revealing an audience composed of faces that bore little resemblance to rock concert fans of an earlier era.

The house lights on the screen faded to black, and Ian Swann and band converged on the stage. The crowd erupted just as I remembered from that night, but I fixed my attention as I sat there that morning on the activities of the backstage crew rather than the performers. Another thirty minutes elapsed and I felt myself move closer to the edge of my leather club chair, knowing from hindsight what was about to happen on the screen.

My attention was rewarded a few minutes later, and I recognized the man in the green shirt and black bandanna in the scaffolding again.

"Freeze it here, please," I said.

The projectionist did so, and I stood and approached the screen, studied the visage of a man in the sidewash of the spotlights, a face as plain and lifeless as a grocery bag but for the deep-set eyes and sculpted sideburns I had seen before. His attention was focused far below him on center stage, his hands gripping a tether or rope of some kind.

"I need a still photo of this shot," I said to Len Kaanan.

"We can't let you do that," Mickey London said before Kaanan could reply. "Footage belongs to the production company."

"The hell you can't," I said.

"Show me a warrant."

"I'll be right back," I said, stepped out of the room and jogged to where I'd parked my truck. When I returned, I was carrying the Polaroid camera I kept in my glove box. Without another word, I stepped toward the screen, framed the man in the green shirt inside the viewfinder, and snapped two photos in rapid succession.

I heard Mickey London coming up behind me and I whirled on him.

"Take one more step and I will drop you," I said.

"Give me those pictures," he spat and reached for the Polaroids I held between my fingers.

"Step back, or I'll cuff you for obstruction," I said to London. Over my shoulder, I addressed Len Kaanan without breaking eye contact with the manager. "I've got what I need for now," I said. "I appreciate your help, Mr. Kaanan. I'll see myself out."

London's pupils were spun down to pinholes, his expression darkened by a mixture of loathing and condescension. He showed me an odious grin and moved to the telephone table in the rear corner of the room. He picked up a paper box and turned, tossing it at me without warning. I caught it with my free hand, set the camera down, and opened it. Inside was a plastic sandwich bag that appeared to be filled with something resembling wood cinders.

"That's Ian's brother you're holding in your hand," London said. "You can take that to the hospital and give it to my client when you see him."

"What the hell's the matter with you?" I asked. "You didn't have the decency to wait and ask anyone what Ian would have wanted?"

"Who should I have asked? Your daughter? Ian's groupie of the month?"

The last word had barely crossed his lips before I dropped him to his knees with a vicious rear hook to the bridge of his nose. Viscous blood streamed over his upper lip and stained his teeth an ugly shade of pink, his eyes quivering inside their sockets as he recovered his focus. He attempted to rise to his feet but I knocked him backward with the sole of my boot, then knelt and crammed the butt of his soggy unlit cigar into his mouth.

"Stay on the floor, you mouth-breathing shitstick," I said. "If you don't, what happens next is really going to hurt."

London spat the shredded cigar on the carpet, ran the back of his wrist across his face, and smeared a trail of blood and saliva along his cheek. I smiled as he winced when he discovered his nose was broken.

"If you say something like that again, London," I said, "I will peel off your skin and nail it to my office wall. If you don't believe me, give it a try. Do it now. I'm standing here in front of you."

Len Kaanan stepped up beside me, and to his credit said nothing about what had just happened.

"My apologies for any damage to your carpet, Mr. Kaanan," I said. "Send me the bill if it requires special cleaning. As for this inbreeder, I'll let the doctor in Meridian know Mr. London will be coming in. The physician's name is Dr. Carlton. The doc's young, but he's done this kind of repair work for me before. He'll know what to do."

I DROVE to the Cayuse Motel in hopes I'd catch Dewayne Gomer and show him the Polaroid of the man I suspected of sabotaging the lighting rig that cost three men their lives and put a fourth one in a coma. The midday sun shone through the pines at a low angle, spears of gold threading the forest and illuminating a small herd of deer as they climbed a steep switchback in single file.

I parked in the dirt lot of the building labeled BAR, pushed through the heavy steel door and into the darkened interior. Dewayne Gomer was seated at the rail much like before, but this time, he wasn't alone, conversing with a painfully thin, sinewy woman sitting beside him, a tanned dishwater blonde who looked like low-rent trouble, and whose sudden rupture of laughter resembled the bray of a frightened jackass. Dewayne Gomer shook a cigarette out of a pack on the bar top, lipped it while he tore a match out of a cardboard matchbook.

When he rose out of his stool, I noticed that he'd tucked his blue jeans into the tops of his work boots, weaving unsteadily between the tables to come meet me, like a man standing up in a canoe. He exhaled a heady exhaust of beer breath and tobacco and flopped into a chair at the vacant two-top I was standing beside. I sat down, threw a glance toward the bar as I did so, where the leather-skinned blonde was busy helping herself to Dewayne's cigarettes. I recognized a pair of inexpensive pasteboard boxes stacked next to his half-empty beer bottle and figured I'd discovered the source of the suffering he harbored in his watery eyes.

"What are you doing, Dewayne?" I asked.

He followed the direction of my focus, noticed I'd seen the two boxes containing the ashen remains of his friends stacked on the bar—the boxes that looked identical to the one Mickey London had tossed at me.

"Having a drink with my traveling buddies," Dewayne said when he turned back to me.

"Getting yourself pickled isn't going to make it any better."

"Likely won't make it no worse, either."

He pursed his lips and looked away, the unshaven planes of his face washed in the purple neon of an illuminated beer sign. He took a deep drag off his smoke and crushed it in a plastic ashtray already filled to overflowing with discarded butts.

"I'm glad you're here, Sheriff," he said. "I wanted to thank you. For the room and the hot shower. And the drinks, too. That was a kindness."

"I'm sorry for what happened here, Dewayne. I truly am."

"We got off to a rocky start, you and me, but I don't blame you none," he said. "I'm catching out tomorrow, though. Nothing to stick around for. Gonna take my boys with me and sprinkle them along the track out there between Pendleton and Missoula. We had some good times together out thataway."

"I've got a favor to ask you before you go, Dewayne."

"Name it."

I dipped into my shirt pocket and withdrew one of the prints I had snapped from the screening room. I handed it to Dewayne and he angled it into the meager light, squinted, and made a sucking sound with his teeth.

"That's him," he said. "The man I was telling you about. That there is Bigfoot. Or Esau. Or whatever it is he's calling himself today."

"You're sure?"

"No two ways about it. See that black bandanna he's wearing around his neck?"

"What about it?"

"It's shows he's a 'high rider' with the FTRA. I told you about them guys."

Freight Train Riders of America. I remembered.

"High riders run the rails between the Midwest and Northern Cal," he said, then stood up and waddled to the bar to retrieve his beer. I waited until he sat down with me again, took a long pull from the bottle, and belched under his breath. "Mid riders operate across the Midwest and wear blue kerchiefs; low riders run between Texas and California and they wear red. Every one of 'em's bad news, Sheriff, make no mistake. I don't care what color neckerchiefs they wear."

"You told me before you weren't sure Bigfoot was FTRA."

"I *wasn't* sure. Not until now. I never seen him wear that thing before."

"What does it mean that he's wearing it now?"

"Nothing good."

"You suppose he had anything to do with tuning up Ian Swann?"

He shrugged and let the photo drop to the cracked veneer tabletop, slid it across to me. I tucked it back in my shirt pocket and stood up; Dewayne Gomer stood up with me. He swayed and placed one hand on the backrest of his chair for balance, offered his free hand to me. I shook it and thanked him, peeled off a fin from my billfold and reached out to pass it to him.

"I probably shouldn't be giving this to you," I said. "But I understand that you need to button things up with your old pals. Promise me you'll stay out of trouble today, Dewayne, and that you'll sleep it off before you try to hop on a moving boxcar."

He reached for the bill that was tucked between my fingers, but I pulled it away, beyond his reach.

"Tell me we got a deal first, Dewayne. I mean it."

"We got a deal," he answered and I handed the cash to him.

The last sound I heard as I stepped out the door was a blast of donkey-bray laughter, and I knew that the wake had officially begun.

I WAS heading into the first curve of the pass, halfway back to the substation, when the radio mounted on the underside of the dashboard crackled to life. I recognized Jordan Powell's voice through the static, adjusted the squelch, and turned up the volume.

"Meridian Base to Unit One," Powell repeated. "Meridian Base to Unit One, respond."

I lifted the mic from the hook and thumbed the transmit button, something in Powell's tone of voice sending cold chills up the back of my neck.

"Meridian Base, go for Unit One," I said. "Make it quick, I'm about to lose you in the pass."

"Ten-twenty-five to County Hospital, Sheriff. Code Two," he said.

Powell didn't ordinarily use police codes on the radio, which troubled me nearly as much as the content of his message.

"Repeat, Meridian Base," I said.

"Roger that. There's a ten-twenty-five at the hospital, Sheriff. Code Two," he said. "You better haul ass, sir."

CHAPTER TWENTY-EIGHT

BY THE TIME I arrived at the hospital, Ian Swann's bed had been wheeled out of the room. The only thing that remained was the vast array of medical devices, electronic monitors strung with tangles of detached ports and cables, and IV poles with empty bottles dangling from their hooks, a forest of mechanical equipment that had proved themselves unequal to the task.

Jesse and Cricket stood in silhouette before the window, holding hands and looking out toward the oxbow of the river. I stepped into the room and waited quietly, unwilling to disturb the silent communion of mother and daughter. I heard the low squeak of crepe soles approaching from down the corridor and I stepped out to find the charge nurse waiting for me a short distance from Ian's door.

"I tried to reach you at the station," she whispered to me.

"I appreciate that you did, ma'am."

"They removed Mr. Swann to the ER a few minutes ago. He had gone Code Blue—heart failure. The staff tried to restart his heart, but Mr. Swann didn't respond, so they rushed him downstairs to Emergency. I'm very sorry, Sheriff Dawson."

"Is he—?"

"No," she interrupted. "They're doing everything they can for him right now. But, honestly, the young man is at risk of catastrophic organ failure. To be candid with you, I am amazed he held on for as long as he did, considering the extent of his injuries. If they can't stabilize Mr. Swann's heart, his other organs will begin to fail, one after another."

Her expression seemed genuinely woeful, and I wondered at the quality of character it required to face potential catastrophe and loss, and the grief of her patients' loved ones, every day she showed up for work. In that moment, I hadn't time to recognize the irony contained in that contemplation. It was conceivable she wondered the same thing about my occupation.

"How much of what you just told me do my wife and daughter know?" I asked.

"Probably very little. They were both in the room when the patient's monitor alarms sounded, but they were rushed out before the doctors put hands on him. Regardless, I have no doubt it was upsetting for them. Would you like me to speak with them, Sheriff?"

"No, ma'am. I'll take care of it."

She touched me on the arm and started to say something, but stopped herself. Nurse Fields averted her eyes, shook her head at whatever she had been thinking, and walked slowly away.

Cricket heard me come in when I returned to Ian's room, ran to me, and buried her face against me as she held me tight. When she pulled away, I could see her eyes were dry, but her complexion was drawn and sallow, her expression emotionally depleted to a point near vacancy.

"His heart quit beating, Daddy," she said. "It happened all of a sudden."

I hadn't heard Cricket refer to me that way in years, her tone laced with a fragility she had so infrequently evinced, even as a little girl, and every parental cell in my possession wished I could reach out and erase her pain.

"Is he going to be okay?" Cricket whispered to me, less a question than an entreaty.

"I don't know, sweetheart," I lied. This was not the moment for hard truths; they would come in their own time, and we would deal with them when that time arrived.

I looked across the room to Jesse, who appeared as drained and anxious as my daughter did. She crossed the room and threw her arms around Cricket and me, and the three of us held one another in the hush of the vacated room for long moments, until I felt my daughter's unshed well of tears finally break loose and let go.

IAN SWANN was pronounced dead by the lead surgeon an hour later, a sterile, callous announcement mismatched to the void that remained in the wake of the declaration. Jesse drove Cricket back to the ranch, but I had a couple of stops to make before I could go home.

I LOCATED Nurse Fields in her tiny office on the first floor, hunched over her desk in the dull light of a banker's lamp, her brow furrowed as she concentrated on some sort of form. I unintentionally startled her when she noticed my shadow in the doorway, dark half circles underscoring her eyes.

"I'm very sorry," I said. "I didn't mean to scare you."

She put down her pen, looked at me, waiting, a bottomless measure of sorrow in her eyes.

"I have a favor I need to ask of you," I said. "I'm sorry, but it can't be helped."

"What sort of favor, Sheriff Dawson?"

By the time I finished explaining it to her, the expression that she wore had transformed into something approaching incredulity.

"That is a highly irregular request," she said.

"I am aware of that, ma'am. Can you do it?"

She considered what I'd asked her as I watched the second hand on her wall clock sweep its face.

"I will take care of it," she said.

I KNEW my next stop was not likely to go easily. Big Jim Belnik did not traffic in accommodation or concession, being neither in his line of work nor in his nature. Like Captain Chris Rose of the state police, Jim Belnik was another Texas transplant; twice divorced with no kids, he was a man whose devotion to his craft had always won out over all else in his life, and the price he'd accepted had often been dear. As his nickname suggests, Jim Belnik is a large man, in voice, presence, and physicality.

He'd arrived in Meridian almost a decade ago, leaving Dallas and a prominent newspaper job in his rearview to purchase the struggling local weekly, the *Post*. Big Jim turned it into a daily newspaper and rechristened it the *Daily Post*. Though the business still struggled to remain above water, it had earned a revitalized level of journalistic respect under Belnik's hardbitten and boisterous leadership, and all with a payroll that numbered fewer than a dozen souls. While Big Jim and I didn't always agree, we had developed a working relationship defined by mutual respect and a modicum of trust, something I was about to ask him to lean upon blindly if he proved to be willing to assist at all.

"Well, here comes trouble," Jim said as I stepped into his office and closed the door behind me. He gave me a once-over with his seen-it-all eyes, scratched his chin through his dense growth of beard, and dropped into his rolling chair. "Jesus, Dawson, y'all look like you could use a little bottom-drawer medicine. Pull up a pew."

I didn't disagree; taking off my hat, I sat down in the only other chair in his cluttered office that wasn't piled with stacks of folders, photographs, and loose sheets of type-written papers. He came up with two jelly jars and a fifth of Jim Beam from his desk drawer, poured two fingers into each of the glasses, and pushed one across the desktop to me. He knocked back half of his with one slug and I did the same, the warm whiskey burning a welcome path all the way down to my stomach.

"So what brings the sheriff of Meriwether County to the fourth estate's untidy hovel?" he asked.

"I need to ask a favor of you, Jim."

He squeezed his lips into a flat line and swirled the liquor in his glass.

"You know I don't *do* favors, right?"

"I think you might be willing to consider this one."

"Okay, tee it up," he said, making a go-ahead gesture with his left hand as he leaned his elbows on his desk. "Let's hear what you got."

I told him nearly everything I'd learned about Ian Swann, plus a few things I surmised, and my thoughts with regard to the incident that had now claimed four lives. He listened with genuine interest as I spoke, the calculations of a seasoned story-teller lighting behind his eyes as I dropped the final shoe.

I watched him evaluate my proposal in studied silence, then he uncorked the whiskey and refilled his glass. He looked at me from under his shaggy eyebrows and made a move to refill mine, but I declined.

"So the long and the short of it," he said, "is you want me to sit on a story."

"I'm asking you to *delay* a story for a couple of days. After that, you tell it any way that you want to. Like always."

Big Jim sipped slowly from his jelly glass this time, gazing out through the slats of his dusty Venetian blinds and into the hive of activity in the bullpen beyond.

"I only need a couple days," I said. "I've already been given reasonable assurances that the hospital has me covered."

"Good," he said. "It'd be a deal killer if they didn't."

He leaned back in his chair, knitted his fingers across his ample gut, and stared at me, the rhythmic clatter of the teletype and the hammering of last-minute copy fused with the susurrus of forced air from the floor vents as I waited him out.

"If I agree to this, I have to be there," Big Jim said finally. "Personally."

"No," I said. "Too unpredictable. Too dangerous."

"I'm a newspaper man, Dawson," he said and leaned forward to drive home his point. "You're asking me to lie."

"I'm asking you to *wait* for *a couple of days* before telling the truth."

He looked at me like he'd just eaten a bad clam.

"Listen," I said. "I'm offering you an exclusive on the real story here. If it comes out too early, the whole thing caves in."

"It's only a story if what you've told me proves to be correct, Dawson."

"I'm right about this," I said and rose to my feet. "I know I am."

"I still need to be there," he said. "I can't write it if I'm not there to see it."

I picked up my hat and thanked him for the drink, turned and pulled open the door.

"I'll think on it and get back to you, Jim," I said. "Deal?"

"Call me in the morning," he said as I pulled his door closed behind me.

* * *

I WAITED for the security gate to swing open and rolled down my window, a line of rain clouds mizzling along the foothills, the cool evening air laced with the sweet scents of cedar and petrichor enveloping the cab of my pickup. The atmosphere was unnaturally quiet at the Half Mountain compound as I parked and climbed out of the truck. I called out to the groundskeeper, the only other person in sight, and inquired as to where I might find Len Kaanan. The groundsman gestured in the direction of the amphitheater without slowing his gait as he propped a rake handle across his shoulders and proceeded to the landscaping shed.

I followed the footpath I had come to know all too well, located Kaanan seated alone in the front row of the cavea, gazing at the vacant platform he'd built, at the scars, divots, and scorch marks that were the irrevocable proof of the death that had plunged down from the battens. But Len Kaanan seemed unaware of my presence until I sat down beside him. One look in my face told him more than he wanted to hear, and he nodded his unspoken understanding. His response was straight-faced and unreadable at first, perpending on his most private thoughts. He tapped my knee as a gesture of gratitude, rose without saying a word, and deliberately made his way to the edge of the stage. He looked into the rafters, then he turned away, tipped his face into his hands, and wept.

CHAPTER TWENTY-NINE

JESSE WAS SITTING by the fireplace when I arrived home that evening, the blood light of sunset reduced to a thin trickle along the mountaintops. I could tell that my wife had not been there long, seated as she was, warming her palms in the nascent flicker of freshly lit logs.

"Where's Cricket?" I asked as I bent down to kiss her.

"I drew her a bath," Jesse said. "I expect she'll be soaking for a while. You taste like whiskey."

"I stopped off to speak with Jim Belnik on my way home."

"What for?"

She scooted away from the heat of the firebox and arched an eyebrow at me.

"Long story."

"I believe this might be a night for long stories," she said.

"I have a suspicion you're right."

I crossed the room to the bar cart, slipped the cork from a bottle of cabernet and decanted a glass for Jesse, and poured a tumbler of Beam on the rocks for myself.

"How's she doing?" I asked, casting a glance in the direction of our daughter's room.

"She's her daddy's daughter," Jesse said.

"Sorry to hear that."

"She'll talk when she's ready. Like I said, she's her daddy's daughter."

Jesse patted the stone hearth beside her and I took a seat next to her. The heat from the fire was a balm to my aching back, and I watched the lingering color like a stain on the sky beyond the window glass.

"Where did you drift off to just now, Tyler?"

"Just thinking."

"This isn't the time to be secretive," she said.

Jesse had no way of knowing in that moment that her choice of words had cut to the quick of my psyche, an unwitting surgical strike. I had just spent the better part of the past two hours constructing a scheme based on little more than decades-old secrets and rumors, suppositions, whispered confidences and vague recollections, the entirety of which was dependent upon the reputation I had earned as the sheriff of this county. That, and the trust being placed in my personal judgment. I had not lied to anyone, but innocent people now found themselves in positions of potential personal compromise that would and should land squarely on me if I proved to be wrong. The burden was solely mine to carry, but I owed my wife a measure of truth.

"I went to see Ruth Brawley yesterday," I said.

"Oh really? What about?"

"About an old case that I couldn't recall. From back in the sixties."

"I hope you didn't upset her," she said as she sipped her wine and studied the firelight reflected in the facets of her glass.

"No, turns out Ruth's a pretty tough cookie. But it's a goddamned unpleasant story. Do you remember the young girl they found at the old McEvoy farm, back in the day? The story at the time was that she committed suicide, hung herself."

"At the McEvoy farm?"

"At the time, the place was owned by a family named Swanson."

"Vaguely rings a bell. What about it?"

I took a deep draft of Jim Beam and rattled the ice in my glass, then recounted the story I'd heard from Ruth Brawley: the antipathy that existed between the Lomax and Swanson families, the budding teenage romance between Paul Swanson and Heather Lomax, and the inexcusable combination of apathy and ineptitude that had tainted the investigation in the aftermath of Heather Lomax's death.

The longer I spoke, the more Jesse receded into herself, and I felt guilty about having brought up the subject at all, reconsidering whether I had unintentionally shifted my millstone to her. The whiskey in my tumbler had turned mostly to water. I stopped speaking, drank off the dregs of my drink, and crossed the room to the bar cart, where I made myself a fresh one and brought Jesse's wine bottle with me back to the fireplace.

She was staring into the firebox when I returned, shoulders hunched, hands clasped, leaning into the heat from the flames. I resettled myself, and I saw my wife startle when a log slipped from the andiron and sent a shower of sparks up the flue.

"Tell me the rest of it," Jesse said.

"That's it," I answered. "That's all of it."

"I can tell that there's more to the story. I'm not made of porcelain, Tyler."

I refilled her wineglass and set the bottle on the mantel beside me; I looked into the face of the best woman I know.

"Apparently, there was some evidence the girl had been abused before she died," I said.

"She was raped?"

I nodded.

"Ruth Brawley believes Heather Lomax might have been pregnant at the time of her death."

"Poor thing. That's horrible."

"Yeah, it is."

"She wouldn't be the first girl to think she was out of options," Jesse said.

"I said the same thing, but Ruth seemed to think she was okay, that she had a plan of some kind."

"The girl must have been terrified. Who was the father?"

"Miss Ruth didn't know. But she was reasonably sure it wasn't the girl's boyfriend. Seems the Swanson boy drove Heather to Doc's office that day, very concerned about her, and not in the way that you'd expect."

"If he wasn't the father, then who was it?"

"Lloyd Skadden's investigation never got that far. And Doc Brawley never got the chance to follow up. But Heather Lomax lived alone with her father, by all accounts a bitter man and an angry, volatile drunk. Caleb told me he knew the man."

Jesse shivered.

"Good god," she said. "People can be such animals."

"Once Skadden had it marked down as a suicide, both families skipped town in a hurry. Seemed the whisper mill here was throwing around a lot of unpleasant speculation, and both the men thought there'd be repercussions of some kind."

"They were probably right. Anybody know where they went?"

"Gavin Lomax disappeared off the map. Had family in Tennessee according to Miss Ruth. Nobody around here ever saw or heard from him again."

I stopped talking when I noticed our daughter padding down the hallway. She was barefooted, wearing a flannel nightgown with an unbuttoned wool sweater wrapped around her shoulders. Her hair was still damp, disheveled and unevenly parted;

the overall effect of her appearance put me in mind of the sole survivor from a ravaged pioneer wagon train.

"You don't need to stop talking just because I walked in the room," Cricket said.

"Have a seat by the fire and warm up," I said as I stood and offered her my seat on the hearth.

Wyatt the dog heard Cricket's voice and wandered in from the mudroom and planted himself on the floor beside her bare feet. She leaned down and scratched him behind his ears and she smiled at him as he squeezed his eyes shut in canine bliss. Our daughter looked up at me, and then at her mother, stitched her lips tightly together, and gazed out the window into the deepening color outdoors.

"I'm not naive," she said softly, her focus lingering outside somewhere in the woods. "I knew Ian wasn't going to make it. I saw the whole thing, watched it happen right in front of me. Nobody could live through something like that."

Jesse started to speak, but Cricket continued as though she was thinking aloud, or perhaps solely to hear her own voice. She stopped scratching Wyatt and he curled into a ball as she settled herself closer to the flames.

"It's just that you never think that the day will ever come," Cricket said. "The day when it actually happens, and he's just . . . gone."

"I'm sorry, Cricket," I said. "Very sorry."

"Ian liked you," she said, and a wistful smile touched the corners of her mouth. "He thought you were cool."

"I don't believe I've heard that word applied to me very often," I said and watched my daughter turn inward again. "He was a decent young man, Cricket. He didn't have it easy, did he?"

"No, he didn't," she said. "How do you know that?"

"People talk. Did he say much to you about his life?"

"A little," she said. She turned toward her mother and held out a hand for Jesse's wineglass. "May I have a sip?"

"You can finish it off," Jesse said. "Might help you sleep."

"Ian moved somewhere outside of Chicago when he was a teenager," Cricket said. "At the time, it was just Ian and his brother and their dad."

"Moved from where?" I baited and noticed the look Jesse shot at me.

Cricket shrugged and tipped the wineglass to her lips.

"I don't know," she said. "He said they lived in an apartment above an old lady's garage. Ian's dad did chores and handyman work for the lady in exchange for rent. Then Ian's dad died in a car crash not long after they moved there. Ian said he and his brother started using new names after the insurance got paid out. He was terrified that Child Services would find them and take his brother away from him. Anyway, the authorities found his dad's car in a lake, but they never found his dad's body. Creepy. Really did a number on Ian."

"He was only a boy himself at the time," I said.

"That's terrible," Jesse agreed.

"It pretty much messed up Ian," Cricket said. "He wasn't even sixteen yet and he had to take care of his brother—his brother's handicapped, you know. They had a little money from their dad's life insurance, but it wasn't much. Ian quit school and bussed tables at a diner. He learned to play guitar and busked in the street for money. That's where the record people found him. Playing guitar on the sidewalk for loose change."

"Ian never mentioned that to me," I said.

"He didn't talk too much about it," she said and looked into my face. Her expression had grown brighter as she spoke of Ian's life. "I guess they had some big reveal planned during the Saturday concert. Some big thing for the film."

"What was it?"

"I don't know. Ian never said. It all seemed very hush-hush."

The hair on the back of my neck stood on end, and the blood in my veins rushed cold.

"Did Kaanan ever say anything about that to you, Jesse?" I asked.

She shook her head and eyed me with that special look she held in reserve for when she wanted me to know that we'd be talking about this whole thing later on.

"First time I'm hearing about it," Jesse admitted. "But Len is the director. There's no reason he'd feel compelled to tell me everything. Why?"

"Just curious," I said, but Jesse knew I was prevaricating, and one more cog clicked into place in my head.

I FINISHED my Jim Beam on the gallery, the ridgeline now reduced to a shadow against a sky of deepening blue, a final gasp of golden glow showing along the rim. I heard Drambuie nickering inside the barn not far away, saw the incandescent light come to life behind the cupola as Taj Caldwell and Paul Tucker fed and watered the horses before they retired to the bunkhouse. I leaned a shoulder on the porch stanchion and passed my eyes across the dense tangle of forest. The musky smell of equine sweat, leather, and trampled sweetgrass lingered in the air as Jesse stepped outside to join me.

"Want to tell me what that was about in there?" she asked.

"It's probably nothing, but if I turn out to be correct, I'll be sure to let you know," I said and winked at her.

I was about to head back indoors when something in the tree line captured my attention. I cupped my free hand to my face and squinted into the woods.

"What is it?" Jesse asked.

I thought I'd seen a flash of light in the shadows of the trees, like a twinkling on metal, or perhaps the reflective surface of binocular lenses. I stood on the gallery and stared into the vegetation until my eyes watered, wondering whether my fatigue and imagination were playing tricks on me.

"I thought I saw something out there," I said.

I dipped into my shirt pocket and showed Jesse the Polaroid photograph of the stagehand from Half Mountain.

"Who's this?" she asked.

"I was hoping you'd know."

"Looks like one of the riggers out at the studio. What's going on, Ty? Why are you carrying that man's picture in your pocket?"

"He's just somebody I'm trying to find," I said. "But if this guy ever shows his face on this ranch and I'm not around, shoot him."

Jesse cut her eyes to the rifle case in the living room and the row of lever-action rifles lined up behind the display glass. She took another look at the photograph, passed it back to me, and nodded.

"I'd shoot that guy whether you're here or not," she said and returned to the kitchen.

CHAPTER THIRTY

BIG JIM BELNIK called me at home before I'd finished my second cup of coffee. I had stayed at home that morning to cook breakfast for Cricket and Jesse, an attempt to return a little normalcy into our lives. The aroma of frying bacon and drop biscuits filled the kitchen, and I'd already set the table for the three of us when the phone started to ring.

"I saw Len Kaanan's statement on the TV news this morning," Belnik said without preamble when I picked up. "Looks like I'm coming along with you, Dawson. You said you'd think on it. Just say the word. Tell me when and where."

I had seen the newscast, too. Len Kaanan had come through, had done exactly what I'd asked of him, and made a statement to the media that Ian Swann's miraculous recovery would see him released from the hospital no later than tomorrow morning. I could tell that it had taken all that Kaanan had in him to stand before the cameras and lie outright, and I recognized that I had now used up every last chip of credibility I possesssed to garner the cooperation of these men, and that of Nurse Fields. I knew I had to allow Big Jim to be with me today. My hunch would either prove right or wrong, and the outcome was about to fall squarely on me.

"Saddle up, Jim. We had a deal," I said, and gave him the details as to where to meet me.

CHAPTER THIRTY-ONE

I WAITED UNTIL the evening shift change at the hospital, intending my clandestine activities to get lost in the transitional commotion. The sign fixed to the wall outside Ian Swann's room still had his name printed on it, but the room's door was closed, and inside, my deputy Jordan Powell was being costumed in a hospital gown, taped with counterfeit IV tubes and wires, and wrapped with gauze from head to foot like Ian Swann had been. I watched him climb into the bed, his service weapon tucked between his knees, one eye exposed beneath the bandages, thin blankets tucked under his chin. I could see that Powell was grinning as we turned out the lights inside the room, the only window in the room exposing the closing moments of dusk outside as the hospital shifted into the quieter modality of evening.

BUSINESS PROCEEDED as usual for the authentic members of the medical staff, serving the needs of real patients suffering real afflictions, while Jim Belnik, dressed in surgical scrubs, pretended to be working, reading articles he'd clipped out of the Portland newspaper and taped onto a clipboard, his brow etched with a scowl. I, too, was incognito, a doctor's white lab coat obscuring the revolver I carried underneath, a stethoscope draped across my shoulders and a plastic badge with a name I didn't recognize pinned to a pocket bulging with ballpoint pens.

Minutes stretched into hours, the hours into increasingly muted spans of unmarked time that overtook the building and commenced to mock me when the hall lights began to dim and the snores of slumbering patients drifted down the empty corridors as the clock passed midnight and crossed into the wee hours. Belnik shot a look at me, his confidence in my scheme visibly diminishing as we sat side by side in the nurses' station, sharing that emotional no-man's-land that is known so well by soldiers and the condemned, that crimson-gray borderline that marks the space between the haze of boredom and the sudden terror of incoming fire; a grenade of razor wire concealed inside the velvet temptation of slumber, the fright that wakes you from your torpor like a blast of Willy Pete and turns your bodily fluids to ice and forever after fills your skull with spiders and disinherits you of any expectation of peace.

I could sense that Belnik had all but given up on me when I looked up and noticed the man I'd been waiting for all night prowling furtively along the corridor. He was attired simply in blue jeans, white T-shirt, and khaki jacket; he carried no weapon that I could detect, which meant little to me under the circumstances. If this man was here with the intentions I suspected, his errand could be accomplished with a simple pillow pressed over an unsuspecting and slumbering face, or a swift and decisive wrench to the head, a broken neck and a severed spinal cord. His shoe soles made little sound as he moved along the deserted passage, his attention focused and unblinking. I averted my eyes from his direction and pretended a flagging concentration on reading from a stack of medical journals at my elbow.

He trailed an odor of stale tobacco, sweat, and creosote, the telltale scents of his personal pursuits, so pungent it was as if they'd been infused into his skin. He shot a quick glance left and right, saw nothing to discourage his objective this time, and, confirming that Ian Swann's name still appeared on the placard, slipped inside the darkened hospital room he'd come so close to entering once before.

I tapped Jim Belnik's foot and woke him, held a finger to my lips to make sure Big Jim remained silent while I unbuttoned my white lab coat and tucked the open flap behind the handle of my Colt. I held an open palm between Belnik and me, gestured for him to stay right where he was as I crept my way along the wall toward Swann's room, one hand tracing the wainscot and the other ready on the grip of my Peacemaker.

I could hear no sound at all emanating from within as I approached the door, risking exposure as I peered through the narrow opening between the doorjamb and the door. The dim glow of the medical devices inside lit the intruder's plain features, and I watched him withdraw a small clamshell box from his jacket pocket and snap it open. I recognized the shape of a syringe as he extracted it from the box, one he'd likely copped from among his junkie FTRA brothers and was now about to employ to commit murder on a man who appeared to be slumbering helpless in his bed.

I noticed the bedsheets stir slightly as the trespasser drew back the plunger, his eyes compacted to slits of concentration as he charged the cartridge with deadly air. All at once, the prostrate body in the bed sat upright, head bandaged like a mummy, a Navy Colt 1911 clutched in a fist and aimed only inches from the bridge of the would-be killer's nose. The intruder spun toward the door, but I now stood in his way. He gripped the syringe firmly in his palm and made a move to stab me in the eye with it, but I juked sideways and felt the breeze of a near miss.

He, too, feinted from one side to the other, then tried to

shoulder past me through the doorframe, but there were two of us for him to deal with now, Jordan Powell now standing behind him in a Weaver stance. Powell thumbed the Colt's hammer with the distinctive mechanical click that anyone with a familiarity with firearms recognizes as the last sound you'll hear on this earth if you choose not to yield.

The would-be killer halted in his tracks and I shipped my Peacemaker and drew a bead on the man's forehead.

"Go ahead and hook this man up, Jordan," I said.

When I looked into Powell's face, I could see that he was grinning, peeling away layers of fake bandages and winking at Jim Belnik, who had appeared in the doorway behind me.

"Best take a few steps backward, Jim," I said. "You don't want any of this man's gristle on you if he forces me to pull the trigger."

"I'm not moving," the intruder said and dropped the empty hypodermic to the floor.

"You cannot publish a word about this until I interview this guy," I said to Belnik. "You can join us at the substation, but I can't let you listen in. What'll it be? Coming or going?"

Belnik showed me an expression shot through with adrenaline and sleep deprivation.

"Call me when you've got something I can use, Dawson," Big Jim said. "I'll be in my office. I've got about three thousand words of hard copy buzzing around my head and dyin' to get out."

JORDAN POWELL drove the man I knew only by his railroad name, Bigfoot aka Sasquatch, to the substation while I wrote a long explanatory note addressed to Nurse Fields and slipped it beneath her office door. The suspect was cuffed and chained to a D-ring bolted to the table in the interview room by the time I got back to the office, and Powell was nowhere to be found.

Lamar Dewey, my night man, looked at me with an expression like that of a ruminant animal, one part confusion and another part utter vacancy, a simplemindedness that I chose to chalk up to lack of sleep. I had hired Lamar because he'd been the only one to answer the ad I'd taken out for the job, bringing him on for graveyard shift, mostly to answer the phone in case it rang and to feed the prisoners if we happened to have any in the overnight cage.

"Where's Jordan?" I asked him.

"He took off," Lamar said. "Said he had something he had to do."

"Did you happen to ask him what it was?"

"No, sir. He just said to wait for you and keep the interview room locked."

Outside the window, the morning sky was salmon pink, a pale predawn that struck me as oddly wistful and out of phase with the nature of the day I was about to have.

"May I go home now, Sheriff?" he asked.

"Hell no, you may not go home. We have police work to do, Lamar; that's what we do here."

I regretted my tone, but I was running on a volatile chemical cocktail of adrenaline, fatigue, and frustration, a potentially combustible concoction that could become a problem for the man chained to the table in the interview room.

"I want you to phone the DA's office," I said to Lamar. "Leave a message for Bridger Midland and have him get his ass down here as soon as he can. Tell him to bring along a jail deputy and a prisoner transport van."

"It's still pretty early, sir."

"That's why I asked you to leave a message for him, son. Anything else on your mind?"

"No, sir."

I poured myself a fresh mug of coffee and brought a Dixie cup of ice water with me into the interview room, whose stale confines had already been subsumed by the suspect's distinct body odor. He looked at me with the fragmented focus of a man who had spent his life inside a carnival attraction and appeared to be motivated by things outside the influence of gravity. His face was like the blunt edge of an axe, eyes dull as pewter, his skin deeply creased, lined by exposure to the elements, tough and lifeless as a pair of old leather chaps.

I placed a tape recorder on the table, tested it for sound levels, rewound the tape, and started over again.

"My name is Sheriff Tyler Dawson of Meriwether County," I announced into the microphone and glanced at my wristwatch. "It is 5:21 a.m. on Wednesday, April 14, 1976. This interview is being conducted at the Meridian substation, interview room number one."

The suspect glanced down at his cuffs, indicating I should remove them. I shook my head, left him chained to the table, but I slid the cup of water within his reach.

"Let's start with your name," I said to the man.

"They call me 'Sasquatch,'" he said.

"I didn't ask about your hobo handle, I asked you for your name. The one your mother gave you."

"Jacob."

"Do you have a last name?"

"Jacob Swanson is the name on my birth certificate," he said. "But I call myself Esau as a reminder."

"As a reminder of what?"

"That I valued my own appetites and hunger more than my father's blessing and birthright. I disrespected it and I threw it away."

"What does that mean?"

"None of your business."

There is a strange light that frequently shines in the faces of the clinically insane. I had seen it in hospitals and medical tents, and in places where men subjected one another to the unspeakable. Self-delusion was something else, perhaps even more dangerous, a moral vacuity that carries no glow, but a stench, and this line of conversation was an enormous red flag. Before I allowed it to veer into the incomprehensible, I confronted the man with more recent and tangible events.

"What were you doing in Ian Swann's hospital room this morning?" I asked.

He gazed at me with lifeless eyes, his expression blank as slate, the hair on his head shaved down to graying stubble.

"Finishing what I'd started," he answered.

"What had you started, Jacob?"

"You know what I'm talking about."

"You defaced Ian's car," I said. "You ordered him to be physically assaulted. Ian must have been aware you were here."

The man who called himself Esau picked up the paper cup with both of his manacled hands and drank, his attention drifting to the tape reels rotating in slow circles.

"What were you doing in Ian Swann's room?" I asked again.

"That's not his name. His name is Paul Swanson. I was his father."

"*Was?*"

"I died a long time ago."

I recalled what Cricket had told me of Ian's life as a teenager in Chicago and pressed Jacob for more.

"You faked your death and left two young sons to fend for themselves," I said. "Why would you do something like that?"

"Don't waste your time feeling sorry for them, Sheriff. They got by."

"Your boy, Dowd, was mentally handicapped. He was only a child."

"His name is Shane," he said. "And he should have been euthanized after his accident."

I had walked into the room believing I had witnessed the breadth and depth of evil of which mankind is capable, the savage brutality and solipsism that reduces a person to something far less than human; but I had never before heard such cold, cruel, and sinister words uttered by a father concerning his own child. I felt a sudden rush of blood in my ears and I had to jump to my feet and step away from the table before I gave in to animal impulses of my own.

"What made you leave Meridian back then, Mr. Swanson?" I asked.

"Why do you ask me questions that you already know the answers to?"

"What made you leave Meridian?"

"I already told you. I am a sinner."

"We all fall short," I said. "What kinds of sins have you committed that would induce you to murder your own flesh and blood?"

"The kinds I will never be absolved of."

I was tiring of his game, his narcissistic insolence, and his world-weary self-pity.

"Tell me about Heather Lomax," I said.

The glazed expression that had defined his expression unexpectedly flickered to life, and he licked his lips as if his mouth had gone suddenly dry.

"I'm not talking about that girl," he said. "I want a cigarette."

"Give me answers, and I'll give you a cigarette."

He cocked his head and studied me for the first time. I could see he was deciding whether to hold, raise, or bluff.

"Her daddy was a very strange man," he said finally. "A bad man."

"Your son cared for her, Mr. Swanson. He loved Heather Lomax."

"We all did. Everybody in town loved her. Heather was a special girl."

"Were you aware that she was pregnant when she died?"

His face revealed no surprise, nor much of any reaction at all. He slumped into his chair and returned to feigned boredom and resignation. But it was clear to see he was acting, the vein on his left temple twitching like a worm.

"Heather was not that kind of girl," he said. "If that's what you're implying."

"You didn't answer my question. Were you aware Heather Lomax was pregnant?"

"Her father was a selfish, evil man. A violent man; a bully and a thief. He hurt that girl. More than once."

"And you decided it was your job to protect her?"

"The whole situation was unnatural. You appear to have some familiarity with the Bible. Isn't that so, Sheriff?"

"I don't believe I understand your reference, Mr. Swanson."

"I shouldn't have expected you to, Sheriff," he said. "And your beliefs are of no consequence to me."

I stood and switched off the tape recorder and tucked it beneath my arm, collected my empty coffee mug, and moved toward the door.

"I'm going to make you a onetime offer, Mr. Swanson," I said. "I'm about to walk up that street outside and buy you a pack of smokes. When I come back, I'm going to restart that tape recorder and you are going to clear your conscience. The district attorney is going to meet us right here in this room later this morning, and if you're a smart man, you'll quit talking in riddles and cut a deal with him and me. It might just save you what's left of your life."

He showed me an expression of boredom, rubbed his stubbled pate with the palm of a manacled hand.

"I'll bet you didn't know this state dealt with death penalty cases with a noose and gallows until as recently as 1931," I said. "These days, people like you go to the gas chamber. They call it the Smokehouse. You ever witnessed an asphixiation, Mr. Swanson? I honestly don't know which is worse."

I rechecked his cuffs and the chain that secured him, and I reached for the doorknob, his expression having maintained an unreadable blank. There had been a time in my life when I would have bounced a man like Jacob Swanson off the cinder blocks, but I had grown older and wiser since my days as an MP. Even so, this man was testing my last nerve, and I needed a few minutes of fresh air to clear my head.

A DOE and her twin fawns, their tiny haunches still spotted with white, strolled unmolested down the center of Clark Street as I strode up the empty sidewalk, where the Cottonwood Blossom's front door had been propped open with a brand-new chalkboard sign announcing Lankard's revised breakfast hours. The clack of billiard balls echoed down the block, and the smell of bacon frying on the grill reminded me I hadn't eaten since yesterday morning.

I stepped through the batwings and spotted Lankard Downing taking an order at a table in the corner beneath a mounted elk head and Leon Quinn grinning proudly at me from his post behind the bar.

"'Morning, Sheriff," Leon said. His eyes were clear, his complexion ruddy from the heat drifting out from the kitchen. He lowered his tone and stepped closer to me, leaned his torso across the bar. "I wanted to say thank you for the other day," he whispered.

"No problem, Leon. Who doesn't need a good game of checkers every now and then?"

He winked and touched an index finger to the side of his nose, and I changed the subject.

"I need a box of Marlboro Reds," I said.

"I thought you quit."

"It's for somebody else."

He slid a pack out of the wire rack on the backbar and passed it to me.

"On the house," Leon said.

"You know I prefer to pay my own way, Leon."

He dipped into his pocket and came out with two quarters, popped the change drawer, and dropped the two coins in the register.

"It's on me, Sheriff, I insist."

I thanked him and stepped back outside into the cool morning, my stomach still growling. The salmon sky had long since faded to misty blue, white tufts of cumulus sliding along the slipstream as I took my time making my way back to the office. I had no way of knowing in that moment that the next several hours of my life would be spent listening to one of the most tawdry, wretched, and heartbreaking stories I had ever encountered.

IT WAS past dinnertime by the time I got back to the ranch that night. The atmosphere was dull gray, blunted of reflected light, the sun a bloodred angry hole in the sky. My body had moved beyond hunger, my system operating on overdrive, fueled by a feeling of rage and distress that was diluted only by grief, and I was unwilling to walk through the door of my own home in that condition.

I heard the radio playing a song by Hank Snow as I stepped up and knocked on Caleb Wheeler's front door. He was still dressed in his work clothes, his hair pressed flat on his scalp from a day in the saddle.

"What's got you all puckered up, son?"

"I just spent the better part of a day locked in a room with one of the sickest and most evil bastards I have ever been forced to share oxygen with."

He inhaled a deep breath and I watched him take my inventory before he took a step back and invited me in.

"And why does that experience bring you to my house instead of your own?"

"I'm not prepared to interact with decent people yet," I said. "I feel like I need to scrub out my skull with a bucket of lye and a wire brush."

"I don't know whether I should take offense at that remark," he said. "I believe you came here for some other reason."

"You weren't completely square with me before, Caleb."

"Get the grits out of your mouth, Tyler. Say it plain. What's on your mind?"

"Jacob Swanson, you remember talking to me about him?"

Caleb narrowed his eyes and slid his hands into the pockets of his jeans.

"I remember telling you his leaving this county was good goddamn riddance."

"It's not that simple, Caleb, and I think you know it."

"Say it out loud. Tell me what you think I didn't say to you."

"Jacob Swanson raped that teenage girl, Heather Lomax. Might have killed her and hung her from his own oak tree, too, though I'm not completely sure about that last part yet. Even if Swanson didn't strangle her, the poor girl lost her life because of him, and because her own father was an abusive, incestuous pile of horseshit and everybody around here suspected it. Either way, the responsibility for her death falls on this entire town."

Caleb cut his eyes outside the window and something nearly tangible departed from him.

"That's not how people dealt with things back then, Tyler."

"That's it? Really? This whole damn town gets to pretend it never happened?"

"No. That's *not* it."

Caleb crossed the room and opened his liquor cabinet. He poured two glasses of rye and handed one over to me without a word.

"A tragedy like the one you just described to me is the exact reason you are here, Tyler," he said. "It's the reason you're the sheriff and Lloyd Skadden is dead and buried and forgotten. Most of us figured he was inept. And the man was most surely an asshole, perhaps even corrupt. But he's all we had at the time. Meriwether County was the Wild West back then. Hell, it still is."

I stood there mute, not knowing what to say as Caleb tossed back his rye and eyed me.

"You don't understand what I am telling you, do you?" Caleb asked, passing his shirtsleeve across his damp lips as he set his empty glass on the lamp table.

"I don't believe I do," I said.

His eyes dropped to the liquor I held in my hand, untouched, my knuckles white as I held on to the glass.

"You better take a lick of that whiskey, son. You're gonna want it."

I did as he recommended and tasted the heat on my tongue, in my throat, and all the way down to my empty stomach and felt a little bit sick. His eyes were unblinking as he looked at me, and I thought I saw something else there, though I wasn't sure what it was.

"I'm telling you that this town needed absolution, son," Caleb said, his tone softer than a moment before. "Needed it for a very long time. And you, my friend, turned out to be it."

"That's not the job that I signed on for, Caleb."

"Maybe not, but it's the goddamn job you ended up with."

CHAPTER THIRTY-TWO

"WHERE THE HELL were you all day yesterday?" I asked Jordan Powell as I stepped through the back door to the office the next morning, still irritable from the evening before. Powell looked as though he'd been there for a while already, and I heard something stirring upstairs.

"Didn't Lamar tell you what I was doing?"

"Lamar Dewey barely knows what *he's* doing from one moment to the next," I said.

"I take it you haven't been upstairs this morning?"

"I just got here, Jordan."

"I got something you might want to have a look at," he said and led the way to the stairwell, where he stood aside and allowed me to ascend first. As I took the first steps of the incline, I noticed Sam Griffin grinning down at me from the landing at the top of the stairs. In the years I had worked with them—both at the Diamond D and as my deputies—these two cowboys had spent more time nitpicking each other than they did doing anything else. On those stray occasions when they were in cahoots with each other, I had acquired good reason to be highly suspicious.

"Come on up, Sheriff," Griffin said. "We got something to show you. Well, Powell does."

"We got 'em, Cap," Powell said, gestured toward the two men who'd been locked in the cages. "The fat one on the left drove all the way out here from Wyoming. He's the one who likes to kill eagles from a seat in a helicopter. His pal over there is his personal taxidermist, and he lives not far up the road outside of Lewiston. Learned his trade in the pen and makes extra cash stuffing endangered species."

"Assholes," Griffin said.

"Where's the chopper pilot?" I asked.

"These two are holding out for a deal before they give up his name," Powell said. "Bridger Midland is on his way down here as we speak."

I stepped closer to the older suspect, a florid-faced over-weight man I placed in his midfifties, wearing an expensive haircut, pressed jeans, and Bally loafers. The khaki jacket he had tossed on the bunk had his name embroidered on the label of a private tailor with a Jackson, Wyoming, address.

"Pruitt Blankenship," I said, reading the hand-stitched calligraphy. "You're quite a ways off your home turf, pilgrim."

"I'll be back home in Wyoming by the end of the day."

"Oh, I doubt that very seriously," I said. "You're facing a federal beef. A couple of Oregon statutes, as well. You should make plans to stick around for a bit."

"A slap on the wrist and a few thousand in fines," Blankenship said. "Just let me out now and save yourselves a passel of trouble."

"A *passel*? My, my. That seems like a lot," I said. "I believe I'll take my chances though, chief. Something tells me you've got a room full of illegal hunting trophies at home in Wyoming, and I bet my two deputies here already called up a federal warrant to search your place. You could be looking at serious prison time, Pruitt. A *passel* of it."

The man in the other cell went suddenly pale, his eyes wide as saucers. He crossed the length of his cell in three strides and hooked his fingers through the welded crossbars.

"I only do side work for this guy," he said. "I'm—

"Save it for the DA," I said. "Tell him all about it, and I'd be willing to bet you'll be the one sleeping at home tonight, not Mr. Blankenship. Just tell the DA everything you know."

I led the way back downstairs, listening to the murmur of expletives being traded between the caged inmates fading away behind us as we retreated from lockup and reentered the office. I took a seat at my desk and looked at Powell, whose expression was like that of a man who'd landed a world record blue marlin.

"How'd you catch this guy?" I asked him.

"Something you mentioned about Lily Firecloud's husband being an amateur taxidermist. I made a few calls."

"This is what the two of you have been cooking up the last couple days?"

"Roger that, Sheriff," Griffin said. "But it was all Jordan. I just came along for the ride."

"One thing: How'd you get Blankenship to drive all the way out here from Wyoming?"

"I had the taxidermist call fatso and tell him he couldn't ship a mounted eagle through the mail, 'cause it would be a federal crime. He had to drive out here to pick it up personally."

"What kind of crime did that jackass think killing a federally protected animal was?"

"Rich people think they know everything, Cap," he said. "Assholes."

I TOLD Powell to gather up his hat, coat, and gear and ride with me out to Jim Belnik's office at the *Daily Post*. Fifteen minutes later, Powell was recounting the story to Big Jim's crime reporter from his seat in a comfortable chair in the conference room, while a staff photographer snapped candid photos of my deputy's interview. Belnik and I walked down the hall to his office while Powell was enjoying his well-deserved fifteen minutes of fame. I set the reel-to-reel deck I'd brought from the substation on Belnik's cluttered desk and plugged it in.

"What's this?"

"I promised you the story," I said. "One caveat, though."

Belnik hitched an eyebrow and leaned back in his swivel chair.

"I'm going to ask you to use some discretion here," I said.

"What's that supposed to mean?"

"This is ugly stuff, Jim. These are real people. Some of them still live here in town."

He drummed his desktop with his fingertips while he considered what I'd just said.

"What's that quote from the John Wayne movie?" Big Jim asked. "'When the legend becomes fact, print the legend'?"

"That was from *Liberty Valance*," I said. "And, yes. That's pretty much what I'm talking about. I'll play you the final few minutes of my interview. It's all you'll need. Frankly, it's all you'll want to hear."

I cued the tape toward the end of the reel, to the recap of Jacob Swanson's statement to me, but I still wasn't prepared to hear his voice or his story again.

"Everything was fine," Swanson said on the tape. "And then the kid had to go and get famous. Next thing I hear, they're making a damned movie about him. I had set up a life for those two boys, sacrificed for it by erasing myself off the earth; now here it was about to blow up in my face."

Swanson stopped talking and I could hear myself lighting a cigarette for him on the tape and handing it over to the man. I remembered he exhaled a cloud and gazed up at the ceiling, his face twisted into an expression of disgust.

"Local boy makes good," he continued. "Comes back to town a big hero. What would you expect me to do? Everything that happened back then was dead and gone. Sleeping dogs, and all that. Now, if it all comes back to light and people start looking for me again, I'm going straight to prison, no quarter, no questions asked."

He'd paused and taken another pull on his smoke, shook his head and looked at me with an expression of incredulity, as though his actions were the normal response of a man to his son's unexpected success.

"Heather Lomax died with my child inside her," Swanson admitted. The flicker of pride in his eyes had turned my stomach. "Shane knew it, too. Damn kid saw me with the girl. I told that boy I'd gut him if he ever said a word about what he'd seen, and I know he believed me. But there was no doubt Shane would talk about it once 'Ian Swann' started whining about their pathetic young lives all alone in Chicago without a mommy and daddy . . ."

The man had nearly spat as he ground out the stub of his cigarette, a man wronged and mistreated by the world. For some, an interrogation is a way of placing their sins on the altar. For this man, it was nothing more than a recitation of self-pity.

"Goddamn Shane," Swanson said. "I told you before, Sheriff, that boy should have been put to sleep after his mother's car accident."

I had heard enough, but I could see Big Jim was rapt, as mortified and appalled as I was, and the tape continued to unspool as Belnik took furious notes on a yellow legal pad.

I stood and began to pace in Belnik's office, the drone of Jacob Swann's voice driving my mind down a path of its own.

I gazed out the window into a small town spring day, where everyday people proceeded with everyday chores and routines, unknowing of the evil that might walk right past them on the sidewalk or the grocery store aisle, the wickedness being revealed in this room.

For seven years, the boy that had renamed himself Ian Swann and his brother survived on the largesse of others; busking on the streets and El stations of Chicago, keeping the rent current in the tiny room the two shared using the dwindling insurance proceeds their father's counterfeit death had provided them.

Once Jacob Swann had been declared legally dead and the insurance money paid out, Ian and his brother lived with the self-created myth that their father had died as an act of self-sacrifice, another single-car accident, his vehicle salvaged from the river, but his body never recovered. In truth, the man's disappearance had been driven by cowardice and paranoia. Jacob Swann believed he was in the clear from his crimes, but another part of him could never seem to let go of the looming possibility he'd be discovered; that one day his son, Shane, would reveal what he'd witnessed, and the manhunt for Heather Lomax's killer—a rapist and sexual predator—would ensue in earnest.

Jacob Swanson had convinced himself of the need to rescue Heather Lomax from an abusive father—a mission he viewed as unfit for his fourteen-year-old son, Paul—and Jacob Swann's psyche began to twist itself into a knot, his quest rapidly degenerating into obsession, rape, and murder.

"You got my confession right there on your tape recorder," Jacob Swanson said as the interview wound to a close. "I told you I got the stain on me, Sheriff. Now, I'm finished talking."

Jim Belnik's office fell into silence as the empty tape reel continued to spin. I stepped away from the window and clicked off the machine.

"You can't unhear that shit, can you?" Belnik said. His complexion had gone pale, and a dark ring of sweat had appeared on his collar.

"When you write your story, go easy on the hospital for fudging the time frame of Ian's death," I reminded him. "Whatever they did, it was because I asked them to."

"What about the record producer?"

"Him, too. I don't know if we would have caught Swanson if Kaanan hadn't agreed to talk on TV."

"So, what's it going to be, the truth or the legend?" Big Jim asked me.

"Like always," I said. "A little of both."

CHAPTER THIRTY-THREE

I DROPPED Jordan Powell at the substation and saw the DA, Bridger Midland, had already arrived and was speaking to the poached eagle's taxidermist in the interview room.

"You got a call from Captain Rose," Griffin said and handed me a pink message slip. "He says he's got something for you on those prints I rolled on the kid at the hospital."

I didn't have the heart to inform Rose that his information was already superfluous, so I let him tell me that the prints had come back to a California resident named Paul Ian Swanson. He went on to tell me that this person was the musician who went by the stage name Ian Swann, though he hadn't had it legally changed. I told him I appreciated the rush he had placed on my request, thanked him, and hung up without letting him know it was a day late and a dollar short. He'd find out soon enough on his own.

I picked up my keys and drove back to the ranch, leaving Griffin and Powell at the office with the DA and their two captives. They still had a long day of processing ahead of them.

I parked in the shade of the larch at the back of the barn and looked up at the mountains, where the white sun shone across ribbons of wildflowers blooming in the creases cut into the high slopes. I walked down the path toward the corral and saw

Caleb with his shirtsleeves rolled up past his elbows, repairing the pump on a water trough. He looked up when he heard me come up behind him, then stood and shook a knot of green moss from his hands.

"What brings you back here at this time of day?" he asked.

"Knocking off early," I said. "Felt the need to apologize to you for last night."

He pushed back the rim of his Stetson and knelt down on a haunch and returned to his work on the water pump.

"You know," he said. "I think I might've hit my head in my sleep last night. I don't recall much about yesterday evening. But we got a stretch of fence that needs mending up on Amantes Camp. Want to come along and give me a hand?"

THE EVENING SUN illuminated a rooster tail of fine dust from the caliche road as I was setting the table for dinner. I left the dining room and stepped outside just as a white Chevy Suburban rolled to a stop in my driveway. I waited as the driver climbed down from the cab, recognized Len Kaanan as soon as he moved into the light.

"Sorry to drop in unannounced," he said. "But I wanted to come by in person to thank you."

"Thank me for what?"

"For catching Ian's killer."

The look on his face was not exactly a smile, but it was as close as the situation allowed.

"Word travels fast," I said.

"Someone from your local paper called me for some background on a story they're doing on Ian. They mentioned you'd caught the man who killed him."

"That's a fact," I said. "Won't likely get out before he meets the cold lonesome."

A cluster of jays erupted in a noisy outburst from the underbrush beyond the house. Kaanan ran a hand through his silver hair and looked like a man who had nowhere to be.

"We were about to have dinner," I said. "Would you care to join us?"

"I believe I would like that very much, Sheriff."

"Here at home, I'm just Ty," I said. "Come on inside."

Jesse and Cricket prepared a dinner of chicken and dumplings, with a side of fresh vegetables from the garden. We drank wine and spoke of Len Kaanan's plans for the film he intended to make about Ian, an artist frozen in time; a generational anomaly whose life was at once ascendant and abbreviated, as gentle and open as he was enigmatic.

As Jesse and I cleared the table for dessert, Kaanan excused himself and went out to his truck. Cricket brought in a peach pie from the kitchen and placed it on a trivet as Kaanan returned to the table carrying a hardshell guitar case with Ian Swann's initials embossed on the side.

"This is for you," Kaanan said to Cricket. "Ian would want you to have it."

Cricket knelt to the floor, tripped the locks on the case, and folded open the shell. Inside was a vintage Martin D-35 acoustic guitar resting on a bed of crimson velvet.

"This guitar was his favorite," he said.

I expected my daughter to burst into tears, but I should have known better by now. Instead her eyes appeared to light from inside, her lips touched by a smile that looked like a new memory had sprung to life.

"He played this guitar for me once," she said softly.

She ran her fingers along the instrument's smooth body, laying the palm of her hand across its strings and holding it there.

"I can't keep this," she said. "It belongs in a museum."

"I beg to differ, young lady," Len Kaanan said. "Museums are for strangers. This guitar belongs wherever you are."

THAT NIGHT I slept without dreaming.

EPILOGUE

NEW CHAUTAUQUA

IF THERE IS such a thing as mercy in this world, I hadn't seen much of it that year, only echoes of quixotic impulses I wish I could have ignored. Even so, there was no denying that in the long and often pitiful account of human advancement, mankind has yet to tire of ignoring its own history, much less learn anything from it.

MY GENERATION was conceived and born during the Great Depression and came of age in its shadow. Its effect on our collective emotional and spiritual psyche is imprinted on our faces as clearly as a tribal tattoo. There is a distance between what we want, what we need, and what we receive in life, and in the gap is where we spend our years.

Most of all, however, mankind is fickle, most especially in its bestowal of respect or praise. Ian Swann knew the truth of this, I was certain. At first they had ignored him, then they considered him, and they finally honored him; in the end, they would likely forget him entirely, as people most usually do.

But insanity is insanity, and hard as we try to understand its origins and motivations, they escape us, and we are left to our own devices when it comes time for us to cope with the losses dealt out by the harvesters of chaos, pain, and violence. The reapers among us know no boundaries, and the victims no solace. Some are born to push the stone of Sisyphus, others experience the fates of Icarus or even Midas; nevertheless, the gods had been merciful enough to leave humankind with hope, and I have chosen to accept that tender mercy as reward enough for this life.

TWO DAYS later, the story about Jordan Powell and the fallen eagle went public and afforded the town of Meridian the opportunity to celebrate the efforts of a truly good man. That same day, Cricket extended her college spring break and elected to remain with us at the Diamond D for an extra week before heading back.

Cricket never strayed far from the ranch in that time, spending most of her days on horseback, or hiking the deer trails that crisscrossed the hills, or exploring the banks of the Knife River bend and the blue bottleflies in the bulrushes where a young eagle had been so mercilessly slain. But the creature's short life had not been without value, for in death it had revived the flagging spirit of my young deputy, and it perhaps even provided blood atonement and the restoration of hope for an entire town. The workings of fate are unpredictable at best, its origins and outcomes operating well beyond my pay grade.

That afternoon, Cricket found me in my ranch office, happy mischief in her shimmering blue eyes.

"I saw the flies hatching up on the Knife," she said. "Want to come fishing with me?"

I folded away the ledgers I had been studying and slid them into my desk drawer. I laced my fingers behind my head and narrowed my eyes at her.

"Do we have to talk?" I asked.

"Nope," she answered, grinning.

"I'll get my stuff and meet you at the truck."

ACKNOWLEDGMENTS

My sincere gratitude to two great friends who provided me with some invaluable insight and background for this book. The first is my author pal, Bruce Robert Coffin, whose expertise with police protocols is profoundly appreciated; Bruce is also hell of a gifted (award-winning) author. Secondly, another great author buddy, Rich Zahradnik, who helped me understand some of the finer intricacies of the newspaper profession. Rich is a Shamus Award winner and fantastic author. Thank you both for your expertise and your generosity with your time. I don't know why these guys let me hang out with them.

As always, to my family, for their endless supply of enthusiasm, love, and encouragement. Christina, to whom this book is as lovingly dedicated as I am, and to Allegra, Britton, Christan, Nick, Ashton, Kheler, Liam and Declynn. . . . *Aloha pau ole!*

To my agent, Peter Riva, whose efforts on my behalf are indescribable; and to Mara Anastas and Emma Chapnick at Open Road Media; and to my editors, Laurie McGee and Sidney Rioux, and all of the great professionals at ORM for being in my corner. I couldn't be more grateful that you're all on my team.

Regarding the soundtrack: Ironically, though this book is more directly about the workings of the music business, the story structure didn't allow for section heading/song titles this time around. But it doesn't mean that my usual immersion in music wasn't a part of its creation. The "soundtrack" this time around would include: "Fallen Eagle" (Stephen Stills and Manassas), "Two Trains" (Little Feat), "Song from Half Mountain" (Dan Fogelberg), "Looks Like Rain" (Grateful Dead), "Krikkit's Song" (Poco), "New Chautauqua" (Pat Metheny), "In Memory of Elizabeth Reed" and "Stormy Monday" (Allman Brothers Band).

Thank you once again for trusting me with your time, and I hope you enjoyed this visit to Meriwether County—I am more grateful for the privilege of taking you there than I can properly express.

Until next time, "May the Four Winds blow you safely home . . ."

Baron

ABOUT THE AUTHOR

Baron Birtcher spent a number of years as a professional musician, and founded an independent record label and management company. His first two novels, *Roadhouse Blues* and *Ruby Tuesday*, are *Los Angeles Times* and Independent Mystery Booksellers Association bestsellers. Birtcher has been nominated for a number of literary awards, including the Nero Award for his novel *Hard Latitudes*, the Claymore Award for his novel *Rain Dogs*, and the Left Coast Crime "Lefty" Award for his novel *Angels Fall*. He was the 2016 Silver Falchion Award winner for his novel *Hard Latitudes* and the 2018 Winner of the Killer Nashville Reader's Choice Award for his novel *South California Purples*. Birtcher currently divides his time between Portland, Oregon, and Kona, Hawaii.

THE TY DAWSON MYSTERIES

FROM OPEN ROAD MEDIA

INTEGRATED MEDIA

INTEGRATED MEDIA

Find a full list of our authors and titles at www.openroadmedia.com

FOLLOW US
@OpenRoadMedia

EARLY BIRD BOOKS

FRESH DEALS, DELIVERED DAILY

Love to read?
Love great sales?

Get fantastic deals on bestselling ebooks delivered to your inbox every day!

Sign up today at
earlybirdbooks.com/book